Blame it on the Onesie

CJ MORROW

Tamarillas Press

This book is written in British English.

Cover artwork © primo-piano/istock.com
Cover design: ©CJ Morrow 2022

ISBN: 978-1-913807-29-0

For Amy, Sophie, Jenny and Chloé –
beware sleaze weasels.

Other books by CJ MORROW

Women's Fiction/Romantic Comedy:
Save the Date
Escape to Christmas Cottage
It's Pamela Rigby Actually
Sooo Not Looking for a Man
We can Work it Out
Little Mishaps and Big Surprises
Mermaid Hair and I Don't Care
Blame it on the Onesie
A Onesie is not just for Christmas

Psychological Thriller:
Never Leaves Me

Fantasy:
The Finder
The Illusionist
The Sister
The Family

Party Time

One

'The thing is, Ella.' Gwynnie leaned in as though about to share a secret. 'You earn more than my husband and he's got a mortgage to pay.' Gwynnie stood up, moved her Barbie doll body across the room and grasped the door knob, signalling the end of the meeting. 'It's just not appropriate,' she continued, 'if I give you a pay rise, everyone will want one. And let's face it, you have had rather a lot of time off.'

Gwynnie opened the door and waited for Ella to walk through first. Ella squeezed past Gwynnie and the two exchanged gritted-teeth smiles. Ella could see the remnants of Gwynnie's macrobiotic lunch nestling along her bottom gum line. Good, thought Ella.

'I love these one-to-ones,' Ella said as they walked back to the main office. 'Such a good opportunity to get to know each other.' Ella had given up arguing all the right and just reasons why she should be paid more. Instead she took pleasure in watching Gwynnie stroking her hair flat in an attempt to stop its natural curl winning the frizz battle – a losing battle. Ella allowed herself to delight in that, even though the bile of spite tasted bitter.

Gwynnie Palmer styled herself on her near namesake, but there the similarities ended. For Gwynnie's hair was not baby-soft and super-smooth and her body was not boyish and lithe. Behind her back she was known as Barbie and she had all of Barbie's attributes – an abundant chest, snake hips and overlong legs. But it was her penchant for pink which had probably earned her the nickname – Gwynnie just loved her pink.

Gwynnie had been Ella's manager at Gubbins Wholesale Stationery for a whole glorious month now and Ella could still feel her anger rise every time she remembered her first day back in the office. She'd only been away for seven weeks – and five of those were unpaid – and it wasn't as though she'd been enjoying herself. The timing couldn't have been worse. There was Ella, confident that she was next in line for the manager job – hadn't Don Perkins promised it to her more than once – then suddenly he vanished and Gwynnie appeared in his place and during Ella's absence.

Gwynnie was well ensconced by the time Ella came back, introducing new initiatives almost weekly. Very few of them had anything to do with the actual work – they already had efficient processes for that, a lot of which had been designed by Ella. That was why she fully believed, especially when Don Perkins repeatedly promised her, that she was next in line. And then, while Ella was off nursing her sick mother on her deathbed, Gwynnie was parachuted in from the offsite warehouse and put in charge of the whole department. It made Ella feel sick.

'How did it go?' Tiffy asked, as Ella returned to her

desk. Tiffy liked to keep tabs on everybody's one-to-ones; it allowed her to pass on accurate gossip later as well as keep up-to-date with everybody's business, even though it had nothing to do with her. She wasn't a manager; she was the same grade as Ella, though she was paid considerably more. Tiffy was another new face, originally brought in as an agency temp to cover Ella's absence. She'd been made permanent by Gwynnie as soon as she took over.

Ella made a *mind your own business* face at Tiffy. Tiffy made a *get stuffed* face in return. Ella sat down and pulled her chair up tight to her desk then opened her bottom drawer and reached inside. She rummaged under the smelly, unwashed old cardigan that had been Ruben's bed – poor Ruben, a great stinky beast of a dog, her mum's dog, who'd pined away and died in the middle of the funeral tea – he'd died on that cardigan. Ella tightly scrunched the head of the blonde Barbie doll she kept rolled in the cardigan. Ah, that felt better, nothing like a squeeze of Barbie's head to relieve stress. And did she just imagine Gwynnie wince?

'You all right, Gwynnie?' Ella smiled mock sympathy over her computer.

'Bit of a head,' Gwynnie mouthed quietly. 'Just come on.'

'Ahh, poor you,' Ella said and pushed the Barbie's face flat before letting go and closing the drawer.

'God, what's that smell?' Tiffy said, her nose up like a sniffer dog.

'Can't smell anything,' Ella said, confident that the sweaty dead dog smell had been wafted over the desks by the air-con and was now languishing on Gwynnie and Tiffy's side.

'Oh, it's vile. It's making me feel nauseous.' Tiffy

stood up and looked around for the source, staring across the office before finally giving up and dropping back down. Then Ella twisted the head of the ugly little green rubber troll she kept on her desk. Tiffy Troll.

'Ow,' Tiffy yelped, rubbing her neck.

Just coincidence, Ella thought to herself before giving the troll's nose a quick flick, she saw Tiffy flinch and touch her nose. Pure coincidence.

The day, like most days in Gubbins now, wore on. Ella wished five pm would hurry up, just like she did every day. What a waste, she thought, I'm just willing my life away – this is no life. She thought about her poor mum who would have given anything for time to pass slowly, to live longer, but cancer had made that impossible. I mustn't waste my life, I mustn't, Ella chanted internally. Even if only for my mum's memory I must make it better.

Finally, it was home time; she switched off her computer and stood up to get her coat.

'Oooh,' Gwynnie said, suddenly jumping up, *she* already had her coat on, her bag over her shoulder. 'I meant to tell everyone, tomorrow is Pink Day. Should be fun.' With that Gywnnie turned and strutted down the office, her frizzy bob trailing behind her.

'Oh fab. I know just what I'm going to wear,' Tiffy said, following in Gwynnie's wake. Ella watched the two of them as they scuttled away, Gwynnie so tall, Tiffy so squat. Barbie and the Troll.

'So, Ella, what are *you* wearing?' The voice came from behind her and there was a hint of smirk in it. She turned and smirked back at Ben who stood next to Kevin who was also smirking. These two worked at the back of the office, reported to Gwynnie and had already learned how to keep out of her way.

'The trouble with you,' Kevin said, as the three walked out together, 'is that you challenge her. It's much easier if you just play along.'

Ella looked at Ben and Kevin. So far as she could see they pretty much did as they pleased while pretending to do as Gwynnie told them. They laughed behind her back as much as they smiled and nodded to her face, and she hadn't caught them out yet.

'Yes, well that's easy for you to say, easy for you to do. She doesn't understand the inventory or how you control it. She thinks she knows all about my job and tells me frequently how I should do it.'

They reached the car park; as they parted Ben patted Ella on the back. 'Ella,' he said, 'you've had a shit time. Don't make it any worse by letting her get to you.'

'Thanks,' Ella said and forced a smile. She knew Ben was right, but it really didn't help. Ben knew how to play the game, in his mid-thirties he'd been at Gubbins for years, he'd survived several managers, good and bad and he was training his apprentice Kevin to master the same techniques. They were each other's allies. Ella didn't have an ally, not in her own department anyway.

She drove home through the rush hour traffic, cussing at every traffic light, cursing every other motorist. Before her mum's illness she had enjoyed working at Gubbins and liked the people she worked with – just Don, Kevin and Ben. But now, well now she struggled to force herself out of bed every day. She dreaded walking into the office because no matter how early she arrived, Barbie and the Troll were always already there, watching, keeping tabs. Ella hated the way the whole situation made her feel so angry and bitter. It wasn't a good way to feel; yet she couldn't stop it.

She turned into her street, drove all the way down to the end and back again before struggling into a parking space. Shame it couldn't have been closer to her home, because just as she got out of her car the heavens opened. Great.

Once inside her studio apartment – huh, that was a laugh, bedsit with its own shower was a better description – she sat down and wailed.

'What the hell am I going to do?' she cried through snot and dribbles. Then she glanced around the sorry little room, its miniscule kitchen at one end, the sofa bed at the other and the stack of cardboard boxes in the corner. And that made her wail even more because the contents of those boxes were all that remained of her mum.

Finally, she stood up, grabbed a tissue, blew her nose, pulled herself together, wrestled her phone from the bottom of her handbag.

Hi hun, you free tonight? xxx she messaged her best friend Samantha who worked in Gubbins HR department.

The reply came straight back. *Hey hun, you okay? Sure. Charlie's going out. Come at 7 xxx.*

Wine? No. Just for me then. Lol. xxx Ella smiled as she messaged, not just because at four months pregnant Samantha couldn't drink, but also because she would be glad to see her friend alone.

Bad day? ☹ Samantha's next message said.

Kind of. See you later. xxx. Ella put the phone down, went to the kitchen end – not a long walk – found a pasta ready meal in her mini-fridge and whacked it in the microwave, simultaneously taking her top off and unbuttoning her trousers. One good thing with such a tiny place – you could do everything at once. Multi-tasking in a mini-world.

* * *

'It's Pink Day again tomorrow, Sam,' Ella said after they'd exchanged greetings and Samantha had filled Ella in on how she felt and how the baby was growing. Ella felt thrilled for her friend and a little bit envious. They were the same age – twenty-seven – but their lives couldn't be more different. Sam lived with her husband Charlie in a designer three-bed semi they owned, while Ella lived in a grotty rented studio hovel.

'Pink Day. Oh God, not again. What is that about?' Sam laughed and sipped on nausea suppressing soda water.

'I don't know. I really don't. God knows what she hopes to achieve by it. Even Ben and Kevin have to comply.'

'Want another wine?' Sam reached for the bottle and started to pour Ella another glass.

'Hey, be careful. Just because you can't drink doesn't mean I have to drink for two.' They both laughed.

'I have to eat for two.' Sam reached for another *Marmite* twiglet. 'Can't get enough of these now. I used to hate *Marmite*.'

'I've always loved it. Work, urgh, I don't know what to do.' Ella sighed and despite her protestations took another gulp of wine. 'I did think, with my mum dying, that they might have been a bit...' she stopped speaking and caught her breath, 'kinder. Instead I have to put up with this shit. And her. That job was mine. I've worked really hard. I used to love coming to work; now I hate it.' Ella stifled a sob before continuing. She'd started, so there would be no stopping her now.

Sam gave her a sideways glance, a little smile of sympathetic encouragement. Ella knew Sam was humouring her, because they both knew it all had to come out, even if it was a repeating loop. Grief and bitterness are not good emotions.

'When I think of all the times I stayed late, all the effort I put in. It just makes me so angry. And sad. It was me who designed the best processes in our office; remember I even got a prize for that?'

Sam nodded vigorously.

'How many times did Don tell me I was next in line? Dozens, that's how many.'

'He probably shouldn't have said that,' Sam offered.

Ella shot her a quick look. 'Don't use your HR speak on me. Where was I? Then the minute my back's turned… and they didn't pay me when I was off; said I should have got a doctor's note for depression. Two weeks compassionate leave – that's all they paid me, then five weeks with nothing. I must have worked all those hours twice over during our system change – do you remember?'

Sam nodded. 'It's at the manager's discretion,' she said, sounding rather meek.

'No HR speak. No HR defence,' Ella said, a bit too sharply before continuing. 'And do you know what Gwynnie the Barbie doll said to me? She said that she saved the day when I was off, what with Don leaving so suddenly. Everything was fine when I left, Don was there and everything was normal. Then I'm off, he leaves and it all goes wrong. Anyway, why did he leave so suddenly?' Ella turned to Sam and waited.

'You know I can't comment.'

'Huh. Anyway, Barbie tells me that everything was a

shambles and she had been brought in to save the day. Bitch. It's not even true. Nothing has changed, we're still doing things the way we have been since the new system, yet she claims credit for everything. She actually said I was lucky to still have a job.' Ella took a deep breath. 'Do you think I've got grounds for a complaint against her?'

'You shouldn't ask me that. See someone else in HR,' Sam said, then added quietly, 'but maybe.'

'Anyway, there's more. Today I asked for a pay rise. I know it was pushing it a bit, but after Tiffy Troll left her payslip lying around and I saw what she was getting…' Ella took a big breath. 'Six grand more than me,' she said, almost shouting to make the point. 'And she's younger and she doesn't know what she's doing and she's only been there five minutes, well... She constantly asks me how to do things. Why is she getting paid more than me? She was an agency temp then suddenly she's permanent and earning more than me. How can that be right? I've been back a month now so I thought what the hell. I asked Barbie for a rise. Do you know what she said?'

Sam shook her head.

'She said, "you earn more than my husband and he's got a mortgage to pay." Can you believe it? Bitch Barbie.'

Sam grimaced.

'Do you think I've got grounds to make a complaint about that?'

Sam shrugged her shoulders slowly, looked away, embarrassed.

'I know, I know, you can't say. Just give me a clue.'

'Maybe,' Sam said quietly. 'But you need to think about the long-term damage it might do.'

'What to Barbie? I doubt it. She's flame proof.'

'Not her – you. Your career.'

'Huh, what career?' Ella took another mouthful of wine, looked at the glass then knocked the rest back. 'I suppose I'll have to leave. I can't see any other way for it. I can't work with Barbie; she seems to have it in for me. I don't know why. Bloody Barbie and her pinky-pink-pink days.'

'Careful you don't call her Barbie to her face,' Sam said, trying to lighten the mood.

'What, like it's any worse than her real name – Gwynnie Palmer? She styles herself on Gwyneth Paltrow but that's a joke, she's nothing like her.' Ella poured herself another glass of wine. 'Her parents must have been psychic to name her after a celeb when the celeb wasn't even a celeb then. Anyway, Ben and Kevin call her Barbie too.' Ella drank from her wine glass again; then glanced at Sam.

'Gwynnie isn't her real name, is it?' Ella said. Suddenly it had dawned on her; of course it wasn't her real name.

Sam shrugged.

'I know, *you can't tell me*,' she said, half mockingly. 'Hey, I'll do a Derren Brown on you.'

Sam reared back from her friend and frowned.

'It'll be fine. I'll just say a few names and I'll watch your face for a reaction.'

'No,' Sam almost shouted. 'No.'

'You don't have to react. What I mean is, if I hit on the right name, you'll give it away without meaning to. You know how Derren Brown can tell…'

'You're not Derren Brown.'

'Humour me. Does it begin with A?' Pause. 'B?' Pause. 'Oh, G? Yes, I saw a twitch. It's G, of course it is. Should have started with G. Obvious really.'

Sam got up. 'I need the loo,' she said, half sighing, half laughing.

'Well, we've made progress,' Ella said, pouring the remainder of the wine into her glass, though it only filled half the glass this time. She pulled a sad face, then drank the wine down in one go. Had she really drunk a whole bottle?

When Sam returned she was carrying two large glasses of water. She placed them on the coffee table in front of Ella.

'Sit back down; I want to get on with Derren Brown-ing you.'

Sam sat and nodded at the water. 'Drink one of those first.'

Ella harrumphed but downed one, then faced her friend again. 'Right. Gillian?' Pause. 'No. Um, I can't think of any names beginning with G. Oh, Glenda?' Pause. 'No. Gerty?' They both laughed. 'I can't think of any. Griselda? No. Ger, Ger, I can't think of any. Give me a clue.'

Sam shook her head and nodded at the other glass of water. Ella picked it up and drank.

'Thought of one, thought of one. Gladys? Oh. Gladys. You twitched. I saw your left eye flare.'

'No it didn't.'

'It's Gladys, isn't it? Gladys. Ha ha ha. Her parents weren't psychic; they were cruel.' Ella fell about laughing. 'Gladys. I love it. Now *I* need to go to the loo, you've made me drink too much water. Gladys. Ha ha ha.'

In the toilet, Ella felt alternate waves of sickness and dizziness roll over her. When she came out she felt herself sway a little. Sam was waiting for her in the hallway. She had her coat on and she was holding Ella's.

'Shall I give you a lift home now?'

'Oh, I'm going now then? Good job I didn't drive, eh? The walk here did me good and it had stopped raining when I came round. I could walk home, if you're tired.'

'I'm fine and it's raining again now,' Sam said, steering her friend out into the night.

'This is such a lovely house and you've got a drive, so lovely,' Ella slurred as they piled into the car. Sam replied with a patient nod and a half-smile.

'So,' Sam said, once they were off the drive, 'what are you wearing tomorrow, for Pink Day?'

'I don't know.' Ella threw her hands up in the air theatrically. 'Can't pretend I don't know like I did last time when I turned up head-to-toe in black. You should have seen Barbie's face. Gladys's face. Ha ha. Love it.'

'Just stick to Gwynnie.'

'Might. Might not.' Ella wiggled her head about, laughing. She knew she was drunk and she suspected she was being an irritating drunk.

'You've got plenty of pink stuff. What about that nice dress you wore last week when we went shopping?'

'I'm not wearing that to work. Why should I? It's too good for work. I've got work clothes for work and they're not pink.'

'Be careful,' Sam said, as Ella almost fell out of the car. Once she reached her front door, Ella turned and waved to her friend. Sam looked back and smiled but she looked sad. After Ella had fumbled her way into her place she sent Sam a message.

Sorry hun. Have I made you sad? xxx

The reply took a while to come back, after all Sam had to get home first, Ella reasoned. It simply said: *I'm fine Ella. Sleep well.*

That was a bit cold, Ella thought, as she dropped her phone on a chair.

Ella didn't sleep well; she tossed and turned, got up twice for the loo and a drink, and slept right through her alarm. When she awoke with a start and saw the time, she jumped out of bed and stubbed her toe. Great, it was going to be one of those days.

She just had enough time to shower and dress. Pink Day. Oh damn it. She threw her wardrobe door open where everything was crammed in tightly because there wasn't enough space, and fished around for something pink and suitable. She was *not* going to wear her nice dress to work. Finally, she spotted a bright orange top and toning leggings in a darker shade – an outfit she'd never worn because it had been one of those impulse sale buys that seemed like a good idea at the time. It had languished in her wardrobe for two or three years, always threatening to take itself off to the charity shop.

Perfect, Ella thought, then out loud, practising. 'Gladys, I'm colour blind.' She'd have to be careful not to say Gladys to Gwynnie's face. Ella sniggered at the prospect. Oh, it was tempting.

She dragged a brush through her hair, grabbed her keys and coat and dashed for her car. She hoped she had some painkillers in her desk drawer because her hangover was starting to kick in now. Ouch.

As expected everyone else was already at their desks when she arrived. She sidled into her seat and waited for Gwynnie to comment, but she didn't. Nobody said a word, not even hello. Ella glanced over at Ben and Kevin; Ben looked up and caught her eye, offered a quick smile, a nod. Ben and Kevin were both wearing pink shirts, and pink ties. They were definitely pink, yet somehow, they didn't look right. Ella screwed her eyes up to see better. There was a patchy quality to them, almost swirly. Oh dear. The hangover was really kicking in; maybe she'd better find those painkillers now.

An hour passed and no one spoke; there was furious tapping on keyboards then a meeting request popped into Ella's inbox. It said, *Team Meeting, 10.30am*. Great, thought Ella. Two minutes later an email from Ben arrived entitled *Team Meeting*; under it just two words – 'Can't wait'. Ella replied, 'Ditto'.

Just before the meeting was about to start Ella got herself a cup of tea and took it into the meeting room, she was first there.

'You're keen,' Gwynnie said, coming into the room behind her.

Ella gave a quick smile in return; suppressing the urge to call her Gladys.

'Are you all right? You look a bit peaky.' Gwynnie's eyes scanned Ella's face.

'I'm fine, thanks.'

The others came in; Tiffy shone like a diamond, all flashing teeth and sparkly eyes. Yuk. Ben and Kevin just looked weary. Now that Ella was getting a better view of their shirts she could see why they had looked strange earlier; they were white shirts that had been through the washing machine with something red, hence the streaks. The shirts were hideous, so were the ties, but the trousers, some old chinos that had also been through the wrong wash – hideous.

'Like your uniforms,' Ella heard herself say as they sat down.

'Well, I'm pleased you brought that up Ella,' Gwynnie pounced. 'Because I'm quite concerned about your clothing. It's Pink Day, not Orange Day.'

Ella looked down at her clothes then made a show of looking around at everyone else's.

'I don't have any orange clothes so I'm really *glad* it's not Orange Day.' Ella placed great emphasis on the word glad and thought she saw Gwynnie wince.

'Is that some sort of joke?'

'What do you mean?' Ella frowned; worried for a minute that Gwynnie had cottoned onto the *glad* joke. She saw Ben and Kevin both look away; Ben was actually biting his lower lip.

'You're wearing orange.'

'I'm not. Am I?' Ella looked down at her clothes. 'Oh. You know I'm colour blind. I thought this was pink. I'd be *glad* to go home and change if you think I should.'

'Oh. No. I didn't realise that. Well, no. At least you tried, I suppose.' Gwynnie forced a thin smile but her face was thunderous.

Despite her victory Ella's heart was racing. She couldn't quite believe she'd had the nerve to say *glad* twice.

'Let's get on with the meeting.' Gwynnie tapped a pencil on the table. 'First, I'd like to commend everyone for getting into the spirit of Pink Day, especially Ben and Kevin, I realise pink isn't a boy's colour, but it does help you get in touch with your feminine side and think outside the box.'

'And the ties are a nice touch, Gwynnie,' Tiffy added.

Boys. Ben was a married father of two and Kevin played rugby every weekend. How could they stand it? Ella was incensed on their behalf. Why didn't they say something? But they didn't, they just stared ahead and kept their faces blank.

'I think it's important for us all to get out of our comfort zones, to make the shift into the unknown, to allow our creativity to come to the fore…' Gwynnie continued, but all Ella heard was 'blah, blah, blah…'

No one said anything as Gwynnie gabbled on. Ella wanted to point out that Gwynnie wasn't out of her comfort zone; she always wore pink, every damn day.

Gwynnie wittered on some more, used a few more stupid pseudo-management-speak words and finally stopped, rounding up her speech with a question. 'Does anyone have any other creative ideas for creative days we could have to make us more creative and productive?'

'I'm been thinking,' Tiffy said.

'Yes?' Gwynnie smiled sweetly at Tiffy.

'What about…Think Day?'

How stupid, thought Ella. Idiot. Just wait until I get hold of that desk troll.

'Think Day. How would that work?' Even Gwynnie was struggling.

'Well, on Think Day, we could all think of a way we could do our job differently, better.' Tiffy smiled brightly.

And that, thought Ella, gets paid more than me. Ben's pen rolled off the table and onto the floor, he bent to pick it up, fumbling down on the carpet longer than he needed to. Ella could see his shoulders shaking.

'Well, thank you, Tiff. We'll give that some thought. What about you Ella, any suggestions?'

Ella had several ideas – she'd thought them up in bed the previous night, probably before the effects of the wine had worn off. Dandruff Day – because Gwynnie did have a bit of a problem in that area; Long Lunch Break Day – everyone would enjoy that; but her favourite was Laxative Day – but only for Gwynnie and Tiffy.

'Ella?' Gwynnie said, tapping the pencil on the table.

'What about Smile Day?' Ella said and saw Ben bite his lower lip again and suck in his cheeks. Kevin's face was still a blank canvas, his eyes staring off into the distance, glazed and unfocused.

'And how would that work?' Gwynnie said.

Tiffy gave a little scoffy cough.

'Well,' Ella said, wishing she hadn't started this. 'If we smile when we're on the phone, especially to a customer, we'll sound happier, and that makes it better. Doesn't it?' What rubbish.

Gwynnie tilted her head and pursed her lips. 'Well, maybe you have something there. Would you like to write up a proposal for that, so I can consider it?' She smiled at Ella. It wasn't a question; it was a command.

Ella swallowed. Serves me right, she thought. She waited a few seconds before replying, made it look as though she was considering her reply. 'Okay.' Ella smiled. 'I'm *glad it's* worth your consideration.'

Gwynnie definitely winced that time.

* * *

'Why are you fighting them?' Ben asked, later over lunch.

'Yeah, you'll never win,' Kevin said, undoing his tie and stuffing it into his shirt pocket.

'What do you two clowns look like?' Ella laughed. 'Look at you.'

'The irony is, she doesn't even see it,' Ben said. 'Why don't you do what we do? We're almost enjoying ourselves.'

'I can't. I just can't. She's got my job. She treats me like dirt. She implies that I've been off on a jolly – I was nursing my mum on her deathbed for God's sake. And she's got that Tiffy – who's incredibly thick as well as a Gwynnie suck-up – on a higher salary than me. I can't see the humour in any of it. I just can't.'

Ben and Kevin looked away, embarrassed. Then Kevin looked at his watch, made a comment about the time and stood up.

They walked back to the office in subdued silence.

Gwynnie and Tiffy were waiting for Ella; Gwynnie stood up as she approached.

'We'll take our lunch break now you're back,' Gwynnie said. 'We're going into town.' She smiled a smile that was more like a grimace.

'I'm ready, Gwynnie,' Tiffy Troll said, and Ella watched the pair prance down the corridor and out of the office.

She waited five minutes.

Then she opened the drawer where stinky Ruben's old cardigan lived and pulled it out. She walked around to Gwynnie's desk where Gwynnie had left a half-drunk cup of water. She tipped a little out and used the smelly cardigan to dab it up. The smell induced Ella's gag reflex; wet wool. Wet stinky wool. She wiped Gwynnie's desk all over with odour of dead Ruben, including the keyboard, then repeated the process on Tiffy's desk. Finally, she stuffed the stinker back in her drawer, closed it firmly then went to wash her hands.

On her way back she called into HR to see Sam. She wanted to tell her all about it, but Sam wasn't alone in the office so she couldn't.

'That's not very pink,' Sam said.

'No. I'm colour blind.'

Sam raised an eyebrow but didn't comment, or laugh. 'Were you all right this morning?'

Ella made a *don't go there* face.

'Come out with us tonight. The band's playing down The Swannie.'

Ella thought about the band. Charlie was lead singer; he said it made a nice change from his job as a management accountant. Then there was the silent drummer – silent because he rarely spoke – 'I speak through my drums,' was the only thing Ella had ever heard him say. There was Steve on bass guitar; much older than the rest, he claimed he'd once jammed with Status Quo.

Then there was Nathan.

'I don't know.' Ella shook her head.

'Oh come on. Keep me company. You can drink lime and soda with me; cheap night and we can have a laugh. Come on.' Sam gave Ella puppy dog eyes.

Ella thought of Nathan.

'Okay.'

Two

Ella didn't stick to lime and soda. She lasted twenty minutes before she went to the bar and bought a bottle of wine. She came back with three glasses - one for Steve's wife and one for the drummer's friend. But she ended up drinking most of it herself.

'You should have seen their faces,' Ella said, explaining for the fourth time how Gwynnie and Tiffy had reacted. She'd told Sam all about the dog cardigan. 'Tiffy actually gagged. Said she was calling the building manager about the smell. Gladys just looked white all afternoon. Ha ha ha.'

Sam shook her head, but she laughed anyway.

'It was funny, Sam.'

'You should be careful. You really should,' Sam whispered, but she had tears in her eyes from laughing.

Ella went to the bar again but this time she did buy lime and sodas; Sam was right, it *was* a cheap drink. She picked her way back to the table now, the carpet was sticky and the air, though not smoky – because smoking was banned – still had that air of nicotine and tar about it.

'Why do they play here?' Ella asked, as she sat down. 'It's such a dump.' She looked around her at the knocked about chairs, the tatty tables.

'Because it pays well and they're the star band,' Sam said, taking a sip from her drink and frowning. 'No ice?' she asked, when Ella queried.

'Run out. Says it all really. How long until they're on?' Ella checked the time on her phone, nearly nine. They'd been there over an hour and Charlie's band hadn't even played yet. So far they'd listened to a pair of teenage lads doing a bad impersonation of One Direction and a country and western singer, complete with yee-haa boots and a Stetson, murder Dolly Parton's *Jolene.*

'Soon. I hope. I'm getting ridges in my back from this chair.'

Ella looked around the pub again: thirty-year-old swirly carpet, mock beams, yellow stucco (a contrast to the dirty grey stucco outside), dark stained wooden bar, postcards of pop stars from another century, *Formica* tops on every horizontal surface. Tonight it was crowded – it was usually crowded – the drinks were cheap and there was entertainment most nights. In an age when pubs were closing every week, this one thrived, maybe because it had so few rivals. But it was still horrible.

'They should demolish this place and start again,' Sam said, eerily echoing Ella's thoughts.

Ella wondered how she'd feel when the band finally did come on. The last time she'd seen them or even been in The Old Swan was New Year's Eve and that had ended in disaster. Not for them, for her. She cringed at the memory.

'So, which one of you is pregnant?' The drummer's

friend turned a gappy smile in their direction. She looked from face to face. Ella looked down at herself, she was wearing jeans and a top, both fairly fitted. She didn't think she looked pregnant.

'I am,' Sam said. Ella glanced at her, and saw the irritation in Sam's face, evidently as insulted as Ella was.

'Don't show,' the drummer's friend said. 'When I had my first I blew up like a whale. That's what they called me, sperm whale.' She laughed loudly at her own joke. 'Hardly showed at all with the second. But number three, well, I nearly exploded.' She threw her arms out, made a sound like an explosion.

'I wish she would now,' Ella whispered in Sam's ear, as she turned away.

Sam, ever the diplomat, smiled benignly.

'You dames want a drink?' The drummer's friend stood up. She was rake thin and very tall. She wore a silver vest which shimmered in the pub's stark fluorescent light, and heavy gold chain necklaces. A tiny bow-tie tattoo lay across the base of her throat. 'We could share a pitcher of BomberZong. I didn't like that wine stuff you got.' She glared at Ella and flared her nostrils.

'That's kind,' Sam said. 'But no thanks.' She patted her stomach to make the point.

'Oh you can have a couple, don't hurt 'em. Have a Guinness, good for you.'

'No thanks.'

'You?' The drummer's friend nodded at Ella.

'I've had enough. Thanks anyway.' Ella forced a smile.

They watched as the drummer's friend walked towards the bar, her black jeans impossibly tight, the outline of a cigarette packet in the back pocket. Her bare arms were yellow white, her shoulders pushed through her skin like a coat hanger.

'Where did he find her?' Ella whispered. 'She's scary.'

'Says the person who wiped down her colleagues' desks with a dead dog's blanket.'

'They deserved it, they really did.' They both laughed. 'And what's with calling us dames? Do we look like drag queens?'

Steve's wife smiled over at Ella and Sam, then pulled her chair closer to them.

'You're looking well, Sam. Everything good? Haven't seen you in a while, Ella.'

'Yes. Great.' Sam replied.

'What's your new friend's name?' Ella asked, after glancing round to make sure she wasn't on her way back.

'I don't know. I haven't asked. She just turned up and said she was with the drummer. She at the bar?'

'Yes, gone to get a bucket of something toxic.'

All three made a face.

It was a while before the drummer's friend came back and as she drew nearer they knew where she'd been from the overpowering stench of stale cigarettes. She carried a tray which she almost dropped onto the table.

'Here,' she said, putting a pint of Guinness in front of Sam.

'Oh, no thank you, not for me. I don't even like it.'

'You have it then, chubs,' she said to Ella. 'Me and her'll have this.' She took the jug of vibrating pink BomberZong and plonked it in front of Steve's wife. The three women opened their mouths in disbelief and exchanged glances. Ella was about to object to being called fat when the drummer's friend sat down, leaned back, fanned herself with a beer mat, complained she was hot then pulled her dirty blonde hair up away from her neck. A skull and cross bones tattoo wrapped itself around the top of her spine. Everyone saw it; no one said a word.

'Okay people…settle down.' The landlord was up on stage with the microphone. The crowd, who hadn't been paying attention to the performers so far, quietened. 'This is what you've been waiting for, this is the act you all came to see, put your hands together for Stone Cats.'

Exaggerated clapping was followed by hoots and whistles. Someone burped loudly.

'Steve says there's a scout here tonight.' Steve's wife leaned over and shouted above the roar.

Ella and Sam smiled enthusiastically and nodded. Steve always said there was a scout in the audience. Nobody believed it; bands didn't get discovered like that anymore, they put themselves on YouTube, built their following online – if they were lucky.

Stone Cats came on, bowed gamely, took their places. Ella looked over at the drummer; his head was down showing his thinning hair scraped into a high pony-tail. He wore his trademark black vest pulled tight over his paunch. Ella pictured the drummer and his friend together: Laurel and Hardy, but gritty, dirty.

She watched Steve give his wife a wry smile and a wink – Steve was the daddy of the band.

She saw Charlie, handsome and elegant with his office-worker hair-cut, his on-trend shirt. He picked the mic up, said, 'This one's for my beautiful wife,' then they started to sing a Beatles' cover. Charlie's voice was good; melodic, smooth, but it was Nathan, the quiet one of the group, on lead guitar, who stole the show.

Ella tried hard not to look at Nathan. Tried very hard.

When they'd finished their first song, the audience cheered and clapped and Ella's table clapped the loudest.

'First time you've seen them?' She leaned over and shouted above the noise to the drummer's friend, who was smiling and clapping.

'No,' she said. 'Saw 'em a couple of years ago. They've improved.'

Ella wondered again how long she'd been the drummer's friend.

It soon became evident that they were showcasing their versatility; they played covers of The Stones, Elton, The Killers, Busted, even a bit of Ed Sheeran. They could play anything. Then Charlie announced that they were going to play an original, a new song written by their very own lead guitarist. Charlie urged the modest Nathan to step forward. Ella watched as Nathan reluctantly stepped into the spotlight, nodded. She watched his hair – long, straggly, rock star hair – flap forward as he moved. Saw his dark brows knit together in modesty. Is that what it was? Saw his eyes – dark and soft and definitely reminiscent of a spaniel – flash across the audience before he stepped back into anonymity.

The song began with a guitar intro – well it would if Nathan had composed it. Then the drummer joined in, tapping out a soft, slow beat, not his usual whacking style normally akin to Animal from the *Muppets*. Charlie stepped forward, gripped the mic softly, kept it on its stand. He started to sing. Ella smiled, watched Sam swell with pride; Charlie had such a good voice.

The words were about a girl, a girl glimpsed in the distance, met socially but always too far away. Ahh, Nathan had written Charlie and Sam's song, for hadn't they danced around each other for two years before finally getting together. The chorus was about love and loss and stupid mistakes. It was catchy and touching and quite mesmerising. The audience loved it, paid full attention, no clinking of glasses or rustling of crisp packets. The drummer's friend was tapping out the slow beat on the table, softly, as though she were playing the piano. She was smiling, focusing her gaze on the drummer who looked up and flashed his eyes at her. Ella knew what that meant; the drummer wouldn't be silent tonight, or alone. Everyone was smiling, everyone was listening – they couldn't join in, they didn't know the words which suddenly became dark and angry. And Charlie turned in a wonderful performance showing hurt and anger as he sang about mistakes and regrets.

It wasn't Sam and Charlie's song.

The words were getting darker – no longer the sweet love song it had begun as – *drunken fumbling in a pub car park, icy breath that tastes of gin, an angry girlfriend in the background.*

Ella swallowed hard. She could feel a lump in her throat, feel her heartbeat quicken. Her hearing became acute, she zoned out the tapping fingers of the drummer's friend, tuned out the lilting guitar, blanked out the drumming and the base, focused in on the words coming out of Charlie's mouth: *a violent face slap, a half-thrown punch, regrets, mistakes, regrets.*

Ella felt sick. She had to get out. She stood up, knocked the untouched Guinness flying across the table. She had to get out. Knocked her chair over, stumbled over it. She had to get out. Pushed her way through irate drinkers. She had to get out.

Outside the air was cool; she gulped, filled her lungs. She turned her face up to the sky welcoming the light drizzle that soothed her burning skin.

How could he? The bastard. How could he?

The smokers, huddled together under their awning, turned as one to stare at her. That's when she realised she was howling, like a banshee.

'You all right, chubs?' a voice said from behind her.

Ella flung round, knocking into the drummer's friend – who was wearing a cerise leather bomber jacket and a knitted donkey hat, complete with long flappy ears -

'Don't call me chubs, right,' Ella snapped back annoyed, but also mesmerised by the outfit.

'Fine. Here, I brought your stuff out.' She pushed Ella's bag and coat at her. 'D'you want a lift home?'

'Why?' Ella snapped again.

'I'm going. Just offering.' She shrugged, started to walk across the car park.

'Yes. Please. Thanks.' Ella followed her to her car, was astonished when they got into a new Lexus.

'Where to?'

Ella gave her the address. She still felt sick. And stupid. And embarrassed. She felt she needed to explain.

'About that…' she started.

'None of mine and happy to keep it that way.'

So they drove in silence and Ella was dropped at the end of her road with little more than a 'bye.' And it seemed the drummer would be alone tonight.

When she got in she messaged Sam. *Sorry, had to go.*

Sam didn't message back.

Ella changed out of her clothes, put on the bright

green frog onesie her mum had given her for Christmas, their last Christmas together. She was cold so she pulled the hood up, the eyes sat atop her head. She forced her face into a wide grin to emulate the frog's mouth, it looked like a grimace and she just felt sad and angry and betrayed.

She made herself a cup of hot chocolate, sat down with it on the sofa. Looked over at the stack of boxes in the corner, her mother's things, reproachfully screeching *sort me out.*

'How has it come to this?' she said aloud; her voice sounded gravelly and rough like she'd smoked forty fags or been crying for hours. 'I hate my home, I hate my job, I hate bloody Nathan. Bastard.'

She took a comforting sip of the hot chocolate then slopped some down her front. She took a tissue and dabbed it off, it had stained but that would come out in the wash.

She dozed off only to be awoken suddenly by the main door intercom buzzing furiously. She jumped up, stupefied for a moment, not remembering where she was, where she'd been. Finally, she stumbled the three feet to the intercom, picked up the phone.

'Ella, it's me.'

'Sam.' Ella buzzed the external door open then opened her own front door and waited for Sam to appear. But it wasn't Sam she saw first, it was Charlie. Suddenly Ella felt stupid in her onesie. She watched as Charlie saw it and forced himself not to snigger.

'You okay?' he asked. Before Ella could answer, Sam stepped out from behind him and rushed towards Ella and hugged her.

'I'm sorry about the beer,' Ella said, once they were inside and squeezed a bit too snugly on her sofa. Thank

God, she hadn't opened it out into a bed yet.

'Don't think it touched any of us. The drummer's friend just calmly picked it up before it completely emptied and the rest of it just slid off the far end of the table onto the carpet – it must have been on a slope. The carpet's just a bit stickier there than usual now.' Sam laughed lightly.

'That's good.'

'So what was all that about?'

Ella glanced over at Charlie who was already looking uncomfortable and embarrassed and said, 'Oh just a misunderstanding that happened months ago.'

Sam raised her eyebrows and waited for more, then Ella noticed her elbow Charlie in the ribs. Charlie jumped up.

'Shall I pick you up in about an hour?' he asked Sam, who immediately jumped up too. The pair exchanged lip pecks, then Charlie was gone and Sam was still waiting for an explanation.

'Well?' she said. 'I'm waiting.'

'It was the song. That's all.'

'It was a good song, I could still hum it now…'

'Please don't.'

'So it upset you. Why?'

'Because it was about me.'

'What? I don't think so, Ella.'

'It was. If definitely was. Did you actually hear the words?'

Sam stopped and looked at Ella. 'Yes, something about regrets and mistakes.'

'Yes, and a drunken fumble in a car park, a slapped face…didn't you hear that part?' Ella's face was flushed; she felt hot and unzipped the onesie a little.

Sam shook her head. 'That was about you? You and

Nathan?' She shook her head in disbelief. 'How? When?'

'New Year's Eve, when you went home early.'

'Oh yes. I was a little bit pregnant, not that anyone knew.' A secret smile swept briefly over Sam's face. 'So what happened?'

'Just like in his song. Bastard.'

'Well I didn't get all the words so I doubt many others did.'

'Those who witnessed will join the dots, make the connection. And Charlie knows all the words; he's probably already worked it out.'

'Charlie won't make the connection; he came home early with me that evening. Just tell me what happened. It can't be that bad.'

Ella shrugged, wished she hadn't started telling Sam about it. So much had happened since that night that she'd put it right to the back of her mind. She took a deep breath.

'Me and Nathan had a drunken fumble in the car park, just like in the song. You know I sort of fancied him. He said he liked me. It went from there. It was going okay too until his girlfriend showed up. Big scene in the car park. She slapped his face, then turned on me. Tried to punch me, I got out of the way. The smokers had a ringside seat. It was awful. I didn't know he had a girlfriend; I'd never have gone near him. Anyway, I wasn't in the wrong, he was, not like I was seeing anyone. Then he writes that horrid song about it, about me, making me out to be a slapper.'

'He didn't actually say that.'

'Might as well have,' Ella said, getting up and pacing as she spoke. 'And he sang that my breath tasted of gin – I don't even like gin, I never drink gin. Bastard. I can't ever go in there again and I don't ever want to even glimpse him again. I know he's Charlie's friend and band mate and all that, but no, never. Never.'

'Well, you probably won't ever see him again anyway. He left the band tonight. He's not very popular with *them* either. Left them in the lurch. You might have noticed he's rather good on guitar and he writes the only original songs they perform; all the rest are covers. I know you think that song is about you, but that aside, it was good.'

'Good, I'm glad he's leaving. They can find another guitarist. I hope he's going far away.'

'Back home, wherever that is. His dad's had an accident and broken his leg and Nathan has to go and help out.'

'Oh, he'll probably be back when his dad's better.'

'He says not,' Sam said. 'But they've left it open for him.' She shrugged.

'He's had a good night then hasn't he – upset us all.'

'I'm intrigued about the girlfriend though. I didn't know he had one. What was her name?'

'Don't know. Don't care.'

'What was she like?'

'I told you, I don't know.' Ella flumped back onto the sofa and sighed. 'Oh Sam, why can't I find someone who loves me the way that Charlie loves you? Why do I always have to want the bastard? Look at that Deano bloke last year. And that other one whose name I can't even remember.' Ella half laughed at herself.

Sam smiled; it was a thin smile that didn't go up to her eyes. 'Come on, it's not that bad.' She reached over and patted Ella's hand.

'Isn't it? Look at this place, I mean, what a dump. Who would have thought? When you think of that lovely flat I used to have, affordable rent, two bedrooms, two bathrooms, overlooking the river. Then I got above myself, didn't I? Thought I'd save for a deposit, buy my own. Moved back in with my mum. And I was doing all right until...' Ella's voice trailed away.

'You weren't to know…' Sam offered.

'I saved quite a bit, then we needed it when my mum got ill. You know all those years she worked there she only ever had a casual contract, so very little sick pay, they did their best but it wasn't enough.' Ella raised her shoulders, trying to shrug off the memory. 'We soon went through my savings, then at the end I wasn't getting paid and hey, here I am, in this shitty shoebox.' She gave off a bitter little laugh. 'The rent here is more than my mum's two bed place; can you believe that? I could have afforded that, well I *was* paying it. But I wasn't on the rent book, didn't have any rights. I had to clear out in two weeks. It's so unfair.

Sam glanced around the room, she nodded; it was hard not to agree.

'Sorry, I know you know all this. I just can't get it out of my head. I do appreciate you looking after those few bits of my mum's furniture in your garage. I will get them out as soon as…' Ella's voice trailed away. Just thinking about her mum's furniture upset her.

'There's no hurry,' Sam said.

'At least, I thought, at least when I get back to work things will improve. I knew Don Perkins had gone, and I thought, well I thought, I'd finally get what was rightly mine.' Ella stopped, took a breath and stood up again.

Sam stood up too, walked to the kitchen sink and ran them both a glass of cold water. She came back, a glass in each hand then looked for somewhere to put them.

'See what I mean; shoebox. Put them on the windowsill,' Ella said before continuing her rant. 'He was a liability Sam, Don. He made stupid mistakes; he drank some lunchtimes. I don't want to speak ill of him, because as a person I really liked him, but he was fairly useless really.'

'He retired,' Sam said flatly, answering a question Ella hadn't quite got around to asking.

'He isn't old enough.'

'For the company pension he was and he'd been there so long that…' Sam shrugged and looked away. Ella was aware that Sam had already said too much. 'Let's just say it was better that way.'

'But why bring that Gwynnie-Gladys-Barbie bitch in? Why couldn't they wait for me to come back?'

Sam shook her head, whispered, 'New broom?'

Ella laughed, despite herself. 'Well, it suits her.'

'Things will get better. Just give yourself time.'

'I don't think it's going to get better at work. I can't see how that situation is ever going to improve. I loathe Gwynnie and I think the feeling's mutual. I can't stand Tiffy either. They drive me mad and I have to take out my frustration on Barbie and the Troll…'

Sam stood up. 'Charlie will be here soon.'

'Yes,' Ella said, but her mind wasn't on Charlie; she was thinking ahead, thinking about what she needed to do. 'I'll ring around some of the agencies next week. Get my CV up to date and out there. That'll be a start, won't it?'

She waited for Sam to agree.

'If I can get a better job I can afford somewhere better than this?' She twirled around with her arms out. 'See, I can almost touch both walls.' Ella gave a bitter little laugh. She was doing that rather too much of late.

'All I want is a new job, a new home and a man. A good man. I want someone to adore me the way Charlie adores you. That can't be that difficult, can it? And I'm not doing internet dating, before you suggest it again.'

'Of course not.' Sam stepped forward and hugged her friend, before excusing herself to use the loo.

The intercom rang and Charlie was outside. Ella buzzed him in, opened the door and watched him come up the stairs. Sam was so lucky, not only was Charlie incredibly good looking – but then so was Sam – but he was kind, generous, sang in a band, had a good job. He was everything Ella wanted for herself. She felt a tinge of jealousy.

'You okay now?' he asked, as he bounded up the stairs. 'Sam ready to go?'

'Yeah. Just being stupid. You know me. Sam's just coming.' Ella watched Charlie's eyes as they flashed up and down her face and body. 'Excuse the frog outfit.' She laughed, expecting him to join in, but he looked away.

'What are you doing over the weekend?' Sam asked, as she said goodbye.

'I've got to tackle my mum's paperwork. I know there are unpaid bills in there; bank accounts that need closing. All sorts. I can't move forward until I've dealt with that lot.'

'That's the spirit.' Sam patted Ella on the back. 'I meant to ask, how did you get home?'

'The drummer's friend gave me a lift. Really surprised me actually, she was driving a brand-new Lexus. It didn't really go with the tattoos.'

'He said he hardly knew her.' Charlie said, helping

Sam into her jacket. 'Said they'd met years ago, then out of the blue she rang up and asked where we were playing tonight. What was her name?'

'She didn't say and we didn't ask,' Ella said. 'She was too scary.'

'So who was she?' Sam frowned.

They looked from face to face, shrugging.

Ella went downstairs and waved Sam and Charlie off. She stood at the main entrance watching them as they drove away. Just before she stepped back inside her upstairs neighbour came in. She'd met him once or twice on the stairs. He was a little older than her and hot, very hot. She knew he lived in a rather more spacious flat than she did; he had at least two bedrooms.

'Hi,' he said, giving her a great big, beaming smile.

'Hi,' Ella beamed back. Well, a smile like that from a hot guy would lift any girl's spirit.

He went up the stairs and Ella followed him. Just before he went up the next flight of stairs he turned and smiled at Ella again, it was almost a laugh.

Wow, that felt good. Who knows, maybe her prayers were being answered already.

She went back into her bedsit, closed the door behind her, locked it, leant on it. Sam was right, things could only get better.

She went into the bathroom, saw herself in the mirror for the first time that night. A big brown stain on her left breast, it looked as though she was leaking chocolate milk. No wonder Charlie had looked so embarrassed and why hadn't Sam told her?

'Oh my God,' she said aloud.

But it was much worse. No wonder the guy upstairs had smiled to the point of laughter. What the hell must he think of her? Frog outfit, chocolate breast and the biggest, brownest, chocolate clown moustache smeared across her face.

'Oh God.'

Three

There were six boxes in the stack. Ella knew what was in the bottom three – she had packed them – mostly bills to be paid, credit cards to be stopped and bank statements. The top three she hadn't packed, just retrieved from the top of her mum's wardrobe and brought them back with her. She'd spotted paperwork and old photos in the top of two of the boxes; the third was taped shut.

It was difficult to know where to start. The taped box was green and someone – her mum she supposed – had drawn a big smiley face in red marker pen on the side. Should she start with that one? Decisions, decisions. This was why she hadn't begun this job already. Which one should she start with? She looked at the smiley face and smiled back at it. Then she watched in astonishment as the box slowly slid off the pile and onto the floor.

'It has to be you then,' she said, dropping down beside it and starting to unpeel the tape. It was thick, black waterproof tape that even when peeled off the box still retained far too much of its stickiness. It managed to attach itself to her hand, and her hand to her jumper. The more she pulled it, the more it stuck; finally it gave way and then rebounded. Suddenly her sleeve was stuck to the neck of her sweater and no amount of yanking seemed to loosen it. If anything, it was getting more stuck; the two sticky faces of the tape were welding together.

'Oh for God's sake,' Ella yelled out. At that exact moment, there was a loud rapping on the door. 'What now,' Ella yelled. She rose from the floor; her hand attached to her neck and peered through the spy hole. It was her hot neighbour from upstairs. What the hell could he want?

She stood behind her front door wishing him away. She cringed at the memory of greeting him the previous night with a hot chocolate clown-face moustache.

He rapped the door again. He wasn't going away. He had probably heard her yelling so knew she was in.

Slowly she opened the door, careful to keep the hand that was stuck to her neck hidden behind it. 'Hi,' she said.

'I took delivery of a parcel for you yesterday when you were out.' He smiled broadly at her; he was even more gorgeous when he smiled like that. He held out a large box.

'I'm not expecting anything.'

He glanced down at the parcel then at the number on Ella's door. 'Definitely for you.'

Ella looked at the parcel and shuddered. She put out her hand and tried to take it from him but it was far too big and heavy for one hand.

'I think you'll need to open the door wider and use both hands,' he said, half laughing.

'Um, right.' She opened the door a little bit more.

'Maybe you could just put it down on the floor and slide it in.'

He looked her up and down for a moment, then suddenly seemed to realise that she might need help. 'I'll bring it in,' he said, all brightness and smiles.

'No. Really. That's okay, just put it on the floor.'

'I'm ready now, Hal,' a seductive female voice called from behind him. Ella looked over her neighbour's shoulder and saw the owner of the voice. She was the proverbial uber-glamorous, leggy blond. Her teeth sparkled when she spoke. 'Oh, sorry,' she said. 'Didn't realise you'd still be messing around with that.'

Oww. Ella suspected the *that* referred to was her and not the parcel.

'It's a bit heavy. I'm just going to take it inside.'

'Well do hurry, Hal, or we'll be late,' Leggy Blond said, pushing up close behind him.

'No, there's really no need. Just leave it on the floor. I'll sort it out myself.' Ella could feel a cold sweat rising along her hairline. Behind the door she frantically tried to pull her hand away from her neck; it just wasn't budging.

Leggy Blond nudged Hal in the back knocking him off balance, he lunged forward and knocked Ella's door flying open. Now Ella stood exposed, her wrist glued to her neck, thick black tape visibly secure.

'Bondage,' said Leggy Blond, laughing. 'Well, whatever gives you your kicks. Come on Hal, dump it and let's go.'

'Sorry,' he said, giving Ella the same look you might give to someone caught with their pants down in a field. 'I'll just leave it here.' He put the parcel on the floor and slid it towards her with his foot.

'Could have done that in the first place,' Ella said,

but Hal and the blond were already halfway down the stairs; laughing loudly together, no doubt at her expense.

She kicked the parcel against the wall and closed the door, then turned to see herself in the mirror.

'Oh God,' she screeched again. Not only was her hand stuck to her neck, but a line of black tape ran down the zip of her jeans and a ball of tape dangled between her legs. How could she have not seen that? She slid down the wall, sunk down to the floor. It seemed she was destined to make a fool of herself in front of her hot neighbour – and his leggy girlfriend.

She sat there for a few minutes, her cheeks burning with humiliation. Bondage. The thought horrified her. Finally getting up she moved towards the kitchenette and rummaged in the drawers for scissors, then cut herself out of the black tape. Once free she went back to the parcel, turned it around and was about to open it, when she read the label. The name of the previous tenant glared at her in bold blue font. All that humiliation for nothing. She'd have to return the parcel to sender later. She kicked it into the corner and went back to her smiley face box.

Rather than peeling the tape now, she used the scissors to cut through it, shame she hadn't done that in the first place. She thought of Hal and his girlfriend, no doubt regaling their friends with the story. Why was life so shit?

Once the box was finally open the contents brought a lump to her throat. Baby clothes. Just a few items, all tiny. What the hell had her mother kept them for? She took them out gingerly and piled them on the sofa. She found a small book underneath, its cover well worn. She opened it. On the first page in her mother's handwriting were the words: Child of Delight. She turned the page. A baby photo. Her mum's smiling, youthful face, and Ella's new-born one, side by side. In the background a hospital bed, clinical green curtains. The date on the bottom of the photo – Ella's birthday – the actual day she had been born. She must have been hours old. Her mother looked radiant; her eyes shiny with happiness. Ella wondered if the photo had been taken by her father. She swallowed the lump in her throat.

It wasn't a proper photo album, more like an old-fashioned autograph book, the photograph was hand glued onto the cream page.

She turned the page. Another photo of Ella, this time taken on a self-printing Polaroid camera, the image faded with age. Ella standing up but not on her own, a pair of masculine hands holding hers. She was laughing, looking pleased with herself. Underneath the photo the date – Ella's first birthday.

She turned the page. Ella on her second birthday, this time both her parents clearly visible, Ella between them being swung in the air. Three laughing, happy faces. In the background, what looked like an allotment. Ella wondered who had taken this snapshot.

Ella on her third birthday – a hat, a cake. Her dad's hands tight around her as he lifted her to blow out the candles.

Her fourth birthday – on her dad's knee.

Her fifth birthday – on a swing, her mum's laughing face as she pushed Ella.

Her sixth birthday – Ella's face squashed between her parents' faces.

Her seventh birthday – a zoo trip, her dad holding her up to see the penguins.

So far, they were just happy family photos documenting every birthday. But there wouldn't be any more with her dad in. Ella remembered that day at the zoo. Remembered the big row on the way home, remembered not understanding why her parents were shouting at each other. Remembered the next morning when her mother told her daddy had gone and there would be just the two of them now. And that's how it had been; Ella and her mum. Now it was just Ella. Why was life so shit?

She turned the pages, a different photo of Ella every year, sometimes with her mum, sometimes on her own. Every year and Ella hadn't known that they were in this little album: Child of Delight. The last photo – a selfie taken on Ella's phone which her mum insisted she download and print – was taken just after her mum had been diagnosed. They'd had no idea then what the future would bring. Just as well.

She hadn't had her birthday this year so there wasn't a picture missing, not yet anyway. Ella turned the page over; there were plenty of empty pages. She closed the book, put it back into the box, piled the baby clothes back on top and pushed the lid down. If she'd had any black tape she would have taped it shut.

The next box had a few framed photos on the top, Ella was more than familiar with these, she'd seen them every day at her mum's, on the mantelpiece, on the sideboard. She thought about that lovely oak sideboard, wished she could have shoehorned it into this miniscule place instead of storing it in Sam and Charlie's garage. She sighed and forced herself to remember Sam's 'things will get better' phrase. She had to believe they would.

There were other albums in there too, ones Ella had

seen before. She flicked through the photos quickly, careful not to linger too long. She loved the photos of her mum laughing with her friends, laughing with Ella – the two on them on holiday, on holiday in a group. Ella's eighteenth birthday party, her mum's fortieth, fiftieth. She slammed the cover closed. 'Must not get maudlin,' she said to herself, her voice sounding croaky. 'Things will get better,' she repeated her mantra.

She pulled out another photo album, an old one she'd never seen before. There were endless pictures of her as a baby, even the typical naked baby shot, the one her mum would have shown to Ella's future husband if there'd ever been one. Her dad popped up in the photos. There was a picture of them both outside an old cottage. Ella had vague memories of it, some relatives of her dad's, visits that her mum dreaded which stopped when he left.

Ella shut the album, put it away.

She stacked the three boxes back in the corner tightly against the wall, she wouldn't need to go in them again, but she wasn't sure just what she would do with them. Then she had an idea.

She went to her wardrobe and rummaged around for the tablecloth she'd brought back from her mum's. It was blue and white, embroidered on the edges, very pretty; Ella didn't remember her mum ever using it. She threw it artfully over the boxes. Perfect. It was just the right height for a table lamp. She didn't have one so she put a scented candle on top. It was the one Sam had bought her as a moving in present – wasted on the grotty bedsit.

'Ta da.' She laughed out loud, holding out her hands. 'That's better, and now I'm talking to myself.' She shook her head, made herself a cup of coffee and sat down to work on the next box.

By mid-afternoon she had cracked open a bottle of wine, probably not the best of ideas but she needed something to help her work through the boxes. Anyway, it was Saturday.

She put on a *Human League* CD that she'd found in one of the boxes. It was one of her mum's favourites and Ella remembered her playing it often during her childhood. She got up to dance, flailing her arms around, enjoying herself, all by herself. *'Don't you want me baby?'* she sang at the top of her voice. She had to be careful not to disturb the carefully made piles of bills and bank statements as well as her to-do list, which now ran to three pages. Finally, she fell onto the sofa exhausted. And dozed off.

When she awoke the music had stopped, the light was fading outside and her stomach was rumbling. In her mini-fridge she found a low-fat yogurt, half a tin of beans and another bottle of cheap wine. She had meant to go shopping. Too late now she thought, and she suspected she might be over the drink-drive limit.

Pizza. That would be good. She could wander down to the place at the end of the road – *DONNY'S PIZZA AND KEBAB HOUSE EAT IN TAKE AWAY WE DELIVER*. The sign always made her laugh, all the letters were the same giant size and in lurid purple with no punctuation. She'd never used Donny's, but there was always a queue, especially late at night.

She pulled on her boots and coat, grabbed her purse and keys and let herself out of the flat.

It was only about seven-thirty but already there was a queue at Donny's. She joined on the end, craning her neck to study the menu through the window. Hawaiian, that's what she would have, with a cheese crust. And cheesy garlic bread. And rocky road ice cream. And lemonade, a great big bottle. Well, it was Saturday night and a girl had to treat herself sometimes.

The man in front of her turned and smiled, he had an array of yellow teeth, two were missing. She flashed him a very brief, polite smile then stared past him.

'You come for your...' he nodded his head from side to side. She wasn't sure if he was drunk. Who was she to judge?

'Pizza,' Ella said, really not wanting to get into conversation with him. She could smell the smoke of a thousand stale fags on him, mixed with old beer and earth and dirt and something else horrible. She felt her throat flinch involuntarily. She tried not to gag.

'And hash brownies,' he said, laughing.

Ella didn't answer. Did he actually mean what she thought he meant? Surely not. She kept looking ahead, ignoring him while trying to make it look as though she wasn't.

The queue moved forward. Smelly, gappy-teethed man was inside the shop. He lit a cigarette. From behind the counter someone shouted at him to put it out. He grumbled, flicked it behind him, it caught on Ella's coat. She jumped and quickly wiped it off her front, burning her hand in the process and squealing sharply.

'Oops, these things happen,' Smelly said, and lurched forward to wipe down the front of her coat. Ella jumped out of his reach. 'I was only trying to help. Sod you, Miss Snotty Gob.'

Oh God, this was what Ella had been trying to avoid. It always happened to her; the freak always found her.

'I said I was only trying to help,' he was shouting

now; his head wobbling wildly from side-to-side.

Ella tried hard not to react, not to show the disgust or the fear on her face.

'Back off,' a voice said from behind her.

'Okay, okay. Just trying to help.' Smelly stepped away, the queue moved forward and he was suddenly at the counter.

Ella turned to see who her knight in shining armour was – not that she needed one, she wasn't completely useless.

It was her hot neighbour from upstairs. Well it would be, wouldn't it?

'Thanks,' she muttered into her boots, embarrassed, yet again.

'My pleasure,' he said. 'Anytime. We keep running into each other, don't we? I'm Hal.' Well, she already knew that. He put his hand out to shake hers.

'Ella.' They shook hands in the queue outside Donny's Pizza and Kebab House. Behind her someone sniggered.

'No doubt we'll meet again,' he said as he walked away.

Ella put her order in. Smelly had gone and so had Hal and the food looked great, and the place clean.

'Hash browns with that? On special,' the guy behind the counter asked. Did he just wink at her? Of course not.

'No thanks,' Ella said, and even to her own ears she sounded indignant.

It was starting to rain as Ella left the take away with two boxes and an ice cream carton balanced in one hand and a large bottle of lemonade in the other. Her purse and keys were stuffed into her pocket. She should have brought a bag, but it didn't matter, she didn't have far to go and the pizza smelt so good her mouth was watering. She put her head down and quickened her pace.

Bang.

She walked straight into Hal's girlfriend.

The lemonade bottle fell from her hand, hit the pavement with a thud and the lid shot off like a champagne cork. The lemonade erupted volcano-like, spewing a sticky fountain high into the air. Ella stepped back and avoided it. Leggy Blond wasn't so quick. The lemonade hit her full in the face and hair. Ella stood staring; she didn't know what to do. Leggy Blond screamed and screamed but seemed unable to get away.

Finally, the lemonade fountain stopped, the bottle now half empty. Hal, who Ella hadn't noticed before, grabbed the lid and put it back on the bottle and, with a wink, handed it to Ella.

'What sort of moron are you?' Leggy Blond screamed.

'Sorry,' Ella said, and scuttled back home, leaving her dripping on the pavement. She could hear Hal trying to soothe his girlfriend.

Ella allowed herself a damn good laugh once she was safely inside her bedsit.

Quite an evening, and Donny's pizza tasted damn good too.

Sunday found Ella back in the boxes. Her to-do list was growing but she was winning the battle. Ella had fantasised that there might be a bit of money stashed away in secret bank accounts – but it turned out, that's all it was, a fantasy. If she was lucky there might be enough in her mum's only account to settle all the bills. If she wasn't, she'd be dipping into her own miniscule savings. She also knew that there was no windfall insurance policy just waiting to pay out either; her mum had never had enough spare cash to fund one. Ella tried hard not to be disappointed, and then felt guilty for even thinking it.

By early afternoon she was at the bottom of the last box. This was the most recent mail; many of the envelopes hadn't even been opened. Ella could clearly remember just taking them from the letter box and stacking them on the hall table. They were from the time her mum had been dying and worrying about mail had been the last thing on Ella's mind.

She began to open them, another bill, another bank statement, another credit card statement. Fortunately, her mum had never been a spendthrift, she'd never had the opportunity to be – there'd never been any financial support from her dad after he'd disappeared. Ella didn't even know where he'd gone or where he was now. Her mum had once told her he'd gone to Australia after he'd left them, but Ella didn't know if that was true. Should she try to track him down, tell him about her mum? What was the point?

She carried on sorting, bills by utility, bank statements, a rubbish pile. Fortunately, the rubbish pile was the biggest.

Then she came across a letter addressed to her: Miss Ella Taylor, it was care of her mum's address. Interesting, whoever had sent it didn't think she lived there, which of course she hadn't until fairly recently. She ripped the envelope open and pulled out the letter. She read it twice before she could fully understand it. It reminded her of the dodgy spam emails she received telling her she was owed money by an African prince.

'Dear Miss Taylor
We believe you are related to Mr Kenneth Stanley Taylor and Mrs Nora Elisabeth Taylor, late of Spring Cottage, Lyffingdon, Wiltshire.
I should be grateful if you could contact these offices at your earliest convenience where you may learn something to your advantage.
Yours sincerely
Evermore Baker

'Evermore Baker,' Ella said aloud, what sort of name was that? She studied the letterhead: Baker, Baker, Baker, Baker and Cake. It was a cruel joke. Who the hell would send something like that to her when her mum was dying? How spiteful. She threw the letter down on the rubbish pile and went back to the box. She was nearly finished, and when she was done, she had promised herself a trip to the supermarket to do her shopping. 'I know how to live life to the full,' Ella said to herself, excited at the prospect of finishing the sorting.

Within an hour the piles were neatly stacked in order of priority, the rubbish was in a bag ready to be taken to work and put through the shredder for recycling. It was nearly three, she just had time to grab her coat, bag and keys and get to Asda before it shut at four.

* * *

'Ella,' Sam called from across the car park just as Ella finished loading her shopping into the boot. Sam came running over, a big smile on her face. 'How's your box sorting going?' she asked.

'Done. Just need to action things now. Big weight

off my mind,' Ella said, laughing.

'Don't suppose you found that crock of gold you were looking for?'

'No. But it could be worse; I didn't find any nasties either. Oh, except for one cruel joke.'

'What?'

Ella told Sam about the letter from Baker, Baker, Baker, Baker and Cake.

'Have you checked them out?' Sam said, pulling her phone from her handbag.

'No,' Ella said, totally unconvinced as to their authenticity.

'What was their address?'

'I can't remember, not local.' She shook her head and started walking away with her trolley, taking it back to the trolley shelter. When she returned Sam greeted her with a big smile.

'Guess what?'

'They don't exist,' Ella said, opening her car door.

'You're wrong. They do. Here's their website.' Sam held her phone under Ella's nose. 'See.'

Ella glanced at it; there wasn't much to see on their mobile site.

'Not convinced,' she said, turning away.

'Ring them in the morning. What have you got to lose?'

Ella shrugged. 'Whatever you say, Sam.' She laughed, gave her friend a big hug and got into her car.

She would not be ringing them in the morning, she was quite certain of that.

* * *

Ella didn't sleep well that night; she never did on a

Sunday night, that Monday morning feeling started early, especially since Gwynnie's arrival. She awoke with a start at 2.30am, sitting up quickly and breathing heavily. She'd been dreaming but she couldn't remember what the dream was about, only that she didn't like it, that she felt afraid. She got up, got a glass of water, climbed back into bed and tried to doze off. But her mind kept returning to the letter from Baker, Baker, Baker, Baker and Cake. She just couldn't believe any company, never mind a firm of solicitors, would have such a stupid name. It had to be a joke – yet Sam had found their website. She'd search for them properly tomorrow.

She kept thinking about the people mentioned in the letter that she was supposedly related to. It had to be on her dad's side because they had the same surname. She thought hard; she had the vaguest of memories of an old aunt and uncle of her dad's who they used to visit. Could it be them?

She tossed and turned and, in the end, gave up trying to get to sleep. She turned on the light and noticed the boxes hiding under the tablecloth. The photo albums were in there. Sighing, she pulled the cloth off and started going through them.

It was nearly four when she located what she was looking for; she knew it was in there because she'd already glimpsed it. Finally she found the right album, the right pictures. An old cottage with a thatched roof. An old man leaning against a spade, smiling, squinting into the sunlight. An old woman hugging a huge mixing bowl, stirring its contents with a wooden spoon. These people looked vaguely familiar but, in all honesty, she couldn't remember their names. She certainly couldn't remember how long ago she'd visited them. Were they the ones?

If it was true, and she still had serious doubts, they couldn't have left her much; surely they would have left anything worthwhile to their own family. She wondered what her dad had got. Wondered where he was.

She kept the album out, but put all the others back in the boxes and covered them with the cloth again. She finally managed to go back to sleep just as the alarm went off. Urgh – Monday morning.

* * *

'Emergency team meeting, emergency team meeting,' Gwynnie screeched, as Ella walked into the office. Everyone else was already there; even though Ella was actually twenty minutes early because she'd been planning to slyly google the solicitors. Gwynnie stood up, she was pink in the face and excited. 'Come on team, I've booked a room.'

Ella shrugged her coat off and switched on her computer and inwardly cursed Gladys the Barbie doll. Everyone else filed out towards the meeting room as Ella picked up her notepad and pen and wondered what could be so important; she hadn't even had time for a coffee and she needed one to get through one of these meetings.

'Well team,' Gwynnie said, grinning and giggling. 'Great news. We've been picked to manage the transition of the Eldorite stock lines into Gubbins' inventory. Isn't that wonderful news?' Gwynnie started clapping her hands like a child at preschool.

'It's just fab news, Gwynnie,' Tiffy said, joining in the clapping.

Ella caught Ben's eye and he winked at her. Kevin

looked away. It was hardly breaking news, they'd been chasing Eldorite for months, and their department would naturally handle stock lines transition, it was what they did.

'So exciting. So exciting.' Gwynnie was squeaking now. Ella almost felt embarrassed for her as she grew more and more excited. Ella zoned her out, thought about the letter rescued from the rubbish and now in her handbag, and wondered when she'd get the opportunity to check out its authenticity and ring the solicitors' office that sounded like a tacky bakery shop.

'So, Ella, that okay with you?' Gwynnie said, and waited for a reply.

'Of course, of course,' Ella said, wondering what the hell she was agreeing to.

'That's settled then. Ella will project manage and Tiffy will be the controller.' Gwynnie tapped the table with her glossy cerise nails.

'Nice nails, Gwynnie,' Tiffy said.

'Thanks, Tiffy.'

'That's quite a responsibility for you, Ella,' Gwynnie said, turning her attention back to Ella.

'Not really. I've done several of these. Anyway, what's a controller?'

'That's Tiffy's role,' Gwynnie said, standing up, signalling the end of the meeting.

'Yes, but what does the controller do?'

'Control, of course.' Gwynnie held the door open and, as Tiffy was walking through it, she turned and gave Ella a sly smile over her shoulder.

Back at their desks everyone was quiet. Gwynnie pinged Ella an email giving her more background and a lot of attachments. Ben sent her one with several exclamation marks and a sad emoji. Ella dropped the troll on the floor and pressed her foot hard down on it. She watched to see if Tiffy reacted, but Tiffy's shudder was probably just a reaction to the air-con kicking in. Then Ella reached into her drawer and bent Barbie's legs backwards right over her head.

'I can smell that smell again,' Tiffy said, her nose going up like a beagle's.

Ella shut the drawer; she wasn't in the mood for one of Tiffy's histrionic dramas.

* * *

It was nearly lunchtime before Ella got the opportunity to go online. She quickly found the Baker, Baker, Baker, Baker and Cake website. It looked very professional and they were listed on their local directory and their reviews were good. Okay, she conceded, the letter could be genuine.

She slipped into an empty meeting room at lunchtime and made her phone call. The voice that answered was female; Ella had an image of some elderly secretary who'd been there since the beginning of time. She left Ella on hold while she checked out the details; she was so long Ella almost hung up.

'Miss Taylor,' the woman said. 'Mr Cake can see you at three tomorrow.'

'I don't know if I can make that. Anyway, the letter is from Mr Baker, Evermore Baker.' She struggled to suppress a giggle.

'Mr Baker is currently incapacitated. Mr Cake is fully conversant with the case. I'm afraid his next available appointment after tomorrow is in two weeks. Would you prefer to wait?'

Ella thought for a moment, could she wait? No, she

couldn't.

'Okay, tomorrow will be fine,' she said. 'Thank you.'

'Miss Taylor, do please bring your birth certificate and passport with you.'

'Why?' Ella didn't like the sound of that.

'So we can ensure that you are who you say you are.'

'Okay,' Ella said, frowning. She supposed they had as much right to verify her as she had them. She ended the call.

Now she'd have to tell Gwynnie that she needed to leave early. But in the meantime, she went and found Sam.

Four

Ella arrived early for work the next day, thirty-five minutes to be exact. She expected to see Gwynnie or Tiffy or both there before her, but she found herself alone. In fact, there wasn't a single person on the entire open-plan floor. Not one. Good, she thought as she waited for her computer to start up.

Once on, she used the time to search through the vacancies on the local recruitment websites. Her heart sank; there wasn't much to tempt her.

'Things will get better,' she muttered her mantra to herself, as she closed down the browser and returned to her work.

Minutes later she noticed two people in the distance. Across the car park Gwynnie and Tiffy had just parked their cars and were heading towards the building, their heads horribly close together. Ella watched them; Barbie and the Troll.

She heard the main office door bang and slumped down into her chair, confident that they wouldn't see her at first. They were giggling together, like schoolgirls. Ella was paranoid enough to think they were giggling about her.

'Oh, hello,' Gwynnie said, suddenly spotting Ella. 'You're in early.'

'Very early,' Tiffy said. If she thought it was under her breath she was mistaken.

'Yes, very, very early.' Ella smiled broadly at Tiffy who blushed, then busied herself at her desk. 'I have to leave early.'

Gwynnie's eyebrows shot up in question.

'Hospital appointment,' Ella mouthed at her, lying though her teeth. She had considered telling Gwynnie the truth, but she didn't want her knowing her business, and she especially didn't want her discussing it with the Troll.

Gwynnie nodded slowly. 'You don't have to make time up for medical appointments,' she said, without any attempt at discretion.

'Just aware of our new project.' Ella glanced over at Tiffy whose eyes had narrowed even though she was affecting not to listen.

'Fab.' Gwynnie took off her jacket; she was wearing a cerise pink top with a soft pink scarf draped around her neck.

'Oh, is it Pink Day today?' Ella oozed mock interest.

'No, no. You can see that I'm wearing pink then?'

Oh shit. 'Not really. I'm colour blind, remember.' Another lie. 'It just looks very bright to me, though I know pink is your favourite colour.'

Gwynnie gave Ella a look that screamed liar but she remained silent.

Ella got on with her work – the exciting project – which as far as Ella was concerned was business as usual. It was her job to check every product before approving it for addition to the Gubbins' inventory.

Then it was over to Ben and Kevin.

At ten past two Ella started making preparations to leave which Tiffy picked up on immediately.

'Ella, could you give me a status update please?'

Ella blinked several times at Tiffy. What the hell was she talking about?

'Well, I am the project controller. I need to be up to speed.' Tiffy glared, she seemed to be daring Ella to challenge her.

'Okay,' Ella said, standing up, wheeling her chair round to Tiffy's desk and sitting up close to her. Ella sniffed. 'What's that smell? Has something gone off in your bin?'

'I don't know what it is. I've complained to the building manager.'

'Oh. It's horrible. Poor you.' That's mean of me, thought Ella, but… 'Okay,' she began to speak very quickly, 'the current situation is that seventeen lines are acceptable and I've passed them for inclusion onto our inventory; six lines are not acceptable because of either quality or ethical issues; and two lines are at question due to source issues. The remaining one-hundred-and-forty-seven lines have not been assessed yet.' Ella waited and watched Tiffy blink as she tried to process the information, before continuing, 'So I've covered quite a few lines for one day – good job I started so early – but at this stage I have to say that I have picked off the low hanging fruit, so progress might not be so speedy on the remaining lines. Is that okay for you?'

'Um, yes. That sounds excellent,' Tiffy said, and Ella could see in her eyes that Tiffy didn't know whether she was being hoodwinked or not. She wasn't. Ella took her work seriously. She knew the processes inside out. She was conscientious. That's why it was all so damn unfair.

'Okay, as controller I expect you'll want a daily update, shall I schedule something?' Ella got up and began to wheel her chair back to her own desk.

'Um. Yes, please. That would be good.'

Ella sat down, tried not to smile to herself as she shut her computer down. Just before she left she squeezed troll's head and dropped it into the drawer with Ruben's smelly rag.

'Sleep tight,' she whispered as she locked her desk.

* * *

It was one of those nice days in spring, chilly but bright. Ella breathed in the fresh air around her as she walked across Gubbins' car park. The drive to the town where Baker, Baker, Baker, Baker and Cake's offices were took less time than she expected and she soon found a parking space on the high street.

She got out of the car and looked around, spotted their offices, then realised she had fifteen minutes to spare. She really didn't want to be that early. Then she spied a quaint department store. She had enough time to pop into their food hall and treat herself to something nice for tea.

If this appointment turned out to be good news, then the meal would be a celebration and if it didn't, it would be compensation. Either way she couldn't lose.

She went through the doors and stopped to get her bearings. It was a large store squeezed into a small space and everything was tightly packed in. The floors were wooden and rickety, ancient ceiling fans moved warmed, stale air around. Time warp, thought Ella, suppressing the urge to giggle. When she saw the sign for the food hall she made straight for it.

Then her phone rang. She kept walking as she fumbled in her bag. Finally finding her phone, she saw that the caller was from work. Was this some sort of joke? As far as they were concerned she was at a hospital appointment. What could be so important, so urgent that they needed to ring her? She thought of Tiffy or Gwynnie needing to know some trivial detail immediately. Well, Ella thought, I won't be answering. How can they expect me to? She waited for the call to go to voicemail then fumbled the phone back into her bag, seething all the while.

Seething so much she didn't notice the little plinth in front of her.

Seething so much she didn't notice the display on the plinth.

Seething so much that she didn't see the mannequin, mistook it for a person and was apologising profusely as she bowled into it before realising what it was. Ella and the mannequin were sprawled across the aisle, their limbs tangled in a grotesque dance. One of the mannequin's fingers poked Ella in the eye.

'Ouch,' she screeched.

'Oh, dear,' a female voice said.

Ella looked up and saw a woman of indeterminate age, her hair, either ash blond or pearl grey – it was hard to tell, especially with a mannequin's finger in her eye – rolled into a neat chignon at the back of her head. Her skirt suit was a lightweight tweed and she wore a heather coloured blouse beneath it. The woman, the epitome of calm respectability, was staring straight at Ella; she had probably witnessed the whole humiliating show.

'Let me help you,' the woman said, offering a hand as Ella struggled to get up.

Up close Ella could see that the woman was probably in her sixties and the fact that she was trying to help Ella up just added to the indignity.

'No, it's all right, I'm fine,' Ella said, wincing as she finally pulled herself from the mannequin's evil, rigid grip. Her eye was throbbing and already starting to close up. Ella swayed. Suddenly a chair was pushed under her and she was being helped to sit. Could it get any worse? Someone had called for the first aider and the other shoppers were either crowding around her or gawping as they passed. Ella did a double take out of her good eye; she imagined that one of those rubber-neckers was Nathan. Of course it couldn't be, could it?

Why is my life such shit? Ella whined inwardly as she attempted to stand up but was prevented by a firm hand on her shoulder, a damp cloth on her eye and a clipboard in front of her face.

'We have to fill in an accident form,' a disembodied male voice said.

'Must we? Really, I'm fine.'

But there was no escape, she was forced to give her name, age, address, phone number, even her email address, then recount what happened. It seemed to go on and on. Ella got her phone out and looked at the time. It was now after three.

'I really do have to go now,' she said, finally able to stand up. 'I have an appointment, I'm already late.'

'Just sign here.' A pen was thrust into her hand and Ella prepared to sign.

'I think not,' a voice said. It was the woman who had helped her up, whom Ella hadn't realised was still there. The woman then proceeded to disperse the crowd and dismiss the store officials. 'I'm Shirley Cavendish,' she said, offering Ella her hand, 'and you are Ella Taylor.'

'Yes,' Ella said, realising that half the staff and customers now knew all her personal details. Hurriedly she shook hands while at the same time looking towards the exit. 'Thank you. I really need to go.'

'Of course. This way.'

Ella cringed as Shirley Cavendish guided her towards the doors. Once outside, Ella turned to thank her and say goodbye, but Shirley Cavendish wasn't leaving.

'Are you quite all right?'

'I'm fine. I need to get to my appointment. I'm late.'

'Don't worry. I've let Mr Cake know you've been detained.'

'What?'

'I work for Mr Cake and the Mr Bakers. We spoke on the phone yesterday. I made the appointment for you.' She offered Ella her arm and Ella just gave in and took it. Together they tottered down the street.

Once in the offices of Baker, Baker, Baker, Baker and Cake, Shirley made Ella a strong coffee and produced an ice pack for her eye.

'You've been very kind,' Ella said, once she was starting to get her composure back.

'The least I could do. I think you will have quite a shiner there.'

'Goes with my luck,' Ella half laughed.

'Mr Cake will see you when you're ready.'

'Thanks. Actually, before I do see him, what's with the name of this place? Is it a joke? Baker, Baker, Baker, Baker and Cake?'

'Not really a joke. More a bunch of men behaving like little boys. They're siblings, except for Mr Cake, he's a cousin. They couldn't agree on a company name, so they listed themselves in age order.' Shirley Cavendish shook her head. 'Ready?'

'I meant their names,' Ella muttered. 'They should run a bakery.'

But Shirley didn't respond, just led the way towards an office, where Ella was left alone with Mr Cake who stood up to shake hands. He was tall, rake thin and wore half-moon glasses perched on the end of his nose. A fringe of steel grey hair ringed his shiny bald head. He peered at Ella over his glasses then waved her into a chair without saying a word. He started looking through the papers in front of him.

Ella sat and watched him. When he didn't speak immediately she glanced around the room. It was panelled in dark wood from floor to ceiling and looked ancient, just like Mr Cake. Age order, Shirley had said, so if Mr Cake was the youngest, how old must the others be? A mahogany nameplate in front of him spelt out his name in bold gold lettering; Aloysius Cake. Like the bear in Brideshead Revisited, Ella thought and, while suppressing a nervous giggle, snorted.

'Ahem,' Mr Cake said, looking at her.

Ella looked back at him and smiled. She didn't expect him to smile back; he was far too austere for that. But suddenly he did and his face lit up. Ella found herself wanting to laugh again.

'I must say, Miss Taylor,' he began. 'How sorry I am to hear of your mishap in the store.'

'Just me being clumsy.' Ella shrugged.

'Mrs Cavendish tells me you didn't sign anything.'

'No, she stopped me. Why?'

'We wouldn't want you admitting any liability.'

'Oh, it was my fault. I wasn't looking where I was going.'

'Nevertheless, we wouldn't want them suing you.'

'What? Why would they?' Ella felt alarmed.

'Oh, I doubt they will. But you can never be sure. And,' Mr Cake leaned across the desk as if sharing a secret, 'they cannot be sure that *you* won't sue *them* now.' He laughed a wicked, knowing laugh.

'I don't think that's likely,' Ella said, not sure where this was going.

'Quite.' He paused. 'Now to the business in hand. You have your passport and birth certificate?'

Ella retrieved them from her bag and handed them over. Mr Cake gave them a cursory glance then rang a brass bell on his desk. Shirley Cavendish reappeared, and took Ella's documents away.

'Just need to check them.' She smiled. 'Don't worry; I'll bring them straight back.'

'Okay,' Ella said, feeling a little anxious.

'Nothing to worry about,' Mr Cake said. 'After all that's happened we just need to be sure.'

'What do you mean?'

Mr Cake gave Ella the briefest of smiles. 'I need to ask you a few questions. Are you the daughter of John Albert Taylor, late of Aberdeen, Scotland?'

'I might be,' Ella said. 'My dad was called John Taylor, it's on my birth certificate, but I thought he lived in Australia.'

Aloysius Cake nodded sagely, but didn't respond to Ella's comment.

'Are you aware of any other siblings you might have?'

'No.' Ella felt sudden alarm. 'Should I be? Are there any?' It had never occurred to her that her dad might have had more children.

'Are you a blood relative of Mr Kenneth Stanley Taylor and Mrs Nora Elisabeth Taylor, late of Spring Cottage, Lyffingdon, Wiltshire?'

'Well, I might be. I vaguely remember an old aunt and uncle who lived in some old cottage somewhere.' Ella shrugged. 'Is that who you mean? I don't really remember much about them.'

There was a tentative knock on the door and Shirley Cavendish came back into room. She nodded to Mr Cake, gave Ella her passport and birth certificate back, then left.

'It would appear that everything is in order and you are who you say you are.'

'Well, actually, *you* said I was who I say I am. *You* wrote to me.' Ella was confused.

'Quite.' Mr Cake shuffled some more papers and looked earnestly at Ella. 'The situation is thus,' he began. 'You have inherited your late great aunt and uncle's property.'

'What? What? I'm sorry, could you say that again?'

'You have inherited Spring Cottage, a substantial property needing some updating, in a picturesque village, together with some freehold land,' Mr Cake read aloud from his papers.

Ella sat stunned into silence, trying to take it all in. 'Well… Wow,' she eventually said. 'I don't know what to say. Why me? Why not my dad?'

Aloysius Cake blinked several times at Ella and appeared to collect his thoughts.

'It's my sad duty to inform you that your father died some years ago in a car accident. I thought you knew. I'm sorry.'

Now it was Ella's turn to blink. She hadn't thought seriously about her dad for years. He was just a blurry memory, a face in a faded photo, a sense of relief after he'd gone.

'I thought he was in Australia. That's what we always

thought.'

'Indeed, he was, but he came back to the UK some ten years ago.'

Ella swallowed hard. 'Did he try to find me?' she said, more to herself than Mr Cake.

'I'm sorry; his family have never given me that information.'

'His family. What family?' Ella felt her heart skip a beat.

'He remarried some years ago. There were, no are, four further children.'

'I have brothers and sisters?' Ella felt both excited and horrified. She took a gulp of air.

'Not blood relatives. They were your father's stepchildren, they took his name, hence the mix up.'

'What mix up?'

'The oldest stepchild is older than you by several months. We had progressed the inheritance a little way before we discovered no bloodline. That was why we had to be sure with you. But we are confident now.'

Ella blinked again. This was all a bit too much. Her father had been back in the UK and never contacted her. It would have been nice if he bothered? And he had a whole other family.

Mr Cake rang his bell again and Shirley appeared with a cup of hot, sweet tea in a bone china teacup. There was a biscuit on the saucer. Ella took the tea and mechanically drank it.

'I expect this has all been a bit of a shock for you,' Shirley said, her face conveying sympathy and understanding.

Ella nodded silently in response.

'Would you like anything else before we continue? A glass of water perhaps?' Mr Cake asked, eager to get on.

Ella shook her head.

'Excellent. Now to your inheritance. Spring Cottage, as I've already said, is a substantial property.'

'How substantial?' Ella cut in too quickly.

'Four bedrooms, several receptions, a cellar, one-acre garden. All has fallen into disrepair, due to the time that it has stood empty, but…'

'How much is it worth?' Ella cut in again, instantly regretting how that question sounded.

'Its value is irrelevant.'

'Not to me.'

'I'm not sure what its value is, but it is irrelevant to you as you cannot sell it.'

'But I thought you said I'd inherited it.'

'And indeed, you have. But there are covenants on the property, quite an extensive list. I can go through it with you now if you feel up to it?' Mr Cake gave her a brief professional smile, which didn't even show his teeth.

'It's not much of an inheritance if I can't do as I please with it. Is it?' Ella's voice sounded horribly petulant even to her own ears.

'Shall we go through the list?' Mr Cake waited.

'Why not?' Ella flashed him a tight-lipped smile.

'It is extensive. I will, of course, furnish you with your own copy. Failure to comply with any of the covenants means that you can be forcibly removed from the cottage and all monies ceased.'

'That's a bit severe.'

Mr Cake drew a breath and started on the list.

'Item one: You cannot sell Spring Cottage. Ever.

Item two: You must live in it while you own it. Owning it is dependent on you living in it.

Item three: On your death, it can only be passed on

to a blood relative, ideally your offspring, but if no offspring exist or survive then another blood relative, preferably from the next generation.

Item four: You cannot cohabit in Spring Cottage with any person/or persons other than your spouse or blood relatives.'

'I don't have any of those,' Ella cut in. 'Does that mean that I can't have friends to stay?'

'No. You may have guests, but not permanent ones.'

'Who would know? Will you be checking up?'

'No, not personally. But these things have a habit of getting back. If I am informed I am obliged to act.'

Item five: You are responsible for the well beneath Spring Cottage and must ensure...'

'Wait.' Ella put her hand up to stop Mr Cake continuing. 'Well? Did you say well?'

'That's correct. The water for the house and some of its neighbours is supplied directly from the spring beneath the cottage – hence its name. The well provides direct access to the spring. You must ensure that the access is properly maintained.'

'I don't have to get the water from the well do I? The house does have taps and things? Doesn't it?'

'Yes, Spring Cottage is fully plumbed, but may need updating.'

'Thank God,' Ella muttered under her breath.

'Item six: You cannot profit from the spring or allow others to profit from it commercially.'

'Like how?'

'That means you cannot bottle the water and sell it.'

'Why would I do that?' Ella laughed. This was all a bit ridiculous.

'Spring water, especially this spring water, is purported to have special…' Mr Cake hesitated,

'…qualities. And you cannot profit commercially from them.

'Item seven: You must allow access to the well by the appropriate people who may need access at appropriate times.'

'Who are these appropriate people?'

Mr Cake flicked through his papers and shook his head. 'It doesn't say.'

'Who wrote this?' Ella leaned over the desk to see the list. Mr Cake was reading from what looked like a page torn from an old school exercise book. The writing was shaky, like a very old person's might be.

'It was copied out by your great uncle with, he told me, suitable modernisations. He also said the original resides in the cottage.

'Item eight: You can only spend the capital on the house for upgrading, repairs, furnishings and so on; you cannot squander it on yourself or give it away.

'Item nine: You will only receive the income from leased land whilst you are living in Spring Cottage. The income is to be treated as taxable.

Finally, Item ten: You…'

'Mr Cake, please,' Ella interrupted again. 'What income? What capital?'

'In the five years since your great aunt and uncle died the income has accumulated and been added onto the capital they already had. The income is derived from the leases on various parcels of land.'

'But how much is it?'

Mr Cake flicked through his papers once again, then jotted an amount on a scrap of paper. He handed it over. Ella looked at it, looked away, looked back at it to make sure she wasn't misreading.

'But that's almost as much as I earn in a year,' she

said. 'And this is just sat in a bank account waiting for me?'

'No. That's the income, per annum. The capital is considerably more. Even after the inheritance tax is paid and...' Mr Cake cleared his throat, 'our invoice for work to date, there is still a considerable sum.' He jotted it down on another piece of scrappy paper and handed it over to Ella.

Ella held the paper in her hand and watched it shake.

Mr Cake rang the bell on his desk yet again and Shirley bustled in and sat down next to Ella and patted her arm.

'Did you know my aunt and uncle, Mr Cake?' Ella asked, once she'd recovered from the shock.

'Yes, I met them on several occasions during the last ten years of their lives. They were very keen to find an heir.'

'I'm sorry I didn't get to meet them; as an adult, anyway. I have only the vaguest of memories. I was a little girl, they seemed very old to me.' Ella thought about the photographs in the albums, they'd looked very old in those photos too.

'I think you would have liked them, and I think they would have liked you,' Shirley said, and smiled.

'Oh you knew them too?'

'Only from their visits here, which were quite frequent towards the end.'

'Ahem.' Mr Cake cleared his throat again.

'Item ten: you cannot build on the land surrounding the cottage, other than to extend the cottage for your own personal use and subject to local planning laws, and you must maintain the garden and ensure the produce is fairly distributed.' Mr Cake stared at Ella over his glasses.

'Maintain the garden? Is it a great big allotment sized garden?' Ella asked, thinking of the photo she'd seen.

'That's right. Though there is nothing in the covenant to prevent you from hiring help. It only says maintain.'

'And distribute,' Ella added. 'What does that mean?'

'I think you're expected to give the excess away to those in need. But you'd do that anyway, wouldn't you? As any good gardener does.' He smiled briefly.

'But I'm not a good gardener.'

'Now onto the second option,' Mr Cake began.

'Second option?'

'The less generous of the two, but I am obliged to apprise you of it. If you choose not to take the cottage and abide by the rules as previously listed, you are entitled to a sum of money but you must sign away any claim to Spring Cottage, the parcels of land and the income.'

'Oh. How much?' Ella sounded mercenary again.

Mr Cake wrote down the sum on a third scrap of paper and handed it over.

'That's two years' wages,' Ella's voice squeaked.

'Miss Taylor, we have everything ready if you wish to sign now.'

'But I don't know which option to take.'

Mr Cake reared his head back and stared at her wide-eyed, then composed himself, smiled very briefly but didn't reply. He produced three copies of a contract and laid them out across the desk in front of Ella.

'Mrs Cavendish can witness if you wish to sign now.'

'But I don't know which option to choose.' Two years' wages would sort out her immediate troubles; give her breathing space to get a new job, allow her to move out of the grotty bedsit. But the cottage might be okay, definitely better long term. But did she want the responsibility? It all sounded very onerous, lots of rules. And the village was miles from civilisation.

'I cannot advise you. I have laid out both options and read out the list. The cottage, the capital and the income are yours once you move in, which must be within three weeks of signing. Or you may choose to take the pay off.'

'What would you do?' Ella looked at Mr Cake. He stared back, his face blank. 'What would you do Shirley?' Ella said turning round to her.

'I would sign for the cottage,' Shirley said softly. 'But you must do what you think best.'

Ella looked from Mr Cake's face to Shirley's and back. Their faces looked anxious. Ella felt anxious. Perhaps she should take the list home and study it before making her choice. She opened her mouth to speak but before a word came out her phone started to ring again in her bag.

'Sorry,' she said, fishing it out and looking at it. Work again, what the hell did they want? It must be important, mustn't it? She answered the call.

'Ella,' Tiffy's voice said. 'We've been trying to get hold of you.'

'Well, you knew I wasn't available.'

'Never mind. You've answered now. Gwynnie just wanted me to let you know that tomorrow is Think Day.'

'Pink Day?'

'No. Think Day. Remember, it was my suggestion at our team meeting.'

Ella remembered; she also remembered how Gwynnie had almost scoffed at Tiffy for suggesting it, yet had seemed keen to implement Ella's own stupid, sarcastic suggestion of Smile Day.'

'Think Day,' Ella repeated. 'So why did I need to know this now?'

'So you can prepare of course. It wouldn't be fair if you turned up tomorrow and weren't prepared.'

'Okay, so what do I need to do?'

'You need to think about it.' Tiffy sounded annoyed now.

'Think about what?'

'Think Day, of course.' Tiffy's voice rose. 'You need to prepare and think about Think Day. Anyway, Gwynnie wanted you to know. See you tomorrow.' She rang off.

Ella looked at her phone and shook her head.

'Where do I sign?' she said.

* * *

Ella sat in her car with a bunch of heavy, old keys on her lap. She picked them up and went through each one, looking at it, wondering what it opened. In her bag was her copy of the contract and the covenant list, together with the full address of Spring Cottage. And she was the owner. It had been a snap decision and she still wasn't sure if it was the right one. But it was done now.

Spring Cottage, Lyffingdon. She could go there now. It wouldn't get dark for a little while yet. She could put the postcode into Google and find her way there. On her own. She didn't want to go on her own. She got her phone out and dialled Sam's number, she should be home from work by now.

Sam's phone went to voicemail. Ella messaged her instead. *OMG amazing news!! Need to talk asap! You about??? xx*. She waited for Sam's reply which didn't come for another ten minutes, during which time Ella googled her new home. It was ten miles away from where she was, which meant nearer twenty from the grotty bedsit.

Hi Hun, oh wow really?? What is it? I'm at the in-laws at the mo and not back till late (yawn) catch up tomorrow?? xx, came Sam's reply.

Ella felt frustrated; she wanted to share her incredible news. Now.

Ah bummer! How about lunch tomorrow? 12:30? xx, she messaged back.

Ella sat in the car for another five minutes debating whether to go to Spring Cottage on her own. No, she wanted company. She wanted Sam to come with her and maybe even Charlie. Who knew what she might find in Spring Cottage, especially if had been empty for five years.

Five

Ella was late for lunch and Sam was already waiting.

'Sorry,' Ella said, sitting down without getting anything to eat. 'Got tied up with yet another issue…' she rolled her eyes to the ceiling. 'It's Think Day today. Have you ever heard anything so damn stupid?'

Sam didn't speak, just gave Ella a sympathetic smile and nod.

'Anyway, rant over. You okay? Mind if I just grab something to eat?'

Sam smiled again and shook her head this time.

When Ella came back she put her plate on the table and started to tell Sam her tale; she talked non-stop and never took a single mouthful of food.

'Wow,' Sam said when Ella had finally finished. 'That's unbelievable. What are you going to do?'

'I need to see it. I haven't even seen it. I want you to come with me. Maybe Charlie too.'

'You've signed the contract and you haven't seen it?'

'That's right.'

'But you have to live in it, don't you? That's what the rules say. Don't they? Although I think you've made the right choice, two years' salary wouldn't last you very long. But it is a lifetime decision.'

'Yes. I know. Maybe I was a bit hasty, but, well…' Ella raised her hands up as though she was about to be shot, 'I was sort of pushed into it.'

'That's unethical. The solicitor shouldn't have done that. I'm sure you have grounds…'

'No,' Ella cut in. 'Not the solicitor. I had a stupid phone call from Tiffy, it just wound me up.'

Now it was Sam's turn to roll her eyes.

'Well, look on the bright side, Sam; I should be able to take my mum's furniture out of your garage.' Ella laughed, she was making light of it; she already had her doubts without Sam's misgivings.

'It's great news, Ella,' Sam said, reaching over and pushing Ella's plate towards her. 'You should eat now.'

'You practising for when you have that baby?' Ella laughed. 'We could go on Saturday, if you're free. In the morning, I thought.' Ella waited anxiously for Sam to agree.

'Yeah, okay. I'll ask Charlie. Even if he isn't free I'll definitely come with you. I can't wait to see what it's like.'

'Me too. To be honest I'm a bit scared. It might be a right hovel.'

'It won't be,' Sam reassured her.

'Well last night I went through all my mum's photo albums again and hunted through them for pictures of it. There were a few shots of bits of it in the distance but nothing I could use to really gauge it by. I still don't know what it looks like, other than that it's thatched. I do, at least, know what my great aunt and uncle look like; there are a few photos of them. Well I think it's them.'

'What are you going to do about your job?' Sam said quietly.

Ella frowned. 'What do you mean?'

'You hate it and you could actually live on that income.'

Ella stopped chewing and swallowed a mouthful of food, it stuck in her throat before it went down.

'It's tempting. Although it's a little bit less than I'm currently earning.'

Sam shook her head slowly. 'Yes, but you won't be paying rent. Mmm, you're right. You probably shouldn't burn your boats just yet. You can wait. At least see the place first.'

'What, in case it's shit, you mean.' Ella laughed loudly. She felt giddy, silly, excited, afraid. Almost hysterical.

'Sshh,' Sam said, frowning. 'Just don't do anything hasty.'

'It's too late for that. I've already signed for the cottage. If I walk away now I end up with nothing. Maybe I should have thought this through a bit better.' She paused. 'You're right. I won't jack the job in yet.'

'No,' Sam said.

Ella glanced up at the clock, took another mouthful of food and set her knife and fork down on the plate. 'I need to go, Gwynnie will be back in a min and I want her to think I've worked through my lunch while she's had an extra-long break having her hair done.'

Back at her desk Ella went on the internet again and googled her cottage. She managed to get a satellite view of it, but the weather was dull and all she could see was a dark thatched roof and little else. She couldn't get a decent street view either, the cottage seemed to be in a dead-end road and the view was obscured by a large tree. Still, from what she could see it looked promising. She felt almost sick with excitement. Saturday couldn't come fast enough.

The door banged at the far end of the office and Gwynnie appeared with Tiffy trotting alongside her. Ella quickly closed her browser and got her head into her work.

'Hi,' Ella said, as they came back to their desks, glancing up and forcing a quick smile. Then she did a double take. Gwynnie's hair was the straightest it had ever been, poker straight and cut into a very short bob. 'Wow, your hair's amazingly smooth.'

'Chemically straightened,' Gwynnie said, running her hand over her head.

'Looks fab, doesn't it?' Tiffy prompted Ella.

'Yes. It's certainly smooth and straight.' Ella, wasn't sure fab was the right word for it. It reminded her of a scarecrow's straw hair, same colour too. She shook herself and got back to her work; she didn't need or want to be bitchy, not now that her own life was improving.

Minutes later an email pinged into her inbox. *Emergency team meeting: Think Day progress.* Oh for God's sake, why?

Ten minutes later the whole team was in a meeting room. Ben and Kevin sat smirking at each other across the table; Ella looked out of the window and Gwynnie and Tiffy sat side by side like matching smiley cats.

'So, how's it going? What are we all thinking? Say whatever is on your mind, whatever you're thinking.'

There was silence as everyone glanced at each other then studiously down at their laps. In the glaring light of the meeting room the whites of everyone's eyes shone brightly, giving the impression of eagerness. The light also glinted off Gwynnie's newly straightened hair. Ella, who'd had the foresight to bring a cup of extra strong coffee with her picked it up and sipped slowly, hoping it would act as a deterrent to Gwynnie and mean she wouldn't be forced to speak.

'Someone must be thinking something. Anyone? It is Think Day. Come on team; get your thinking caps on. Try to be creative. Kevin?'

Kevin, shy by nature and by design stumbled over his words before finally speaking. 'That's a really cool wig,' he said. 'What're you going as?'

Ella's coffee came out of her mouth in a spurt as she coughed it up. Coffee gushed from her mouth and splashed onto her white shirt, it ran in rivulets down her front. Ben dashed off and returned with some paper towels, Tiffy looked on in disgust and Gwynnie gave Kevin the evil eye.

'Sorry, went down the wrong way,' Ella said, when she had finished choking and mopping herself down.

'Mmm,' Gwynnie said, getting up. 'I think the meeting's over; we've all got plenty of work to be getting on with.' She walked towards the door and led the way out, turning only to look Ella up and down.

Ella, Ben and Kevin exchanged glances but didn't dare speak. On her way back to her desk Ella got herself a glass of water, her throat was sore from choking.

An email from Ben arrived: *Kevin wasn't taking the P. He really thought it was a wig.*

Ella replied: *His days are numbered…* When she heard the email reach his inbox, she glanced up at Gwynnie to make sure her super smooth head was down then turned and exchanged smirks with Ben.

Poor Gwynnie, Ella almost felt sorry for her. But

that feeling didn't last long. It stopped when Ella went to the toilet and saw herself in the mirror.

She thought she'd mopped the coffee up, in the harsh white light of the meeting room it had hardly noticed, but now she could see two dark brown stripes down her front ending in big brown blobs over her nipples. No one had said a word; she had sat there most of the afternoon looking like that.

She walked back to her desk with her arms crossed over her chest. She closed down her computer, collected her bag and coat.

'I need to go now,' she said to Gwynnie, daring her to say something. Gwynnie looked at her watch then back at Ella for an explanation. 'Headache,' Ella said over her shoulder as she marched out and 'bitch,' once she was through the door.

Ella drove home annoyed but also pleased at the way she had flounced – yes that was the word, flounced – out of the office. She parked the car in her street and headed for her flat. As she went through the communal door she was thinking about her shirt, she'd have to get it off and soak it straight away, that coffee had been strong; would it stain? She unbuttoned her coat and started to bound up the stairs when she came face to face – if not quite chest to chest – with Hal, the hot neighbour. He gave her the biggest smile. God, he was gorgeous.

'Hi,' he said. Then backed up the stairs to let her pass.

'Hi.' Ella could feel her face colouring; this was ridiculous.

'You're home early.' He stopped at the top of the stairs effectively barring her way.

'Yeah, had a bit of an…issue,' she didn't want to say

accident, 'at work.' She gave him a big bright smile.

'Mmm, so I see.' His eyes alighted on Ella's chest. Oh God. She pulled her coat closed and pushed past him. Yet again she'd humiliated herself in front of Hot Hal.

Once inside she shook her head and laughed. What did it matter? She'd soon be out of here. She'd be just a memory that he might laugh over with his leggy girlfriend; at least *she* hadn't witnessed Ella's stains.

* * *

For the rest of the week Ella had to fight her impatience, she willed Saturday to come, counted off the hours until she could see her inheritance.

'Charlie can't come,' Sam said over lunch on Friday. 'Says he's sorry.'

'That's a shame. I was hoping we'd have a man with us.'

'Ella. Really.' Sam shook her head.

'Might be spiders. Probably will,' Ella said and watched Sam's eyes widen in fear.

'Do you think?' Sam's shoulder shuddered. The last time Ella and Sam had been faced with a spider scampering across Sam's sitting room rug they had both stood on the sofa screeching while Charlie picked it up and put it outside. Even though both Ella and Sam had begged him to kill it, he wouldn't.

'We'll just have to manage.' Ella said sound braver than she felt.

'Mmm. He would have come, but the band's interviewing guitarists to replace Nathan. He's really let them down just going off like that. I told you, didn't I, that he wrote the only original songs they played.

Everything else is a cover.'

'Well if that shitty song they did in The Swannie is an example, good riddance.' Ella felt sick at the thought of it. Nathan. Bastard.

'You sure it was about you? I asked Charlie, he didn't seem to think so.'

'Well he doesn't know what happened.' Ella stopped. 'Does he?' she added, alarmed.

'No, I didn't tell him. Anyway, we've always thought Nathan was gay, so I'm confused.'

Ella thought about the kiss and the fumble in the car park. 'Definitely not gay.'

'Maybe bi then,' Sam said, then saw Ella's chin drop. 'Sorry, didn't mean…'

'Doesn't matter. Forget it. I'm not letting nasty Nathan spoil my new life. I'm so excited. Stupidly excited.'

'What time are you picking me up?' Sam said, clearing her plate onto her tray.

'Nine okay?'

* * *

Ella sat outside Sam's house and messaged her; she didn't want to waste time getting out of the car but after five minutes with no reply and no Sam she switched the engine off. She was just about to get out of the car when Charlie appeared on the doorstep; he held up his hand and mouthed 'two minutes.'

Sam appeared next to Charlie; he gave her a hug and kissed the top of her head, then stood smiling and waving as she got into Ella's car. That's what I want, Ella thought, someone to love me like that.

'Sorry about that,' Sam said, doing up her seatbelt. 'I

felt so sick.'

'Oh, you okay? Something you ate?'

'No. It's…' she patted her little bump.

'I thought you'd finished with morning sickness now.'

'Comes and goes. And it's not just confined to the morning; I don't know who named it that. Anyway fine now. So let's go and see your cottage. How exciting.' Sam put on a big smile for Ella, but Ella could see how white Sam looked, how dark the circles under her eyes were.

'You sure you're okay?'

'Yes. Let's go.'

Getting out of town took a while but they were soon trundling down little country lanes.

'Seems quite remote, this village. What's it called again?'

'Lyffingdon. Yeah, I did wonder about the route but this is the way the satnav is sending us. I bet there's a better way. I'd rather be on main roads.' According to the satnav they would arrive at Spring Cottage in four minutes.

They took a sharp left, then a sharp right and suddenly the sign for Lyffingdon loomed on their left. They carried on slowly, approaching a village green complete with duck pond.

'The Giddy Goat,' Ella read out as they passed the village pub. It looked ancient and welcoming, had real ale and a prominent menu board. 'Maybe we could have lunch there. Oh look, village shop and Post Office. And a butchers, a proper one. Public toilets. Ha ha.'

'Stop, stop now. Quick.' Sam was already undoing her seat belt.

Ella swerved the car into the curb and Sam jumped

out and ran for the public toilets. Ella watched her friend push through the door and heard it bang behind her. She re-parked the car, lining it up properly with the curb and got out and locked it, then turned to look around the village. Everything was green and pretty in the weak spring sunshine. She could see a church tower behind the pub, its stone ancient and weathered grey.

There wasn't anyone about, at least not on foot; then a car passed. The occupants, an old couple Ella thought, tooted and waved from inside the car. Ella raised her hand to wave back, then glanced behind her – it probably wasn't her they were tooting at, how could it be? But there was no one else around.

Sam was taking ages so Ella followed her into the toilets. They were amazing, from a bygone era; shiny, dark green and white tiles, mahogany doors and frames, polished brass taps, pipes and door knobs. A plaque on the wall explained how the village *took pride in the conveniences* and asked people to *respect the premises.* Ella suppressed a snigger and called out to Sam.

'You okay, Sam?'

'Feeling better,' Sam shouted back, although Ella could hardly hear her because the cubicles walls went from floor to ceiling. 'Won't be long.'

'Okay,' Ella shouted. She decided that since she was there, and the toilets were so nice, she might as well use them. Who knows what they might find at Spring Cottage, if it had been empty so long, the water was probably turned off.

Ella pushed open a cubicle door; there was large money box on it with a slot saying *1d.* She wondered how much that was but was glad it didn't seem to need a coin to open it now. The door closed behind her with a reassuring clunk.

Then she heard Sam's door close with a clunk too. Good, Sam must be feeling better.

'Wait for me,' Ella called, but Sam didn't answer.

Ella pulled the chain – also brass, with a porcelain pull on the end – then turned the handle to open the door. Nothing happened. She pulled it harder. Still nothing happened. It was stuck solid, so solid that it felt as though it wasn't a door at all. She tried lifting it up, a trick that usually worked, but there was still no movement. The door was well and truly stuck and because the cubicle was floor to ceiling there was no way to escape. Ella spotted a window, tiny and six feet from the ground, even if she could have reached it, which she couldn't, it would be no good, it had bars across it.

'Sam,' she shouted, filling her lungs with air before shouting again, even louder, 'Sam.' She waited for Sam to shout back. Nothing.

Ella shouted again, then started banging on the door, she banged the door so long and so hard her hands hurt. If only she hadn't left her phone locked in the car.

'Sam,' Ella shouted and banged the door again. Where the hell was Sam? Bang, bang, bang, bang, bang. Ella stopped to get her breath. 'Sam,' she called out again.

'Ella?' Sam's voice was muffled and distant.

'Sam, I'm stuck in here.' Ella banged on the door again.

'Ella. I'll push the door.' Sam's voice was clearer now that she was up against the door. Whether Sam pushed the door or not, it was hard for Ella to tell, because it didn't move, not even a rattle. 'It's no use,' Sam shouted. 'I'll get help.'

Ella put the toilet lid down and slumped onto the

seat. This is a good start, she thought.

Suddenly the door was being rattled; she heard a tiny little clunk and the door swung open. A rosy cheeked man gave her a big beaming smile.

'Sorry it took so long,' he said. 'We had to get *the* penny. It's free to go but you have to spend one to get out.' He chortled away to himself.

'Thank you,' Ella said, wondering what the hell he was talking about.

''I'm Walter,' he said, putting his hand out to shake.

'Oh, do you mind if I wash my hands first?'

'Of course, of course,' he roared, stepping aside to let Ella out of the cubicle. He hovered while she washed her hands, keeping too close and crowding her. When she'd finally dried them, he held out his hand to shake hers again. 'I'm Walter, most call me Walt. And you must be a Taylor.'

Ella narrowed her eyes. 'My name is Taylor. Yes, but… Ah, I suppose someone told you I was coming.'

'No, no. But we've been expecting you. We've had a long wait. Come on and meet some folks.'

Ella followed Walt out of the toilets and was met by a crowd of seven, including Sam who was deep in conversation with a woman called Edna who turned out to be Walt's wife. When Ella appeared they all clapped.

'What have you been telling them?' Ella asked Sam, after she had shaken hands with everyone. 'It feels weird; they're treating me like royalty.'

'I haven't told them anything, well, other than you were stuck in the loo.'

'You told them my name,' Ella said, as they got back into the car.

'No, I didn't. I just said my friend was stuck in the

loo. They said that happens a lot and they had to get the old penny, they keep it in the shop; apparently it's the only one.'

'Mmm?'

'I'm sorry. That was all my fault. If I hadn't been sick…' Sam's voice trailed away.

'No, it was just my typical luck. All I meant was how weird that they knew who I was. That's all. Let's go.'

Ella turned the key in the ignition and waited for the satnav to start up, then they drove two hundred yards around the corner and reached their destination.

Spring Cottage was tucked away on a corner plot with a front garden three feet high in weeds and grass.

'Oh. God.' Ella stared over the steering wheel at it. 'What a dump.' Her eyes took in the peeling paint, the dirty windows, the greying thatch which seemed to comprise most of the cottage, leaving barely ten feet of grubby grey-white painted stucco below. 'And I hate gardening. I did tell that Mr Cake that. What a disappointment.' Ella switched off the engine and took the key out of the ignition. 'I suppose we'd better have a look,' she said, grabbing her handbag and fishing inside for the keys. 'I wonder if it's too late to change my mind and take the money. You ready, Sam? Sam?'

Sam was staring at the cottage too. Her mouth and eyes wide open. She turned to Ella and shook her head. 'Ella, how can you be disappointed? It's the most amazing place ever.'

Ella glanced at Spring Cottage again, still unable to see anything other than a big dump.

'Yes, it probably needs some work,' Sam said, as they got out of the car. 'But just look at it. Just look.'

'I am. It's a shit hole.'

'Oh, Ella, no. How can you say that?'

They reached the front door – green peeling paint, the door handle covered in cobwebs. Ella pointed to them, made a *told you so* face at Sam who went white and Ella worried she might be sick again. Ella fumbled with keys, trying the largest one first, it didn't fit, but the second one did.

Finally inside and leaving the door wide open to let some fresh air in and diffuse the fusty overwhelming stench of damp, Ella took in her surroundings. They were in the hallway – a set of very narrow, rickety stairs in front of them, yellowing rosebud wallpaper which might have been nice fifty years ago (and it was hanging off in places), a set of coat hooks so high on the wall Ella would never reach them, grubby oak doors to the left and right.

'Which way?' Sam asked.

Ella shrugged then opened the door on her left. A big, dark room, beamed ceiling, flaking paint, more revolting peeling wallpaper, sticky carpet to rival the one in The Swannie. There was a shabby, tiny sofa, one chair and a coffee table in front of an enormous inglenook fireplace.

'Wow,' said Sam. 'You should get that exposed, probably even better under the plaster.'

'What?' said Ella. 'How can you say wow?'

'Yes, it needs work. But look at the potential. This place will be amazing. You are so lucky, Ella.'

Ella didn't reply, just walked through what she supposed was the sitting room and went through another door. Another room with some tatty bits of furniture in it, everything covered in dust, another fireplace.

'Does any of it look familiar?' Sam asked, lifting the lid of an oak chest then dropping it rapidly.

'No, not at all. There weren't many photos in my mum's albums of the cottage and none of the inside.' They stepped through into the kitchen; another huge fireplace, an enormous oak dresser complete with floral plates – all thick with sooty dust.'

'Vintage chic.' Sam walked over to the dresser and attempted to blow the dust away.

'Not even shabby chic, Sam. But this looks familiar.' Ella stood next to the Belfast sink and solid fuel cooker. 'I have vague memories of cakes coming out of this.'

'Is that an Aga? They're worth a fortune. You can get it refurbished.'

'It's not an Aga. It's a …' She grabbed a crusty tea towel that was hanging over the taps and used it to rub away some of the dust on the cooker. 'Well, I still don't know what it is, it's ancient. And horrible. Like everything else in here.'

'The dresser is gorge, and that table, look eight chairs. This place is enormous.' Colour had returned to Sam's face and she was smiling excitedly. 'I wish it was mine. Let's see what upstairs is like.'

The stairs were steep, narrow and creaky, the carpet threadbare, the handrail wobbly.

The landing was small and made dark by the five doors which led from it all being closed. Ella quickly opened a door to let light in. A big room, a brass bed, a little fireplace, a neat stack of wood in it, covered in soot. All four bedrooms were similar. The bathroom was tiny, cramped and not at all appealing.

'I'm glad we used the loo before we got here,' Ella said. 'Even if I did get locked in. And humiliated.'

'Me too.' Sam glanced in the toilet and mock-gagged.

'Glad I never gave up my job,' Ella said, as she started to walk down the stairs.

'But you've signed the contract. You have to live here.'

'No. I've been through the contract and if I don't take up residence within three weeks of signing, then everything is null and void, just as if I never even knew about it. Shame I never saw it first, I could have taken the money and run. Too late now.' She paused. 'Stupid me.'

'What's the back garden like? Let's check it out.' Sam took Ella's arm and guided her outside. It was massive, laid out like an allotment. But it was overgrown with waist high weeds even worse than the front garden.

'And, according to the contract I have to get *that* in order. I'm so glad I haven't told anyone else about this. Did you notice there's no heating?' Ella shook her head. 'Let's go. Otherwise I might start crying.'

Sam waited while Ella locked the cottage door.

'Hello again, Miss Taylor,' a male voice called. Ella and Sam turned. It was Walt. Again.

'Urgh,' Ella muttered under her breath.

'Hello there.' Sam smiled over at him.

Walt seized his opportunity, taking Sam's smile as an invitation and headed straight for them.

'Urgh,' Ella muttered again.

'So, Miss Taylor, what do you think? Handsome, isn't she?'

'Who?' Ella and Sam chorused.

'Spring Cottage. Handsome. She's been waiting a long time for you.'

'Mmm.' Ella started walking towards her car, beckoning over her shoulder for Sam to follow.'

'Ella's a bit disappointed. It's very dilapidated,' Sam explained. 'Not quite what she was led to expect. She feels it's too much for her.'

'Get help,' Walt called after Ella, who already had her car door open. 'I hear there's plenty of money for it.'

'Is that right?' Sam caught up with Ella. 'You didn't tell me that bit.'

'Oh yeah. Well, I doubt it's enough for that.' She gave the cottage a withering look. 'It needs pulling down.'

'Why don't you girls come in and have a cup of tea.' Walt gave them his best beaming, apple cheeked grin.

'Said the spider to the fly,' Ella whispered in Sam's ear.

'My wife's just baked a cake. She must have known you were coming.' He gave out a loud chuckle. 'Come on, we're going to be neighbours.'

'Neighbours?' Ella glanced up at him.

'Yes. We live next door.' He pointed to his cottage. Now *that* looked enticing; a beautiful cliché cottage.

'I *could* do with a drink and something to eat, Ella,' Sam said quietly. 'Why not?'

'That'd be great. Thanks.' Ella sighed, shut her car door, locked it.

Walt's wife, Edna, sat at the kitchen table with a big pot of tea, four cups, saucers and plates and an extravagant cake under a glass dome. She jumped up to greet them.

'You made that. Wow.' Sam eyed the cake. 'It looks yummy.'

* * *

'I think your pregnant self got the better of you in there,' Ella said to Sam two hours later, as they were driving out of the village.

'Oh, come on. The cake was lovely. They were lovely. Their cottage is lovely. Don't be such a misery.'

'They wanted to know all my business. They'll always want to know all my business, they're that type.'

'They told you more than you told them. At least now you know a bit about your aunt and uncle. At least you know why they knew you were a Taylor, because you do look like your uncle in the pictures they showed us.'

'Suppose so,' Ella said. She had to admit she did know more; they'd died within days of each other, they were really very, very old. Ninety-five, at least, Edna thought. But then Edna and Walt had admitted to being well over seventy. 'They look good for their age, don't they?' Ella mused out loud.

'That's what it's like in these villages. That could be you.'

'Thanks.'

'Well you know what I mean. I loved their cottage. Their range was just like yours, only clean and working.'

'Yes.' Ella thought about Edna's kitchen, a proper country kitchen suitable for a country cottage. She struggled to imagine Spring Cottage looking like that.

'So, what are you going to do?'

'I'm going to have a shower when I get home, I feel filthy.'

'I didn't mean that. You know what I mean. What are you going to do about the cottage?' To Ella, Sam's voice sounded too upbeat, she was trying too hard.

'I don't know. I need to sleep on it. In the meantime, I'm going to stay in and watch a film, or something.'

'Charlie's out. He messaged me, they've got someone, they want to practice with him tonight. Why don't you come round? We could have a girly night, manicure, pedicure, watch *Bridget Jones* again, again.'

'No. That's okay. I need some time to think.'

'If you change your mind,' Sam said, as Ella dropped her off at home, 'let me know. Offer's still there. We could order pizza.'

'Bye, Sam. And thanks for coming with me.'

* * *

Ella let herself into her bedsit. It looked sad and forlorn. She thought of the bedrooms at Spring Cottage, each one twice the size of this bed-sitting-kitchen-bathroom combo. But so much work. How could she cope?

She had a shower, washed her hair, wrapped it in a towel, pulled on her frog onesie and looked in the fridge.

Someone knocked on her door. She took the few steps towards her front door and peeped through the spy hole. It was that damn Hal. Again. He kept knocking.

'I know you're in there.' He was worse than Walt and Edna. Why couldn't people just bugger off?

He kept knocking.

Ella opened the door enough to show her head.

'Yes?'

'Having a few friends round tonight. Thought I'd better invite you, cos it might get rowdy.' He laughed and his eyes crinkled up and he looked so sexy. 'You could wear that if you wanted.' He nodded at her onesie, even though he couldn't see much of it.

Ella thought about his friends, wondered if they were all leggy and blond.

'Thanks.' She beamed at him. 'Bit short notice for

me. I'm already going out. Don't worry about the noise; I'll be back really late.'

'Oh. Right.' That took the wind out of his sails. 'Only you don't, do you, normally go out on a Saturday night?'

'Not since my mum died, no. I haven't felt like it. But, you know, getting back into it now.'

'Oh. Right. Sorry. Didn't know. Have a good one.'

'You too.' Ella shut the door in his face, found her phone and messaged Sam.

Six

'I'm so glad you changed your mind,' Sam said, giving Ella a big hug in the hallway. 'Are you going somewhere else later?' Sam stood back to admire Ella's outfit.

'No.' Ella shrugged off her little fur jacket and hung it over the banister.

'Oh. Only you look as though you're going clubbing.'

'Hunky Hal invited me to his place…'

'Wow. So you're going there later?'

'No. It wasn't just me. He only invited me because they'll be noisy and he didn't want me complaining. Couldn't let him think I'm a Saturday-stay-at-home-Suzie-saddo, could I? Even if I am.'

'Forget him.' Sam waved her arms in the air as though swatting a fly. 'You haven't eaten have you? I dashed out to M&S when you messaged. Picked up a few things, wine included.'

'But you can't drink.'

'But you can.' Sam guided Ella towards the big squishy sofa that curved around one end of what Sam called her living-kitchen.

It was such a fab room, *modern family living* was how it had been described in the house brochure: enormous, expensive kitchen one end, dining area with glass doors to the garden in the middle, then lounge area around the corner. Ella imagined Sam and Charlie's children running around this room by day, while in the evening Sam and Charlie would retreat to the grown up sitting room next door. She thought about Spring Cottage, grubby and quite horrible with all its conditions attached to living there.

'I'm driving,' she said, when Sam handed her a full glass of wine.

'Stay the night.'

'Won't Charlie mind?'

'Of course he won't.'

Ella took a sip. 'Okay.'

It didn't take long to cook the ready meal. Ironic, thought Ella, this kitchen is amazing but there isn't much actual cooking done in it. Sam loved M&S and Charlie loved takeaways, except when he made non-descript pasta dishes.

While they were eating at the large beech table which Sam had picked – Charlie had wanted black ash – Ella had another two glasses of wine; the bottle was almost empty.

'Don't worry; I've got another in the fridge.'

'I keep telling you I can't drink for two, just because you can't drink. Ella laughed, draining the dregs into her glass.

'We can watch *Footloose* then I've got *Bridesmaids, Bridget Jones* – first, not second or…

'Put *Footloose* on, but we have to dance. Last time I put it on in my bedsit and danced the old lady from downstairs came up and wondered if I was all right.'

'I've got some magazines too.'

'Give me Hello, let's see which celeb is getting too fat this week.'

'I didn't get those mags, I got these.' Sam laid them out on the table in front of Ella; they were decorating and style magazines, tips for country cottages – shabby chic style.

Ella tried hard not to sneer. 'Did you say you had another bottle of wine?' She drained her glass.

'Sure. Shall I put the film on?'

With the new bottle in hand Ella moved over to the sofa and left the magazines on the table while Sam put *Footloose* on. They sang along and danced until Ella fell over on the hardwood floor. She got up again, laughing and grateful that only Sam was there to witness it.

'That'll be another bruise,' she hiccoughed.

'Did anyone at work notice your black eye after the mannequin incident?'

'No one said a word, but I did a good camouflage job on it with make up.'

After the film had finished Sam got up to get them both glasses of water – which, Ella noted seemed to be Sam's new job in life – and Ella idly followed her, stopping at the magazines now fanned out on the table. She picked one up, flicked through it, spotted an ancient range cooker which had been refurbished.

'Hey, that looks just like the one in my cottage,' she called out to Sam.

'What's that?' Sam said, holding a glass in each hand.

'This,' she showed Sam the picture.

'Bit better than yours though.' Sam laughed, taking the glasses to the sofa.

Ella joined her, bringing the magazine with her. She started at the beginning, turning each page slowly, taking in the detail of every photograph. She didn't say anything, just looked. Every page showed someone's multi-million-pound home. Every room was show house perfect, but they were all old cottages; admittedly some were enormous, probably several cottages knocked into one, but basically they were all old thatched places with beams and gleaming range cookers. Ella finished the magazine and went back to the table for another one.

'The bed in this room is like one of the beds in my cottage,' she said, showing it to Sam.

'Oh yeah. Room isn't though, is it?' Sam laughed and pressed play on *Bridesmaids*.

'Do you think it could be?'

'Yes, if you throw enough money at it.'

'There's probably enough money. I just wouldn't know where to start.'

'You can get ideas from those mags,' Sam said.

'Okay, I know what you're doing.' Ella nudged Sam with her elbow. 'I can't do it on my own. I can't imagine this.' She jabbed at one of the photos with her finger.

'You don't have to imagine it; there are so many mags and websites with ideas like that.'

'Mmm.' Ella got up and brought the rest of the magazines over to the sofa. 'Any more wine?'

'No. Afraid not.'

'I haven't drunk two whole bottles by myself. I haven't, have I?'

'The second one was low alcohol.'

'Thank God for that. I didn't notice; it tasted all right. It wasn't yours, was it?' Ella put her hand to her mouth, she felt mean and greedy.

'Don't worry. I drank *no* alcohol. You haven't

deprived me.'

'Do you think I could do this?' Ella pointed at the magazines again. 'I mean renovate that dump. Turn it into something like the ones in here. Which I'm starting to love, I have to admit.'

'Why not?'

'I don't know. It's all seems so...' Ella held her arms out, 'big. The cottage is a big mess. Then there's moving away.'

'What's keeping you here?'

'Well, you. And Charlie. And your new family member,' Ella said, rather upset that Sam should think otherwise.

'It's not that far away, we would come and visit you. Frequently. And you can come here. Even more frequently because I will need a babysitter I can trust.' Sam laughed.

'But it's not the same, is it?'

'Ella, you get in your car to drive around here and it's a five-minute drive. How long is the journey from here to the cottage? Twenty minutes? That's nothing. So don't use that as an excuse.'

'Okay, what about my job?'

'You hate it.'

'I don't hate the job, I've always enjoyed it. It's the circumstances now. That's what I hate.'

'And do you think that's going to change in the near future?'

Ella shrugged. 'Suppose not.'

'But you don't actually need to work. Do you? At least not for the money.'

'I do if I don't live in that place. I only get the money if I live there. I don't want to live there. It's miles from anywhere. I'd be all on my own.' Ella shook her head; the wine was making it more confusing.

Sam tried to stifle a yawn then offered to make Ella a cup of coffee.

'Better not,' Ella said, 'or I won't sleep.' Taking the hint, she started to collect her things together, retrieving her kicked off shoes from under the coffee table, her bag from the dining table. Sam had stacked the magazines into a neat pile and Ella felt obliged to take them up to her room with her.

Sam and Charlie's guest room was far more luxurious than Ella's bedsit. The bed was a proper bed, and king size too, not some grotty sofa bed. She looked around the room and wondered if it would ever be possible to make a bedroom in Spring Cottage look half as good. Of course it wouldn't; this was a beautiful modern designer house, not some ancient old dump.

She used the en-suite bathroom – something else that was definitely lacking in Spring Cottage, a decent bathroom, never mind an en-suite – changed into the elegant PJs Sam had lent her and climbed into bed. She put the light out and closed her eyes.

But sleep didn't come.

* * *

'Morning Ella. Did you sleep okay? Hope I didn't disturb you when I came in.' Charlie's affable, smiling face greeted Ella in the kitchen.

'Morning. No, you didn't. Thanks.' She accepted a cup of coffee and proceeded to sip it. She hadn't slept well, but that was hardly the fault of the bed or any noise, it was entirely down to her own fears and, maybe, hopes. She had tried in vain to sleep but finally gave up; put the light on and starting flicking through the magazines again. They offered such a tempting picture of what could be. But whenever Ella tried to picture Spring Cottage even vaguely like any of the pictures, she just couldn't. It was an impossible task…but what if?

'Sleepyhead,' Sam said, trying to get Ella's attention. 'I was asking if you wanted some breakfast?'

'Oh. Sorry.' Ella pulled herself back to the present. 'Only if you've got some going.'

'There's always plenty of low sugar muesli here.' Charlie shook the box.

'Take no notice of him. I'm weaning him off sugar and he doesn't like it.'

Charlie made a face then grabbed his wife and kissed her playfully. Ella felt like an intruder.

'We're going out for the day,' Charlie said, making Ella feel even more uncomfortable. 'Did you want to come with us?'

Ella glanced between Sam and Charlie's faces. 'No, thanks. I've got some things I really must do.'

'Okay.' Charlie took his bowl of low sugar muesli to the table and sat down to eat.

'Ella?' Sam held up a cereal bowl.

'No. Thank you. I need to get off. Thanks for having me. I really appreciated it and these.' She patted the magazines she was now clutching to her chest.

* * *

She parked the car outside her bedsit and made her way up the stairs.

'Hello again.' The voice was low and seductive. Hal.

'Hi.' Ella smiled at him briefly then moved to pass him.

'You missed a great night. But looks as though you had a hell of a night yourself.'

Ella glanced down at her clothes, yes, she was wearing last night's no-clubbing-clubbing outfit but she'd showered and she didn't have old mascara smeared all over her face.

'Excuse me,' she said, without answering him.

'Sure. I expect you want to get into your frog outfit for some serious slobbing about.'

Ella blinked. Did he really just say that? She didn't answer. What the hell could she say? She pushed past him and let herself into her bedsit, leaning behind the closed door and fighting back tears. How bloody stupid, she told herself, why do I care what *he* thinks?

She did change, but not into her onesie. She pulled on a pair of comfortable old jeans and a top her mum had bought her one birthday.

She'd just finished four slices of her famous meese toast while looking through the magazines again – she was beginning to wish Sam hadn't bought them – when a knock at the door made her jump.

She looked through the spy hole but could see no one. She opened the door and as soon as she did Hal stepped into view. He was holding the biggest bunch of flowers she'd ever seen and a sheepish grin on his face.

'I realised how rude I was earlier and how I may have upset you. It was insensitive and clumsy of me. I hope you'll accept my apologies.' He offered the flowers to her.

'Err. Thanks,' she said, holding her hands out.

Hal placed the flowers in her arms and stepped forward and kissed her softly on the cheek. 'I hope I'm forgiven.'

'Yes. Of course.' Ella was thinking that she should

invite him in, but then she thought about the poky little bedsit, the meese toast remnants on the sofa bed.

'And I hope you'll allow me to take you out to lunch. Today. If you don't have other plans.'

'Err.' That was a shocker. He was so gorgeous. So hot. And here he was inviting her to lunch. Out of the blue. 'Err,' she heard herself say again. Hold on, it was only lunch. Lunch meant nothing. 'Okay. I think I can fit that in.'

'Great. Shall I call for you around one?'

It was only after he had gone that she remembered Leggy Blond. God, what if he brought her with him. Would he? Was that a possibility? Maybe it would be better to cancel now. Don't be stupid, she told herself, whether he brought her along or not, it didn't matter; it was only lunch.

Ella changed into smarter jeans, a different top and found her leather jacket at the back of the tiny wardrobe. She made her face up, careful to keep it natural looking; fortunately, the black eye had faded away. She pulled on her burgundy ankle boots; they had a nice high heel on them. She surveyed the result in the mirror by the front door, stepping back into the bathroom in an attempt to get a full-length view. She nodded approval at her reflection and waited for Hal to arrive.

He was prompt. And he was alone. Unless Leggy Blonde was already in the car.

'You look lovely,' he said when she opened the door. She wanted to tell him that he looked lovely too, and he smelt absolutely amazing. Instead she muttered a humble thank you.

Leggy Blonde wasn't in the car which was an expensive sporty thing. Ella wasn't that up on cars –

she drove a fairly ancient Peugeot herself – but she knew enough to know that someone who drove a car like this expected it to be admired. So she obliged and it was his turn to mutter humble thanks.

He never told her where they were going and she didn't ask. She just sat back in the sumptuous leather seat and enjoyed the ride. He drove them quickly out of town, out into the open countryside then into a small market town. He pulled up outside an attractive pub with a conservatory restaurant.

'I thought we'd eat in the restaurant rather than the bar. That okay?' He jumped out of the car and quickly went round to Ella's door, though she was already getting out by the time he got there. Still, it did show his manners.

When they got inside the restaurant was obviously popular; it was full.

'Sunday lunchtime. We should have booked,' Ella said, hoping it didn't sound like a rebuke.

'Don't worry.' Hal gave Ella's arm a reassuring stroke – it made her tingle – then he smiled over at the waitress who rushed to him.

They were escorted over to a discreet little table for two which Ella hadn't noticed was vacant.

'So you did book,' Ella laughed.

Hal raised his eyebrows then handed Ella the wine menu. She gave it a cursory glance then handed it back saying that she really wasn't too keen on drinking today.

Ella looked through the menu, it all sounded delicious, but the truth was she wasn't hungry. She glanced around at her fellow diners, noticing how large the portions were. Maybe she should have said no to lunch.

'Have you chosen?' Hal said, putting his menu

down.

'To be honest I'm not really that hungry. I had a late breakfast. Four slices of meese toast. But it does all look delicious.'

Hal screwed up his face. 'Meese toast?'

'Oh, sorry. Layer of *Marmite* followed by layer of cheese then grilled, though I haven't got a grill so I have to toast the bread in the toaster then microwave it to melt the cheese. Not as good as the real thing, but…' Ella stopped talking; Hal was smiling broadly at her. Smiling. Not laughing.

'*Marmite.*' He made a yuk face. 'I'm starving, so I hope you don't mind if I tuck in.'

'No, absolutely not.'

'Maybe you could have a starter as a main. Keep me company.'

'Yes. Why not?' Ella felt sure she could force something light down.

Hal ordered a jug of water and Ella had a lime and soda as they waited for their meal to arrive.

'So,' Hal said, leaning towards Ella, 'do you eat this meese toast in that fetching frog outfit?' His voice was low and husky. He gave her a secret little smile. Oh my God, was he flirting?

Ella felt flustered. He was so hunky and so delicious, so tall and well dressed, how could he possibly be interested in her. Anyway, what about Leggy Blonde? Ella gave him a little smile back, one which she hoped showed she was flattered – if he *was* flirting – but not interested in being some sort of backup bit on the side.

Their food arrived and just as the waitress put the plates down on the table Ella said, 'Does your girlfriend mind you taking me to lunch?' She felt the waitress's eyes move from Ella to Hal and back again; she hovered just a little too long, before Ella looked up and smiled at her.

'What girlfriend?' Hal said, without missing a beat.

'Your girlfriend with the long legs.'

'Oh you mean Phoebe. She's not my girlfriend, she's my sister.' He laughed and cut into his steak entrecote. Ella had chosen mushrooms in garlic butter, she now wondered if that had been a wise choice.

Sister; that could make sense. They were both tall, long-legged, had athletic builds. Hal had very dark hair which flopped seductively over one eye and he had a habit of brushing it aside. Phoebe had white blonde hair, but it was unlikely the colour was natural.

'That is, half-sister,' Hal said as though reading the question in her face. 'Same father. Her mother's Swedish, hence her hair. My mother is Greek, hence my hair.' He ran his hands through it, just to make the point and Ella almost swooned. 'What about you? Brothers and sisters?'

Ella thought about the family her father had spent most of his life with, the family that took his name, but they weren't Ella's blood relatives. 'No. Just me.' She ate a mushroom, it melted in her mouth. 'Mmm, that's good,' she said. 'You're close then, you and your sister? She's at your place a lot, or does she live with you?'

'Phoebe most certainly does not live with me. She's got a shoebox in London.' He stopped, looked at her. 'Not that there's anything wrong with living in a shoebox…'

'Doesn't matter. Don't worry. You were saying?'

'Yes, she has a place in London but she's between jobs – actually she's always between jobs – so she drops down for visits. Frequently.'

'That must be nice, to see her so often. What does

she do? For a job I mean?'

'Oh, everything. She's been a model, a receptionist, trained as a nail technician – whatever that is – a PA, a profession lasted about three days. That sort of thing.'

Ella wondered how she managed for money, but looking at Hal's expensive clothes, knowing that his flat upstairs was very large and he probably owned it; she guessed there was money in their family.

'What do *you* do for a living?' Hal was giving her one of his devastating smiles again.

'I work in an office, with a Barbie doll called Gladys and Tiffy the Troll.'

He blinked, screwed up his eyes, which crinkled at the sides, and frowned.

'Oh, long story. Not one I want to bore you with. What do you do?'

'Bit of this, bit of that.'

'Oh?'

'I part own several businesses. We own SmartCars the car valeting company, some property we let out, a share in a restaurant.'

'Not this one?' Ella interrupted.

'Well, yes.'

'That's impressive. No wonder we got a table so quickly. It's lovely here. You must be very proud.'

'Yes. We are. Obviously, I only have a share in it, but it does bring a few perks.'

'And SmartCars – I had my car cleaned there once.'

'Did they do a good job?'

'Yes. But then I had to take Ruben to the vets the next day and he had an accident in the back seat, so…'

'Take it back and get it cleaned again, my treat.'

'Oh, it's okay. It was ages ago. The smell's gone now and Ruben's dead.'

'Oh, I'm terribly sorry.'

'He was a dog, not my dog. He was my mum's, though I grew up with him.' Ella's voice sounded wistful. She swallowed hard, tried not to think about her lovely mum. 'Do you own any other businesses?' she said, changing the subject.

'Aren't three enough?' He looked into her face as though awaiting approval, then laughed. 'Actually, we have just bought a spa. Bit run down now, but we're doing it up, just sorting out the finance.'

'Maybe Phoebe could work there doing her nail thing.'

Now Hal really laughed. 'I wouldn't want to be the next one to sack Phoebe and I'm sure I'd have to.'

'Is she that bad?' Ella was looking at the pudding menu now, despite being full of meese toast, she had seen elaborate puddings being brought to other tables and was struggling to resist.

'Her work isn't the issue; it's her time-keeping. She doesn't really understand work is every day, all day. What are you having?' He tapped the menu. 'Or would you like me to order something we can share?'

'Yes please,' Ella's mouth said, before her brain had caught up.

An enormous glass bowl arrived, carried from the kitchen with a sparkler burning brightly and when it was placed in the centre of their table, the whole restaurant clapped.

'Oh no. Do they think this is some special occasion or something?' Ella could feel her face colouring up.

'It is special. We're finally getting to know each other properly, that's cause for celebration. Tuck in.' Hal offered her a long-handled spoon and took his own.

The pudding was full of strawberries, raspberries, ice

cream, fresh cream, meringue, marshmallows, tiny little cubes of melt in the mouth sponge, curls of white and dark chocolate, and sprinkled with gold dust. They didn't get halfway through before Ella knew she'd had enough. But she did enjoy crossing spoons with him, fighting over the last marshmallow.

'So,' he said, when they'd finished with still a third left in the bowl. 'Tell me about your job again. What was this Barbie troll thing?'

'Barbie troll thing. That just about sums it up.' Ella tried to keep the bitterness from her voice. 'Still, I've started looking for another job now, so I won't be stuck there for ever'

'That's the spirit,' Hal said. 'Don't let the bastards grind you down.'

'I'll drink to that.' Ella raised her glass of lime and soda. 'Anyway, it might not be practical for me to work there anymore.'

'Why's that?' Hal signalled to the waitress to come over so that he could order coffee.

'I've inherited a house, well a cottage to be exact. Well sort of inherited.'

'Sort of?' Hal's face took on a puzzled look. So Ella told him the whole story, about the cottage, its conditions, or at least the ones she could remember, what a dump it was, how she really couldn't see beyond that. It all came out in one very long, non-stop ramble.

'Where is it?' he asked, when she'd finished.

'Lyffingdon. I'd never heard of it.'

'I know Lyffingdon,' he said. 'Nice pub there; The Giddy Goat.'

'That's right. Don't tell me you've got shares in that too.'

'No, no.' Hal stood up to go and Ella wondered if

she'd missed the bill being paid, or if he didn't pay. She wondered what she should do.

'Um, how much do I owe you?'

'For what?' He helped her into her jacket.

'Lunch. My share.'

'Absolutely nothing. I wouldn't dream of accepting any money from you; I invited you out.' His tone suggested he was insulted.

'Thank you. I appreciate it.'

'My pleasure.' He waved a thank you at the waitress and guided Ella out into the car park; he opened her car door for her and waited while she got into her seat. What a gentleman.

'Why don't you show it to me,' he said as he started the engine.

'The cottage? Really?'

'Yes. As I said, we have a couple of rental properties, so I know a little bit about refurbishment. I might be able to give you a few tips.'

Ella sifted through her handbag and found the keys. She jingled them towards him. 'We're in luck. I have the keys with me.'

* * *

They drove into the village, drove past The Giddy Goat, drove past the incarceration toilets.

She directed him to Spring Cottage and when they pulled up outside Ella thought it looked just as shabby and run down as it had the day before. Hal got out of the car and walked round to open Ella's door. This time she waited for him; she wasn't in any hurry to get out.

'You've done well here, Ella,' Hal said. A broad smile spread across his face as he looked at the cottage.

'Huh. You haven't been inside yet.'

Hal offered Ella his arm as they walked up the path towards the front door. She hesitated for a moment, then linked arms with him. It felt good. She put the key in the lock and turned it, the door swung open with a creak. The fusty, damp smell swept across their faces.

'See what I mean.' Ella flapped her hand across her face.

They walked around the cottage and Hal made approving noises and enthusiastic comments about the size of the rooms, the potential; he even admired some of the furniture. But no matter how hard she looked Ella couldn't share his vision. She tried to match the pictures in the magazines that Sam had given her to the dismal rooms she now stood in. In the magazines, there had been beautiful cottage kitchens, but the kitchen here could never look like any of those, no matter how much white paint she threw at it. It was hopeless.

'I told you it was a hovel,' Ella said, although she wasn't particularly talking to Hal.

'I'll admit it'll need a lot of work just to make it habitable and that means a lot of money.' He shook his head slowly and started to walk into another room.

'There's money,' Ella said.

Hal stopped, turned around, stared at her. Then a broad smile spread across his face. 'You have plenty of money? Enough to do this place up?'

Ella shrugged.

'If money is no object – if that's what you're saying – then you could have the most amazing place.'

Ella looked around the cottage, turned her nose up. 'I wouldn't say money is no object.'

'You could gut this place, have new everything, of course you'd want to keep some of the original features, but …'

'No,' Ella cut across him, 'I couldn't cope with it.'

'But why not? You employ people to do it. When it's done, you just move in.'

'No. I have to move in within the next three weeks, actually less now.' She shook her head. 'Or I don't inherit. It's one of the conditions.'

'Okay, so you make one room habitable, then move in and begin the work.'

Ella looked around the room they were standing in, the sitting room with the sad sofa and chair. She'd have to scrub and clean everything just to live in one room. She'd have to get rid of the smelly bits of furniture and clean up the stuff she wanted to keep. And there would be spiders galore hiding everywhere. It was all too much, just completely overwhelming.

'I can't do this on my own,' she said, turning to walk out.

Hal grabbed her arm and pulled her back, put his arms around her and hugged her tightly. 'You don't have to,' he said. 'I can help you.'

Seven

Ella was quiet in the car on the way back. Hal had the good sense not to talk about the cottage either. Ella was thinking. Thinking hard. Would it be possible to live in that chaos? Alone?

Hal parked the car outside their block and held every door open for Ella – ever the gentleman. At the top of the stairs they exchanged cheek kisses, a light hug.

'Let me know when you go again. I'll be happy to accompany you. And I meant what I said about helping.'

'Thank you.'

Ella felt exhausted; it had been a long day. She put the TV on and flicked through the cottage magazines without really seeing them. Her head buzzed. She didn't know what to do. She made a mental list of the pros and cons of accepting her inheritance.

Pros: she could probably give up work – hurray, no more Barbie and the Troll. She would have enough to live on. She might eventually end up with a beautiful cottage – *that* was hard to imagine.

Cons: it would be very hard work. She was on her

own. She would be moving away from her home town, even if it was only twenty miles or so. She didn't know anyone in Lyffingdon. She doubted there was much nightlife there for anyone her age. In fact, she hadn't even seen anyone her age. She was on her own.

She wondered again if she should have chosen the second option. Too late now.

The more Ella thought about it, the worse it seemed. But one thing was obvious, if she'd had someone to share it with it would be easier, it would probably be fun. She thought about her mum and a lump came into her throat. Her mum would have loved that cottage and known exactly what to do with it. Life could be so unfair.

She changed into her pyjamas, opened up the sofa bed and climbed in. She turned the TV off and lay down. It wasn't really that late and she *was* tired but she couldn't get to sleep. Her mind just kept going round and round in circles. The sensible part of her knew that Spring Cottage, no matter how dilapidated, was just too good to turn down. But the doom-laden Ella couldn't face it on her own. She knew, deep down, that she should be embracing the opportunity – how many people her age got the chance to own something so potentially beautiful.

'I'm scared,' a little voice said aloud; her own voice, timid in the darkness.

Ella finally started to doze, several times jumping back from that falling feeling. Then her phone rang, shocking her with its noise and flashing. She blinked herself awake and fumbled to answer it.

'Ella, Ella, it's me,' Sam's voice sounded urgent yet tired.

'Sam. Is everything okay?' Ella sat up, shaking

herself awake.

'Yes. No. Yes. Sorry. Yes, I'm fine. I've been out to a gig with Charlie; we were on our way home when his car started making horrible noises. So now we've broken down. The AA is coming, but we don't know how long they'll be or if they can fix it or anything really. I want to go home, Charlie will wait alone. I was going to get a taxi but Charlie isn't keen on that. He suggested you. Could you come and get me? Say no if you don't want to.'

'Of course I'll come,' Ella said. As if she would say no. 'Where are you?'

They weren't actually that far away, stuck outside *McDonald's* on a main road. Ella got out of bed, went to the loo and considered getting dressed, maybe she could just put a coat on over her pyjamas, then she saw her frog onesie hanging on the bathroom door. It was warm, much cosier that any coat she had. She pulled it on and zipped it up. She pulled the hood up too, buttoned the flap across her chin. Super cosy. She needed some shoes that the frog feet would fit into, she opened her wardrobe. Boots. That would do it. She folded the feet up as neatly as she could and pushed them inside the boots, bit tight and she couldn't do the zips up, but they'd do. She grabbed her keys and phone and started off into the night.

It was cold and the steering wheel was freezing, but fortunately she had a pair of gloves – a left over from a gorilla fancy dress costume she'd worn last year – stuffed into the drinks holder by the radio. She pulled them on and smiled at her own hands, furry on the outside, smooth on the palm, perfect for driving, plenty of grip.

She started the car and headed off to find Sam. It

didn't take her long to reach the road Sam and Charlie had broken down on. She approached a mini-roundabout which gave her a choice of left or right. That was when she realised she wasn't sure which end *McDonald's* was, which way she should turn; left or right.

As she approached the junction she straddled both lanes, keeping her options open. As she got closer she decided on left, then, at the last second she remembered, glanced in her rear view mirror and veered right. She could see *McDonald's* a few hundred yards ahead.

The flashing blue light filled her car, so did the siren, she pulled over to let the police car pass.

It didn't pass. It pulled up in front of her, ensuring she couldn't drive on. She swallowed, gulping air, her heart thumped in her chest as the officer got out of his car and came towards her. He bent down to her window. She lowered it slowly and gave him a nervous smile.

'Would you like to step out of the vehicle please?'

Ella turned the lights and the engine off. She picked up her phone and opened the door.

The officer, mid-thirties and quite dishy in his uniform, looked her up and down as she got out of the car; his eyes finally came to rest on her gorilla hands.

'Is there a problem?' Ella's voice squeaked.

'Have you been drinking?'

'No.'

'If you'd like to accompany me to the police vehicle.' He started walking and at the same time managed to move Ella along without actually touching her. Ella waddled along the road, her boots tight on her feet and flapping around her legs. When they got to the car he opened the back door and invited her to get in.

As Ella climbed into the rear seat a car went by and tooted at her. A loud wolf whistle resounded down the road and someone, somewhere shouted 'ribbit.'

'Friends of yours?' Another officer in the car said. A woman.

'No.'

'Name,' the female officer asked, her tone indicating that it had already been a long night. Ella gave her name, then her address, then her car registration number, but they already had that. 'Blow into this.' The officer passed Ella a breathalyser; the male officer explained how to blow properly.

'But I haven't been drinking.' Ella did a quick reckoning in her head; she had drunk last night, but not tonight. Could that still be in her system? Surely not. She hadn't had that much. Had she?

'You were driving erratically, that usually suggests intoxication,' the female officer said, sighing. 'And you're obviously in some sort of fancy dress, been or going to a party. Just blow.'

Ella blew and the male officer took the breathalyser from her and looked at the reading, he waited, looked up and almost smiled at her.

'Okay, that's fine. You obviously haven't been drinking. What about drugs.'

'Absolutely not,' Ella said.

'Do you usually drive like that?' he said.

'Like what?'

'Erratically,' he said again. 'You appeared to go one way then veer off in the opposite direction. Very dangerous.'

Ella's phone rang and Sam's face popped up. Ella swiped her thumb across the screen.

'Please don't answer the phone,' the female officer's voice droned.

'But that's why I changed direction, I'm picking my friend up outside *McDonald's*, I couldn't remember which end of the road it was. Now she's ringing to see where I am. She's probably worried.'

'And your clothes?' The male officer said. Ella thought she could see a hint of curled lip.

'I was in bed when she called.'

'In that?'

'Not against the law, is it?' Was she pushing her luck?

'Okay, you can go,' the female officer interrupted, having spent the last few minutes looking at her phone. 'Everything's in order. Just watch how you drive.'

'That's it?' Ella was relieved and annoyed.

'Frog outfits aren't against the law, so yes, that's it. You might want to rethink your footwear.' The male officer got out of the car and opened the rear door so Ella could get out. He escorted her halfway back to her car then stood and watched as she walked towards it. 'Bye *Kermit*,' he said, turning and walking back to the police car. As he opened the door Ella heard his colleague laugh and he joined in.

'Bastards,' she hissed, as she turned her engine and lights back on.

'You've taken ages,' Sam said as Ella pulled up. 'The AA is already here. It's not as bad as we thought. I think I'll stay and go home with Charlie.'

'But, I've…' Ella started. Oh, what was the point? 'Okay.'

'Sorry to have got you out in the cold.' Sam leant in to kiss Ella on the cheek, but stooped to look Ella up and down. 'You shouldn't come out in public like that.

Thank God it's dark.' She shook her head and turned to walk away.

'Bye,' Ella called, but Sam was already back with Charlie, his protective arm wrapping around her.

Ella drove home, annoyed, humiliated and thoroughly wound up. She'd never get to sleep now.

* * *

'Been up all night?' Ben said as he walked past Ella at work the next morning.

She looked up and scowled. Had he seen her with the police?

'Only you look a bit pale.' He hastened towards his desk.

Mid-morning an email popped into her inbox: *Friday is Pink Day. Make sure you wear pink to increase your creativity.* It had been sent to the whole team. Oh, for God's sake. Ella deleted the email, then opened her drawer and gave Barbie's head a therapeutic squeeze.

By the end of the day all Ella could think about was getting home. She hadn't told anyone about her police incident, not even Sam, who was oblivious to the humiliation she had caused.

Ella slept well that night and the next morning she awoke refreshed and perky, until she realised she had slept in again. She had little more than twenty minutes to get to work and half of those were needed for the journey. She would not be late, she was determined.

She jumped in the shower, even cleaning her teeth under the hot jets, and towelled herself dry at the same time as flinging open her wardrobe to find something to wear. She grabbed a pair of black trousers and a cosy pink jumper – one she'd completely forgotten she had –

hurriedly dressed herself, scooped her hair up into a quick knot at the back secured by the first clip she picked up, which was also pink and matched her jumper – how lucky was that? Grabbing her coat she was out of the door within nine minutes flat.

'Well done, Ella,' she said as she started the car. Her stomach growled its hunger. 'Shush you, you'll have to wait.'

'Morning,' Ella said to Gwynnie and Tiffy as she slipped her coat off and sunk into her chair.

'Morning,' they chorused back. A quick glance from Gwynnie, but not even that from Tiffy.

Ella felt sickly hungry now. She'd give it half-an-hour then slink off to the restaurant and see what was on offer.

She switched on her computer and waited while it went through its tedious start up process. When finally it burst into life she opened her email and there it was, an email from Gwynnie sent since Ella had arrived.

Is today Friday? That's all it said. No explanation. No context. Just those three words.

No it's Tuesday, Ella replied. She wondered if it was a quiz, but Gwynnie's reply soon told her otherwise.

That's what I thought. So why are you wearing pink?

What. Was the woman serious? They sat three feet apart, they faced each other and they were having this stupid conversation via email. Ella didn't even bother to reply. How dare that Barbie doll dictate what Ella wore? Especially when that Barbie doll wore pink most days herself.

Gwynnie got up to go to the printer, Ella watched her strut across the office. Today Gwynnie wasn't wearing pink. Typical.

Ella watched while Gwynnie came back with several

sheets of paper in her hand and plonked herself back down at her desk. She didn't look at Ella, didn't say a word.

Right, that's it. Ella grabbed her purse and got up, but just before she left she opened her drawer an inch, the drawer with the smelly dog rag in it and she left it open.

Ella could see Sam through the HR office door; she had her head down and was typing furiously. Ella slipped in unnoticed and said a quiet hello but Sam didn't acknowledge her straight away.

'Oh Ella. Hi. Have you been there long?'

'No. Not really. Have you got time for a quick coffee?'

Sam shook her head without even considering it. 'No. Sorry. Bit up against it this morning.' She turned her attention back to her work.

'Okay.' Ella felt deflated. 'What about lunch?'

'Can I email you about lunch?' Sam said, without even looking up.

'Okay. See you later.'

She went down to the staff restaurant and queued up at the coffee station with a surprisingly large number of people who were also not at their desks. Then she chose a large, blueberry muffin.

She found herself a quiet table by the window, sipped her coffee and picked at the muffin. It was raining again and she watched the rivulets running down the glass making grubby trails on their way to the ground. That's what my life's like, Ella thought – grubby trails.

What the hell was she doing with her life? And what the hell *should* she do with it? Spring Cottage reared its ugly head again. If she was honest Spring Cottage occupied her head far too frequently and she spent a lot of time trying to push it out. One minute she was almost homeless – she didn't consider the grotty bedsit a home – next minute she owned a four-bedroomed cottage. The thought of the cottage made her shudder. The enormity of the work just to make it habitable scared her witless. If she was part of a couple like Sam and Charlie it might be an easier decision just to take it on and do the work. But on her own. No. Oh grow up, Ella, a little voice in her head said.

Was she on her own? She thought of Hal. She smiled. He was hot, no doubt about that, and he had a bit of experience with property. What had he said? Oh yes, he had a couple of rental properties so knew a bit about renovation. And he had offered to help; he had definitely said he would help. Maybe, she thought, maybe it's possible. She imagined herself in the cottage with Hal by her side, each holding paintbrushes, dabs of white paint on their faces, laughter in their eyes. Hal in overalls, just overalls, unbuttoned to the waist because painting was hot work. Him grabbing her, pulling her to him. She heard herself sigh.

'You all right?' Ben sat down at her table. 'That bloody woman is mental; she's called another emergency team meeting this afternoon.'

'Oh. Hi. Yeah. I'm fine. Thanks.' Ella was suddenly back in the staff restaurant, back to reality. 'It's probably about me wearing pink today.'

Ben laughed, leaned over and patted Ella on the arm. 'We did enjoy that. Well done. You didn't see her face when you took your coat off; you had your back to her. If looks could kill. It was so funny. You certainly know how to wind her up.'

'I didn't do it on purpose.'

Ben creased his brow and wrinkled his nose.

'Really. I didn't. I woke up late and grabbed the first thing I saw in my wardrobe. I think Sam bought me this.' Ella brushed the sleeve of her jumper. 'And I don't think I've ever worn it before, in fact I'd forgotten I even had it. And I certainly didn't wear it deliberately. I've been so preoccupied lately I must have thought today was pink day.'

'Well, either way, it was priceless.'

'For you maybe.' Ella stood up and scraped her chair back across the floor. Ben winced.

Back at her desk she closed the stinky drawer before sitting down. She hoped they'd savoured the smell. There were several emails waiting for her, among them one from Sam. Ella ignored the others and opened it. *Sorry, can't make lunch today; have to go into town with Sally. Catch you later. No point you coming, no time to talk. xxx*

Great. Sally was Sam's boss; Ella wondered what that was about. She didn't even bother answering.

She didn't speak to anyone for the rest of the morning, just got on with her work, went to the drinks machine at the end of the corridor several times, and, belatedly, accepted Gwynnie's invitation to the meeting, via email. At lunchtime she grabbed a sandwich from the restaurant then went and sat in her car to eat it. At least she could have the radio on; at least she wouldn't have to speak to anyone.

The rain had stopped and the sun came out and it was lovely in the car on her own. She closed her eyes and thought of Hal. Tall and muscular and hot. She liked his clothes too – elegant, expensive. She compared him to Nathan, no comparison. Nathan had grungy long hair and wore black denim; Hal had precision cut hair and wore classy suits, jackets, leather brogues.

Nathan wore brown workman boots.

She shook her head and got Nathan out of it. Why was that snake creeping in anyway? Now Hal, he was something else. He was a gentleman; he knew how to behave. He would never sing a vile song about her in public.

Spring Cottage – it popped to the front of her mind. Again. She pushed it back, but this time it didn't feel quite so daunting.

Back at her desk, calmed and rested after her car break she got on with her work. An email from Tiffy popped up. *I need an update on the Eldorite project before the meeting.* No please; no thank you. It seemed that tone of email was catching. So Ella replied: *All is fine, just as it was yesterday at 4.30pm when I last updated you.* She watched as Tiffy opened it and blinked, but she didn't say anything and she didn't email back. Excellent, thought Ella. That's just how I like it.

They piled into the meeting room yet again and everyone sat in the same seats they seemed always to sit in now. Unspoken allocation.

How very different this was from Don's day. He only called team meetings if there was a major problem. He called them s*hit's hit the fan* meetings. He may not have been much of a manager but he did believe that everyone could just get on with their jobs and speak up if they had a problem. Ella found herself almost wishing he was back. She thought wistfully of the many times she had wished he would leave. Be careful what you wish for.

'Thank you all for coming,' Gwynnie began, as though they had a choice. 'Before we start I just want to remind everyone that Friday is Pink Day.' Gwynnie's eyes drifted in Ella's direction. Ella looked away. She wasn't going to be dragged into an argument; it just wasn't worth it. But it seemed that Gwynnie wasn't going to leave it there. 'I know that some of you don't fully understand the relevance of creative initiatives like Pink Day and Think Day, but they really do focus our attention on our creativity; they help us to see things differently and this helps us to be more creative about how we approach our work and our work ethic and our colleagues.' Another dirty look in Ella's direction. 'Oh, and Ella, I'm still waiting for your Smile Day proposal.'

Ella nodded but did not speak. No one spoke. Ben bit his lip, and Kevin focused on a pencil he was rolling slowly on the table.

'Hear, hear,' said Tiffy, filling the air space. She gave the room a bright smile and pulled up her shoulders, puffed out her chest.

'Thank you, Tiffy.' Gwynnie waited for a moment, smiling around the room, apparently hoping for further affirmations. They didn't come.

'Excellent,' Gwynnie said, as though someone had said something positive. 'Ben, how's your part of the Eldorite project progressing?'

'Yes. Good. We're just about keeping up with Ella, getting the lines on once she's approved them.' He nodded sneakily at Ella.

'Thank you,' Ella mouthed back silently.

'Kevin, are you enjoying the work?' Gwynnie stared at the pencil between Kevin's fingers.

'Yes, thank you,' Kevin muttered to the pencil.

'Very good. Tiffy?' Gwynnie's head tilted to one side.

'Everything is fine and on schedule.' Tiffy said, puffing herself up again.

'That's very good. Now then, I called this meeting

not just to…'

'Excuse me,' Ella interrupted.

'Yes?'

'What about my update?'

'Tiffy's the controller for the project and she's given your update for you.'

'Not really.'

'Oh. Didn't Tiffy ask you for an update?'

'Yes.'

'Well, did you update her?'

'Yes, but only generally. Everything is fine, but I do have a couple of problems with two lines and now would be a good time to discuss those.'

'No, it wouldn't.' Gwynnie looked at Ella and seemed to dare her to answer back. 'I'm sure I don't need to remind you that Tiffy is the controller. You can have a chat about the troubling lines outside the meeting. Now back to what I was saying. We have another fantastic project, which Tiffy here,' Gwynnie turned round and patted Tiffy on the shoulder, 'has agreed to control again. I think that's great news because she's doing such a good job on the Eldorite project.'

'No she isn't.' Ella's voice cut through the air.

Ben and Kevin looked down at the table.

Tiffy blinked several times; her mouth opened and closed.

Gwynnie's mouth opened then closed too.

'Well, she isn't doing anything. I do all the work checking the lines and Ben and Kevin put them on the inventory. I don't know what else there is to do but whatever it is, Tiffy isn't doing it. She doesn't understand the work. Do you Tiffy?' Ella turned to Tiffy whose face had now pinked up and red blotches were appearing on her neck.

'How dare you speak like that to your colleague, your superior, in fact.' Gwynnie's voice climbed an octave as she spoke.

'Okay then, Tiffy. Tell us about the project. Tell us where we are. If you're the controller you know everything. That's right, isn't it?' Oh shit Ella, a voice said in her head. You've gone too far. You shouldn't have started this.

'Tiffy doesn't have to explain herself to you. How dare you try to humiliate her. I think you've said enough. But if you apologise now, and Tiffy accepts it, I think we can move on.'

'I'm not apologising. It's the truth. And, while we're at it, I don't know what you do either.'

'I manage. That's what I do.'

'Manage what? Pink Day and Think Day. Ha.' Oh dear, Ella knew this was the end. Knew there was no going back, so she might as well go for it. She knew she'd regret it later but the feeling of getting all these weeks of frustration off her chest was so good, so liberating it was intoxicating.

'How dare you,' Gwynnie began, but Ella cut across her.

'You're making our department a laughing stock. Pink Day, for God's sake what is that about? Are you mad?'

'It helps our creativity. And you seem hell bent on jeopardising that. Look at you today, wearing pink on the wrong day.' Gwynnie shook her head and her brittle bob rasped against her shoulders.

'We don't need to be creative. We do a process job; we just need to be conscientious and diligent and efficient.'

'There are always opportunities for thinking outside the box, for creative thinking.'

'Oh shut up.'

'I think you'd better go to the toilets and wash your face. You need to calm down. Then you can apologise to the team.' Gwynnie stood up and opened the door.

'I don't need to wash my face, thank you very much. And, just so you know, I won't be apologising. Not to you and certainly not to Tiffy.'

'The meeting's over. Everyone can go back to their desks now. Except Ella.'

Ella waited. Not sure what she wanted to do. Not sure where this was going now. Suddenly she felt she was no longer in control of the situation – if she ever had been.

After everyone had gone Gwynnie closed the door with a bang and turned to Ella. Neither woman sat down.

'That was mean and unnecessary. I'm going straight to HR now and you can go back and get on with your work while I decide what's going to happen to you.'

'No.'

'No? No?'

'Yes. That's right. No. I'm not going back to my desk and getting on with my work.' Ella's head bobbed from side to side, an imitation of Gwynnie's movements earlier. 'And *you're* not going to decide what happens to me.' Ella smiled. Suddenly she knew exactly what was going to happen to her.

Gwynnie's head wobbled but she didn't seem to know what to say.

'You see, Gladys,' Ella said and watched as Gwynnie's eyes and mouth widened in shock and horror. 'I'm going to get much more money than your husband and I *don't* have a mortgage to pay.' Ella gave Gwynnie a sweet little smile, opened the door and skipped down the corridor back to the office.

When she approached her desk Tiffy pretended to concentrate on her work, but Ella could see that her neck was still blotchy. An email pinged into Ella's inbox and for one hilarious moment Ella thought it was from Tiffy, but it was from Ben: *Stairs, now? Pls?*

'I'm sorry I didn't support you in there,' Ben said, as they stood together on the landing, away from eavesdroppers.

'It's okay.'

'I'm ashamed too. Everything you said is absolutely true.'

'It's okay,' Ella said again.

'No, I really am sorry. I can't afford to lose my job; I've got a family to support. But I should have said something. I should have backed you up. I feel really ashamed. I hope you don't lose your job.'

'It's okay.'

'I wish you wouldn't keep saying that.'

'It really is okay. And as for losing my job, I'm not losing it, I'm dumping it. Barbie and the Troll can get on with it. I just hope it doesn't leave you guys in the muck.'

'Barbie and the Troll. Ha ha ha. That is so funny.' Ben laughed now. He looked relieved. 'So what are you going to do? Have you got another job already?'

'No.' Ella shook her head. 'I have a plan B.' She thought of the cottage, she thought of Hal and his offer of help, how she was going to accept that offer. 'I'll tell you about it some other time, when we're away from here. Now I have a few other things to do.' Ella was feeling empowered and she liked it.

Gwynnie was waiting at Ella's desk, her hands on her hips and her lips pursed.

'Would you come with me please?' Gwynnie spoke in a flat, even tone, but she too had a blotchy neck.

'Where?'

'To HR. Where we can talk in private.'

'No.' Ella leaned past Gwynnie and switched off her computer, she didn't shut it down properly and she didn't care. Then she started to collect her personal belongings together. She picked the desk troll up, smiled at it, then set it aside. She collected her coffee mug, though it had never had coffee in it, just pens and an emery board. She tipped the pens onto her desk then stuffed the cup in her handbag.

'What are you doing?' Gwynnie squeaked.

'What do you think I'm doing?'

'But it's not home time yet.'

Ella laughed. 'Well, it is for me.'

'No. I don't think it needs to come to this. I'm sure if we discuss it rationally and calmly we can move on from this misunderstanding.'

'What misunderstanding? It's all perfectly clear to me.' Oh dear, Ella was enjoying this just too much.

Gwynnie backed off, moved round to stand beside Tiffy's desk. Ella looked at the pair of them, Barbie and the Troll, their faces slowly registering what was happening.

Ella opened her drawer, pulled out Barbie then closed it quickly. She took Barbie and the desk troll over to Ben and Kevin.

'One each,' she said, laying them on their desks. 'They are amazing stress balls. Try it when the stupidness gets too much.'

Ben laughed and picked up Barbie, Kevin eyed the

troll and said nothing.

'I'll email you, Ben.' Ella strode back to her desk. She turned to Gwynnie and Tiffy. 'Oh, you haven't moved.' They were static, like a tableau – one standing, one sitting, both with their mouths open.

She pulled her coat on, found her car keys and picked up her bag. Then she opened the drawer and pulled out Rueben's stinky old dog rag. She held it at arm's length, and marched round to Gwynnie and Tiffy – they were already recoiling at the stench.

'Here, have this. You can add it to your repertoire of stupid days. Call it Stink Day.' She threw it at Tiffy, and somehow it managed to drape itself round both Gwynnie and Tiffy at the same time.

She could still hear the horror squeals and gagging as she strutted down the office.

Eight

The message came just as she started the car. She pulled her phone out. Sam. *OMG what have you done?!? You okay hun? xxx*

Ella winced. Of course Sam would know all the details, one of the privileges of working in HR.

Ella considered how she felt for several seconds. Was she okay? Yes. At the moment she was. She thought about ringing Sam, or at least messaging her back. No, she'd wait. Sam hadn't made herself available when Ella needed her, so now Sam could wait for Ella's version of events.

As she drove home Ella thought about what had happened. It had felt so good when she'd challenged Tiffy and told Gwynnie – and everyone else – just how it was. She hadn't said anything that wasn't true. Tiffy knew nothing and Gwynnie didn't know much more. And the look on their faces when she threw the dog rag at them. Priceless.

She wondered what her mum would say when she told her. Ella gasped. She wouldn't be telling her mum anything, how could she? She took a deep breath.

Sam messaged twice more before Ella got home. The last message said that she was popping round on her way home from work. Interesting. Ella's place wasn't on Sam's way home. Was she really so desperate to know the facts.

'What have you done?' Sam gasped, as Ella opened the door to her. No hello, no how are you.

Ella shrugged. 'Only what I should have done weeks ago. And it feels so good.'

'Yes. But…well…you…' Sam was stuck for words, but she soon found them again. 'I did caution you not to do anything you might regret. How will Gubbins be able to give you a good reference after this?'

Ella shrugged again. She didn't want to hear it. She didn't want the sensible voice of reason. She wanted support. She wanted to be cheered. She wanted to be told that she had done the right thing. She wanted congratulations.

'It's not too late,' Sam said, sitting down on the sofa bed, still unmade from Ella's late start that morning. 'I think if you apologise Gwynnie will have you back. You can put this behind you and forget about it.'

'What? What are you saying? I'm not apologising. If there's any apologising to be done it has to come from them – Gwynnie and Tiffy.' Ella folded her arms. 'No way am I apologising.'

Sam sighed quietly. She stood up, folded her arms. 'Well maybe you'll feel differently in the morning. You need a job Ella, it's not as though you've got any other money, or a partner to support you.'

'Well maybe I have.'

Sam frowned.

'Maybe I'm going to go and live in my cottage and live off the income that goes with it.'

'Ha. On your own? Take all that on, on your own. You said you couldn't do it.'

'Maybe I won't be on my own.'

Ella could tell by Sam's expression that she didn't believe Ella had anyone, didn't believe it for a minute.

Sam moved towards the door. 'Message me in the morning when you come to your senses.' She left without saying any more, not even goodbye.

Now Ella did feel bad, but not over of what had happened with Gwynnie and Tiffy but because of Sam, her best friend who seemed incapable of supporting her. One thing was for sure, there was no going back to Gubbins and Ella would not be apologising to anyone.

Ella went to bed happy to the point of intoxication, and she slept the best sleep of the smug.

In the morning Ella woke up early and felt her heart sink. Oh my God, what had she done? *Pull yourself together,* her stern inner voice said. *What's done is done and you had complete control. You did it. Now live with it.*

She dragged herself out of bed, the pep talk still running at high speed in her head. It kept up its constant babble in the shower and as she made herself meese toast – well why not, she had the time – and got dressed. She had done all this before she looked at the clock; it wasn't even eight am. If she left for work now she would be very early. Oh, the irony.

Ella cleared up her breakfast things, tidied and folded the sofa bed away, cleaned the shower room out, put her mini-vac over the carpet and even polished all the surfaces. She glanced around. It was tidy, but still tiny and still little more than a bedsit. She slumped down on the sofa and sighed. What now?

Spring Cottage. That's what now, the stern voice said.

'Okay,' Ella's little voice squeaked aloud. 'Okay.'

The drive out of town was tedious; she was battling the rush hour traffic. Once into the countryside it became calmer. It was quieter for a start, so much so that she could hear the birds sing, even as she drove along. It was a bright, clear day and the countryside was starting to wake up.

'Spring Cottage,' she said, 'it's spring and I'm moving into Spring Cottage.' She laughed to herself, reassurance, affirmation; it was meant to be.

There were more people about in the village as she passed the pub, the shop, the dreaded public toilets; someone even waved at her. She waved back, completely ignorant as to whom they were – probably one of the spectators from her toilet lock-in.

She pulled up outside Spring Cottage; it was her home now, she had no choice. Without a job, without a salary, she couldn't even afford the rent on the grotty bedsit.

It suddenly hit her that she would need to move quickly. She didn't know how she stood financially with work, how much they owed her especially as she had just walked out. She'd have to give notice on the bedsit; she'd have to move into Spring Cottage very soon, before the deadline expired.

She fumbled in her bag for the keys, still wondering what the biggest one was for.

The door opened and the musty smell enveloped her, urgh. Despite being here twice before, this was her first time alone. She turned her head to the side, took a deep breath of fresh air and marched in, closing the door behind her.

It looked just as awful. Just as run down and shabby. *Well*, said the stern voice, *what did you expect?*

'Shut up,' Ella said aloud. 'You're supposed to be on my side. And now I'm talking to myself. Again.'

She pushed through the rooms growing more and more despondent. Without Sam – she felt sick just at the thought of Sam – to point out the possibilities; and without Hal – hot Hal – to make enthusiastic assurances, she couldn't see any hope. She thought of the magazines now sitting on the front seat of her car, how the hell could she ever realise that vision in this place?

Pull yourself together. Get on with it.

Ella slumped down on the tatty sofa in the living room, then leapt straight up, it really didn't smell good – that would have to go.

A loud rap-rap at the door made her jump.

'Saw you here again,' Walt said. He was wearing what Ella thought was a boiler suit, a dark blue canvas version of her onesie. With his head of thick white hair, he reminded her of a *smurf*. She didn't know whether to laugh or cry.

'Hello,' she said, forcing a smile.

'Bit of a job.' He glanced around the room, went into the kitchen and whistled. 'All a bit bad. Very run down.'

'Thanks for that,' Ella said, so quietly that she didn't think he heard her.

'Sorry dear, just stating the obvious, I know.'

She looked around the room, felt the hot pin prick of tears in her eyes. Go away, she thought, but she wasn't sure if she was talking to the tears or Walt.

'Place has been empty for years, so you've got accumulated filth, and they were very old, set in their ways, they weren't much bothered with modern conveniences. I don't think they even had a TV.' He glanced around, his eyes stopping on the strange brown light switch. 'Bakelite,' he said, not that Ella had a clue what he was talking about. 'You'll need a full rewire.'

'Mmm.'

Another rap at the door.

'Here comes the cavalry.' Walt beamed and rushed to open the door. Edna bustled into the room; she wore the same new canvas onesie boiler suit affair as Walt. Behind her were four other people, two men, two women, all very old and all wearing the boiler suits. The women wore flowery turbans on their heads; they carried mops, buckets, all sorts of cleaning materials. The men carried step-ladders, a tool box.

People were introduced but the names washed over Ella. She stood in front of them open-mouthed.

'You might want to put this on,' Edna passed Ella a new boiler suit, still in its packaging.

Someone produced a kettle and a box of mugs. 'First things first,' Walt laughed. 'We'll make tea while you get changed.'

Ella blinked. Felt her mouth drop open.

'Hurry along dear, we need you to make a decision about the furniture. If we get it out front, Gilbert's lad will pick it up in the van and take it down the dump. It's hard to get skips down these lanes.' Edna and the rest went into the kitchen leaving Ella on her own to change. 'He'll be here around ten,' Edna called behind her.

Ella had actually dressed in what she considered appropriate cleaning clothes, she even had an old pair of trainers on, but she could hardly refuse the boiler suit. She took off her jeans and jumper, kept her t-shirt on and pulled on the suit. It was large, very large; she wondered how big they thought she was. She rolled up the sleeves and legs – she was the short *smurf*.

'You might want this too,' one of the old ladies handed Ella a flowery scarf.

'Umm,' Ella said, eyeing it and wondering what the hell to do with it.

'Duck down and I'll do it for you. Reminds me of the land army, I was in the land army, you know. Happy days.' The old lady smiled to herself, a faraway look in her eyes.

Ella wondered what the hell the land army was as she allowed the lady to turban her hair.

'During the war,' Edna said, answering the question on Ella's face. 'When the men were away fighting, the women worked the land, farming.'

'Oh. Right.' During the war? How *old* were these people?

'Phones off,' Walt shouted and everyone pulled their phones out of their pockets and switched them off. 'Especially you, Ella. We don't want you distracted by Facebook every two minutes. We know what you young uns are like.' He gave her a big beaming smile which stopped Ella in her tracks, stopped her from objecting and she obliged, switching her phone to silent.

'Furniture first,' Edna said, corralling Ella as the others drank tea in the kitchen. They marched around the house, Edna making a list as Ella made decisions. The sofa and chair had to go, the dresser was staying, the bed frames could stay but the mattresses had to go, in fact anything vaguely fabric or soft, had to go. 'Mice,' Edna said, 'you've probably got 'em, or had 'em.' She laughed. Ella didn't, it wasn't funny.

Walt and the two old men carried the furniture out and dumped it in the road and Ella found herself in a front bedroom with Edna and assorted buckets and cloths, while the two other old dears – that's what Edna called them, the old dears – worked on the other front bedroom.

'Who's Gilbert?' Ella asked, as they began their mammoth task.

'The man with the van.' Edna chuckled as though she'd made a joke. 'Village builder, might be handy for you.'

'Yes. Probably will.'

They scrubbed and they cleaned, they found the inevitable big spiders but Edna just scooped them up and flung them out of the window.

Ella had just moved onto cleaning the window when she caught sight of 'Gilbert's lad' loading the last item of furniture onto the truck. He was tall, muscular, as you might expect from a builder's son, wore black jeans and a tight, white t-shirt, had very short, dark hair. Ella wondered how old he was, from the back it was hard to tell. She stopped what she was doing and watched him intently; he was alone, so presumably he had loaded everything into the van by himself.

'Ah, he's finished,' Edna's voice said, suddenly standing next to Ella. 'He's a good lad.'

'Yes. It's very good of him. How old is he?'

Edna looked out of the window, studied him. 'Young,' she pronounced. 'Young and fit.'

Ella did a double take, then realised that Edna didn't mean fit like Ella meant fit, she meant able, strong.

'He might be your age,' Edna's parting shot, as she left to get a bucket of clean water.

In the next bedroom the old ladies had started singing, Ella didn't recognize the song. When Edna came back she asked her.

'Oh, I don't know. One of their golden oldies, I expect. They're very old ladies, those two, you know.'

Ella smiled, didn't press it, because everyone here seemed ancient, except maybe for Gilbert's lad, but given Edna's approximation of age, even that was doubtful. He was probably seventeen, or he could be forty-seven. Ella hoped there were some people in the village nearer her own age, desperately hoped it, because she was stuck here now.

The song in the next room changed.

'I know that.' Ella stopped, listened wide-eyed as the old ladies sang *Mr Brightside* by The Killers in their warbly old lady voices.

'No. I don't. ' Edna shook her head. 'It'll be some old war time song.'

'No. It's not. It's The Killers.'

'I wonder where our lunch is?' Edna said, changing the subject and going out onto the landing, calling down to the kitchen. When she came back she informed Ella it was on its way.

'Lunch? I hadn't even thought about lunch.'

'We have to feed the men, and the old ladies will be flagging now, I'm quite hungry myself.' But the old ladies didn't sound as though they were flagging, they moved onto *Jumping Jack Flash* by The Stones and Edna joined in. When it had finished, she laughed. 'Glad they're finally singing one I know.'

Somewhere in the depths of the cottage a whistle sounded and suddenly Edna and the old ladies downed tools and trooped into the bathroom to wash their hands, with Edna urging Ella to do the same.

Downstairs in the kitchen the men were already sitting around the table and tucking into soup and fresh baked bread. The aroma made Ella's stomach growl.

'There's pea and ham or chicken broth,' Walt said, nodding towards the two big vats in the middle of the table.

'Where did they come from?' Ella asked, sitting down and thanking Edna for the bowl of chicken broth she was passing her.

'Pub,' Walt said.

'But who's paid for it. I need to reimburse someone.'

'Oh no,' Walt said, patting Ella's hand. 'They're happy to donate it. It's in everyone's interests that you settle in. Call it a welcome present.'

'Well, I'm very grateful. And I'm very grateful to you all too, giving up your time to help me. You're all very kind.' Ella felt a tickle in the back of her throat. She swallowed hard, she was not going to cry, she didn't even know why she wanted to.

A jug of cider and glasses were produced and Walt proposed a toast. 'To Ella.' He raised his glass. 'The long-awaited, much welcome, young and beautiful new owner of Spring Cottage.' Everyone repeated the toast.

Ella blushed; she was many things but beautiful had never really been one of them.

The men all had second helpings of the soup and soon it was all gone.

'Is there no pudding?' One of the old men asked.

'No. Not today,' Walt said, standing up.

'Well, that's a shame. I was looking forward to a bit of spotty dick and custard.'

'And a good sleep after it.' His wife tutted. 'That's probably why there isn't any.'

The old ladies laughed and gave each other knowing looks, then the meal was quickly cleared away and everyone was back at their allotted tasks. Ella wondered where these old people got their energy from, because she was starting to tire.

By late afternoon all the bedrooms were cleaned and the wallpaper had been stripped off the stairs and most of the downstairs rooms too. Ella stood and surveyed the work. It certainly looked better without the peeling wallpaper. The men had even rubbed down the woodwork. Downstairs required a lot more cleaning, but Ella now realised that upstairs only required repainting since most of the bedroom walls had only ever been painted.

'Which room will you have as your bedroom,' Edna said, as they walked around admiring their efforts.

'The one at the front with the little fireplace. Do you think it works?'

'Might need the chimney sweeping,' Walt said, from the landing. I'll give the man a ring.

'Thank you. But won't that undo all our hard work. Ella had visions of black soot everywhere.

'Better not.' Walt laughed and Edna joined in. 'I've sent the old people home now. It's been a long day for them.'

'It's been a long day for me too,' Ella said. 'I can't thank you all enough.'

'It's been a pleasure.' Walt clapped a big hand on Ella's shoulder. 'It really has. Seeing this old place coming back to life is bringing a smile to everyone's face, the whole village.'

'Tomorrow we'll polish that brass bed up ready for you. So you'll just need to get a new mattress.' Edna pulled the turban from her head.

Ella thought of the beds from her mum's place, the ones she'd sold for a pittance because she hadn't had anywhere to put them. Her own bed had only been a couple of years old. She wandered back into the bedroom, her bedroom to be, looked at the brass bed, it suited the cottage perfectly, but she wondered how comfortable it would be with its springy base. She laid her hands on it gingerly, it seemed firm. She sat on it, laid down; it actually felt okay.

'Better with a mattress on it.' Walt laughed from the doorway.

'Would you like to eat with us or do you have plans?' Edna was starting to unbutton her boiler suit. Ella followed suit and wondered which room she'd left her clothes in.

'No. Really. You've been so kind, but I have to catch up with my friend Sam.'

'Let's have a quick look at the garden before you go,' Walt put his arm out, pointing the way.

The garden. Ella's heart sank. She hadn't even thought of that.

'Stick to the walkways,' Walt instructed, they're not too muddy.

Ella followed Walt up and down the garden. What struck her was the size of it, enormous. It was ten times the size of her mum's garden. Walt was pointing things out, telling her plant names, it was in one ear and out the other for Ella; he might as well have been speaking a foreign language.

We'll need to get started on it soon,' he said. 'We're just in time to get the main crops in.'

'Crops?' Ella could hear the alarm in her voice. 'I don't know anything about gardening, never mind crops. Can't I just leave it for now?'

'Such a waste, it's been wasted for a few years. We did try to keep it up after your aunt and uncle died, but without the…' His voice trailed off. 'Don't worry, it'll be fine.' He patted Ella on the back and turned towards the cottage. 'Oh dear, look.' He pointed to some green shoots which appeared to have been cut off just above ground level.

'What's that?'

'New growth, which is good. But it's been got at. Probably that Feral Billy.' Walt shook his head and marched on.

'Who's Feral Billy?' Ella said to Walt's retreating form, but he wasn't listening.

On the way home Ella stopped off at an out-of-town homewares superstore and, on impulse, bought a mattress and new bedding. The sales staff helped her put the back seats of her car down and force the mattress – a foam one conveniently rolled into a vacuum pack – into her car. She used her credit card to pay for it and then wondered if she'd be able to pay the bill. She needed to find out how much she would get from Gubbins; it might be nothing. She needed to ring the solicitor and tell him she was definitely moving in and ask about the money.

The bedsit seemed even smaller now. And darker, and drearier. Ella sat down on the sofa bed and thought about the new mattress in the car.

'I think I've made the right decision,' she heard herself say out loud.

She pulled her phone out of her bag. Checked her messages. Four from Sam, escalating in urgency from *Ring me, hun. You OK? xx* all the way through to *Desperately need to speak. Where are you?* There were also two missed calls from Sam.

Ella rang her back.

'I've been trying to get in touch with you all day. Where have you been?' Sam sounded annoyed.

'I've been up at the cottage, cleaning.'

'Oh. I see. I suppose there's no phone signal there.'

'No. I think the signal's okay. We had to turn our phones off. I only put mine to silent, but then never looked at it again.' Ella laughed. She'd quite forgotten about her phone during the day, which was most unusual.

'What are you talking about? Who said you had to turn it off.'

'Oh. Don't worry about that. What did you want? Your messages sounded important.'

'Gwynnie's made an official complaint.'

'Bit late for that.' Ella laughed. 'I've left.'

'Not against you. Against me. You called her Gladys and she's put two and two together and worked out that I told you her real name. I'm in a trusted position. I work in HR, it could only have come from someone in HR and she knows we're friends.'

'But you didn't tell me. Not in so many words.'

'But you did get it from me, or rather out of me with your silly Derren Brown thing. Remember.'

'Yes.'

'I don't need this. I'm going on maternity leave in a few months. I don't want all this aggravation.'

'Okay. What do you want me to do?'

'Tell them you didn't get it from me. You need to come in tomorrow to be interviewed. You're my defence.'

Ella thought about it for a moment. The last thing she wanted was for Sam to be disciplined for that. But the truth was she *had* got it from Sam, albeit not verbally.

'Okay. I'll say you never told me, because you didn't. When do I have to come?'

'Three, tomorrow. You won't let me down, will you

Ella?'

'Of course I won,' Ella said, affronted.

'Get here before three; ask for Sally, not me. Okay?'

'Okay.'

'Bye.' Sam's voice was already sounding distant and she ended the call before Ella could even respond.

Well, you evidently don't want to hear about my day, Ella thought, rather hurt. But who could blame Sam, she was running scared. And to be fair it wasn't her fault. If there was any blame, it should go to Ella. But it had been worth it, the look on Gwynnie's face when Ella had called her Gladys was exquisite.

* * *

After a good night's sleep, brought on by the excess of physical work during the day, Ella dressed in the boiler suit, wrapped her hair in the flowery turban – though not as expertly as the old ladies had – picked up a change of clothes and left. In the car she wavered between joy and worry; she felt elated at the prospect of getting Spring Cottage into some sort of shape but equally daunted by the enormity of the job. Then there was what awaited her this afternoon at work. An involuntary shiver ran up her spine.

When she pulled up outside Spring Cottage the cavalry were already waiting, queued up in the spring sunshine with their boiler suits and turbans on.

'You haven't been waiting long have you?' It was bad enough that they were helping her, without her keeping them hanging around.

'Just got here,' Walt said. 'So don't you worry.'

They piled into the cottage, Edna assigned everyone jobs and off they went. Today Edna and the old ladies were giving the kitchen the benefit of their cleaning expertise. Ella rolled up her sleeves keen to get on with it, but it seemed that she wasn't included.

'Ella, we need to look at the spring,' Walt said, his voice almost a whisper.

Spring? Oh yes, she was supposed to maintain the spring, whatever that meant. 'Okay,' she said, cheerily.

'Have you got the key?'

Ella shrugged. 'Why does it need a key? I've got three on this bunch.' She pulled them from the pocket she'd stuffed them in after opening the front door.

Walt selected the biggest. 'This'll be the one. Shall we go?'

'I wondered what that key was for.' Ella walked towards the back door and looked round for Walt; he hadn't moved.

'It's this way,' he said.

'Oh, I was thinking it was outside.' She had imagined a well somewhere in the overgrown garden. 'But I remember now, it's in the basement, isn't it?'

'Cellar,' Walt corrected, leading Ella along a narrow corridor that ran behind the stairs, a corridor she hadn't really noticed before. The door at the end of the corridor was dark and heavy; Walt jiggled the key in the lock several times but it wouldn't turn.

'Oh,' Ella said, 'I thought it was that key too, because the other two fit the back and front doors and I don't have any others. Maybe the solicitor has it.' Ella turned to walk back along the corridor.

'You try it,' Walt said. 'My hands aren't so nimble anymore.'

'I doubt I'll do any better.'

Walt stepped aside and Ella jiggled the key in the lock. It turned easily and the door swung open.

'I knew you could do it,' Walt said, patting Ella on the back as though she had just passed a test. He fumbled inside for the light switch, evidently knowing where it was, but the bulb was ancient and low wattage and the light pale and yellowy. But it was enough to show the steep, narrow staircase that led down into a gloomy cellar.

'I'll lead the way,' he said. 'Be careful as you follow, I remember these steps being very steep. Bring the key, we'll need it again.'

They stumbled down the stairs together, inhaling stale air and dust. Ella tried not to think about how many spiders there might be lurking down there or maybe mice, or other things. She shook the thoughts from her head.

At the bottom of the steps Walt found another light switch, the bulb – much brighter – illuminated the cellar. Judging by the size, the cellar ran under the entire cottage. In the middle was a circular hatch, six feet across and made from the same, dark, heavy wood as the cellar door. It had symbols painted into it, stars and moons, Ella thought. Carved around the rim were other symbols, which Ella couldn't make out. The hatch was secured by six black iron bolts. She could hear water running beneath it.

'We need to get it open,' Walt said. 'We'll need the key again now.'

Ella laughed. 'You are joking. We can't lift that. Just the two of us. It's enormous and it looks very heavy. Let's leave it for another day.' Another day when Hal would be around to help, he was young and fit, and she meant that not in the way Edna would. She certainly didn't want to get the old men down, they had been dispatched to the garden and she thought *that* physical labour was more than enough for them.

'Come on,' Walt said, taking Ella's hand. 'Try the key in here.' He guided her over to a little white painted door in the wall. Ella put the key in the lock and turned it. Inside the cupboard were a large metal switch and a handle. 'Watch the hatch,' Walt said, as he used both hands to push the switch down, it resisted initially but finally gave way and Ella saw the bolts retract.

'Wow.'

'Best is yet to come.' Walt stepped aside and told Ella to turn the handle in the cupboard.

Ella looked for spiders first, couldn't see any so grabbed the handle and started to turn. It was stiff. It creaked. It did not want to move.

'I can't turn it.' Ella let go and stepped aside to let Walt try.

'It probably just needs a bit of WD40,' he said. 'Wait here. I won't be long.'

Ella surveyed the cellar as she waited for Walt. A tall cabinet stood in the corner; Ella could see that it was free standing and not as old as the door or hatch. Considering how stale the place had smelled when they opened the door and how dusty it was it didn't look too bad. It didn't smell damp and she couldn't see any damp patches, or at least she didn't think she could – there was no mould. Everywhere was painted white except the hatch, and the floor, which was red.

Suddenly the cellar was plunged into darkness, the bulb had blown. Ella felt panicked, afraid, then realised that the weak bulb on the stairs was still on and spreading a little light into the cellar. It cast long shadows which seemed to move across the floor. It's fine, Ella told herself. Walt will be back in a minute.

A cold breeze blew across the cellar, wafted up

towards her and made her shiver.

'Walt,' Ella called. 'Walt.'

Then she heard the door to the cellar close.

Nine

The cellar was silent. Ella waited, listened. Why had Walt, or someone – who – shut her in? She clutched the handle and called Walt's name again and again, but he didn't reply.

Her rational, sensible self told her that there was an explanation for the door closing. Her irrational, less sensible self imagined all sorts; she'd been lured down, tricked, locked in. Sensible Ella asked why?

She heard the door rattle.

'Ella, Ella, are you all right down there?' Walt came down the stairs.

'Walt. Yes, I'm fine. What happened?'

'I opened the front door and the draught must have closed this one. It's dark down here. Ah, the bulb's blown. I suppose it's been a long time since it was last used. I've got the WD40.'

'I'll buy some more bulbs later; I need them for the other rooms too.'

Walt moved gingerly towards Ella, spray can in hand. He sprayed the handle, gave it a jiggle, then sprayed again.

'Try that.'

Ella gripped the handle and turned, it was still stiff, but this time it gave and she was able to spin it.

'What's it actually doing?' Ella asked.

'That's what it's doing,' Walt said, nodding at the hatch.

Even in the dim light Ella could see the big, wooden hatch start to lift, it was pivoting across the back. As she spun the handle the movement became easier, the hatch rising higher and faster.

She could hear water running, fast water – she hadn't been expecting that. Finally the handle stopped turning.

'I think that's as far as it will go,' Ella said, as Walt stood mesmerised by the hatch and the gaping hole it had exposed.

'Yes, it's fully open. Come and have a good look. Be careful in this light, you don't want to fall down there.'

She inched towards the edge and peered in. The hole was six feet across. She could just make out the water rushing beneath them; she could smell it, clean, fresh and sweet.

'I wasn't expecting that. I'd imagined a little trickle, something like a wishing well. It's more like a river.'

'Sometimes it does go down to a trickle. But it's good and healthy now.'

Ella watched Walt in the dim light and saw him take great big gulps.

'Breathe it in, Ella. Breathe in the Spring of Life.'

'The what?'

'Can't you feel it? Can't you sense its vitality? Take a deep breath.'

Just to please Walt, Ella breathed in deeply. 'Not really,' she said, smiling.

'Probably because you're young anyway.' Walt laughed, patted Ella on the back and turned away. 'We can close it now we know it's healthy.'

'How can you tell?'

'By the flow and the scent, it's so sweet.' Walt turned the handle and the hatch closed, blocking off most of the noise. 'It's obviously pleased to meet you.'

'Okay,' Ella said, humouring him. 'Does it supply all the houses round here? I'm sure that's what the solicitor said.'

'It supplies this cottage with all its water. It supplies others if the flow is good enough. We have two taps, one from the spring, one from the mains. You don't.'

'So I'm not on the mains?'

'Only for sewage,' Walt said, then added, laughing, 'Fortunately.'

'So you must be using it now, if the flow's so good.'

'We haven't used it for years now, but I tried it this morning, just to see. It coughed and spluttered a bit, then it came through, so I knew it was probably all right, but it's even better than I expected. Well done, young Ella.' He closed the hatch, laughing and chuckling to himself.

'But I haven't done anything.'

'We need a plan,' Walt said, ignoring her. 'We need to make the cellar and the spring our priority. We'll ask Edna about it, she helped your aunt with it towards the end.'

'What? Why?' Ella asked, but Walt closed the wall cupboard door, went up the stairs and left her wondering.

The morning passed and the cavalry carried on cleaning and stripping wallpaper. The kitchen looked incredibly clean, still tatty and old fashioned, but clean.

The old ladies had found a blue and white dinner service – dozens of plates and serving dishes – tucked into the back of the pantry; another door Ella hadn't noticed before. They were washing it up in the big stone sink and laying out the dried pieces on the dresser they had scrubbed clean. It all looked stunning.

'I expect you'll want to modernise all this,' Edna said. 'I think it might all need rewiring too. We plugged the kettle it and there were sparks. The plumbing's a bit clunky as well.'

Ella stared at the dresser and thought about the enormity of the work needed. She sighed, then jumped as the back door sprung open and the smell of food wafted in.

'Lunch,' Walt called and everyone started to wash their hands in readiness.

They ate hot soup and fresh bread around the kitchen table again and washed it down with cider. During lunch the talk turned to Feral Billy and his antics in the village; he had stolen washing from someone's line, had taken cabbages from another garden, had knocked over several dustbins and been seen wearing a dress in the high street. He sounded like a real character.

'He's been in my garden too,' Ella laughed, more at herself for calling it her garden than anything else.

'His days are numbered, he'll be caught. He's evil,' one of the old men said and everyone nodded their agreement.

'Sooner the better,' another added.

Edna's plan for the cellar involved a thorough cleaning, repainting and some fresh flowers. Ella was unclear as to the urgency, but the entire cavalry, as well as Ella went down into the cellar and starting scrubbing and cleaning. The old ladies started singing again, this time it *was* old war songs and the men discussed how much paint it would take to paint it out, then set about oiling all the hinges on the hatch. The old cabinet Ella had noticed in the corner was opened; inside were half a dozen vases. They were quickly washed and arranged in the corners.

'I have some lovely scented flowers I'm bringing on early, we can put them in the vases,' Edna said.

The next thing Ella knew they were in Walt and Edna's greenhouse picking flowers. When they came back a paint roller was thrust into Ella's hands. They had found an unopened can of white paint and had decided there was no time like the present. Ella loaded up her roller and began to paint; the last time she'd done this had been with her mum, redecorating her sitting room. *I wish you could see me now, Mum.*

The whole cavalry was in the cellar, some rollering, some cutting in, Edna arranging the flowers, the old ladies still singing, the men making faces at them.

'Oh my God, what's the time?' Ella shouted.

'Two-thirty-five,' Walt shouted back. 'We'll easily get this finished today.'

'No. I have an appointment at work, at three. I have to go. Now.'

'You go young Ella; we'll carry on until you get back.'

There was no time to change, no time to tidy herself up, Ella just grabbed her bag and ran for the car, jumped in and roared down the road.

She parked the car, badly, in Gubbins car park and rushed into the offices. She still had her pass and no one had thought to cancel it; at least she didn't have to waste time signing in. She dashed down the corridor towards HR, glanced at the clock – just coming up to three so technically she wasn't late.

'Ella, what have you come as? A clown?' Gwynnie stepped out from a meeting room door, almost as though she had been hiding in wait.

Ella glanced down at herself, of course she was still wearing the boiler suit but what she hadn't noticed were the paint daubs on it.

'Before you go in, could I just have a word? In here.' Gwynnie gestured towards the meeting room.

Ella shrugged. What difference did it make now? She followed Gwynnie.

'The thing is, Ella, your friend Sam could lose her job over this.' Gwynnie smiled, she'd been eating that macrobiotic stuff again. 'She shouldn't have told you my name. And you shouldn't have repeated it in front of everyone else.'

Ella didn't say anything.

'But,' Gwynnie said, 'I'm prepared to let the whole thing drop if you agree to come back and behave yourself.'

'What?'

'I'm even willing to forego the apology, even though I do think you owe me one. How does that sound?'

'I don't owe you an apology. So don't ever think you'll be getting one. And why would you want me back?'

'We're a good team; we're doing some excellent work. We're getting recognition, my,' she shook her head hastily, corrected herself, 'our profile has been raised. We shouldn't let this spoil our success. What do you say?'

'No thanks.'

'Are you sure about that?'

'Quite sure.'

'Your friend Sam will lose her job, her reputation, and her maternity pay and her maternity leave and she won't be able to come back. Probably won't be able to work in HR ever again. Do you want that on your conscience?'

'She never told me your name. She's innocent.'

'The evidence suggests otherwise. It'll be hard for her to prove. The thing is Ella, you did nasty things in front of an audience, you're not exactly a person of credit, a reliable witness, are you?'

'And you are?'

'I'm a manager. The company will support me over you and your friend.'

Ella watched Gwynnie's smiling, confident face. Was that true? Would they?

The door opened and Sally appeared. 'We're ready for you, Ella.'

So Ella went with Sally to be interviewed. Also in the room was Misha, the HR administrator taking notes and – sitting silently at the back of the room – the HR Director, a man who only made himself visible during times of crisis; not a good sign.

'So,' Sally began, 'I understand that Sam told you that Gwynnie's real name is Gladys.'

'Sam never said anything of the sort. Not one word.'

'So how did you know?'

'I guessed.' That was true; it had been a guess – a guess made on Sam's unconscious reaction to the names Ella suggested.

'But how? That's a quite a leap from Gwynnie to Gladys.'

'I knew her name couldn't be Gwynnie, especially as she goes so far out of her way to copy Gwyneth

Paltrow, it was just too ridiculous.'

Sally's face was impassive. Misha scribbled down Ella's words.

Ella stopped speaking; she wasn't going to say any more than necessary.

'But how? Why Gladys?'

'I had other names; Barbie was one of them.'

Sally's eyebrows shot up.

Oh, what the hell, Ella wasn't coming back to Gubbins.

'Barbie?' Ella thought she saw Sally's lips curl a little.

'Yes.'

'Still a leap to Gladys.'

'Yes.' Oh shit, this wasn't going to plan. How Ella wished she hadn't done the Derren Brown thing on Sam. 'I said I was glad about something and I noticed that Gwynnie jumped when I said glad. I tried it out a few more times, then put two and two together.' Ella shrugged. It was true – to some extent.

'That sounds perfectly plausible.' Sally stood up, smiling. 'Thank you, Ella. Appreciate your help with this and coming in on your own time too.'

The silent HR Director also stood up, nodded at Sally and left the room, but not before he gave Ella a quick glance, and was that the hint of a smirk?

'That's it?' Ella looked between Sally and Misha who had already put down her pen and closed her notebook.

'Yes. We knew Sam would never do such a thing.'

'Well, why all this?'

'We had to. You understand. A complaint was made.'

'Poor Sam, having to go through this. I'll just go and say hello.'

Ella followed Sally into the main HR office and Sally

gave Sam the good news before leaving them alone. Sally now had the lovely task of telling Gwynnie.

'I'd love to be a fly on that wall.' Ella laughed.

'Don't even go there. Thanks for being on my side.'

'My pleasure. And I only told the truth.'

'I do appreciate it, but, why did you come dressed like that?'

'Oh, the boiler suit, it's a long story. Actually a lot has happened since I last saw you; I'd love a catch-up.'

'Well here's not the place. Maybe later. Have you actually seen yourself?'

'Yes, I know it's a bit big but it was a present so…'

'No,' Sam interrupted. 'I don't mean what you're wearing, though that's bad enough, I mean your face. You need to look in a mirror before you leave the house.'

Ella blinked. That sounded like a rebuke if ever there was one. 'Okay, shall I pop round this evening?' Ella waited for Sam, who seemed to be considering the idea.

'Sure,' she said finally. 'Message me the time, but not before seven and not after nine.'

'Okay, I'll see you later,' Ella said, her voice falsely cheerful.

On the way out she popped into the toilets and saw her reflection. She'd already seen the paint on the boiler suit, but what she hadn't realised was that she had paint on her face, a wide stripe on both cheeks, perfectly symmetrical and a white exclamation mark in the centre of her forehead. It looked like war paint. Ella laughed out loud and considered washing it off, then remembered that she was going back to Spring Cottage to more painting and didn't bother.

In the car she felt a mix of emotions, excited to be going back to her soon-to-be home, relieved that Sam wasn't in trouble anymore and sad that Sam still appeared to be annoyed with her.

When she reached Spring Cottage the cavalry were in the kitchen drinking tea and eating cake.

'Ella, have a piece of carrot cake, it's one of Edna's best. Then I'll show you what we've done in the cellar.' Walt passed one of the newly found blue and white plates to Ella with a large piece of cake on it.

After carrot cake and tea, the cavalry started to leave. Ella was disappointed because she'd missed a couple of hours but she was still immensely grateful. Walt led her down into the cellar, they'd even replaced the light bulb – with a low energy one that took a while to fully light the room.

'We've finished the walls, the floor must have been done just before your aunt and uncle died because it doesn't need doing, and we've found a tin of oil for the wood. Look.' Walt waved an arm at the hatch. It shone brightly, the dark painted stars and moons showed up in sharp contrast to the lighter background wood.

'It looks amazing. Thank you so much for all the hard work you've done. How can I ever repay you?'

'It's an honour to help you.'

An honour? Ella shook her head and looked closely at the hatch. The carving around the rim was now much clearer and she could see that what she had previously thought were symbols were in fact words.

'What does it say?' Ella twisted her head to follow the writing, then read it aloud. '*WHEN EVIL VISITS, WELCOME IT. WHEN SORROW VISITS, REPEL IT. FEED THE SPRING OF LIFE, RESPECT THE SPRING OF LIFE.* Spring of Life; you called it that earlier. What does it mean?'

'Oh, who knows? These old words get written on

these old things. Pay it no heed.' Walt gave a muted laugh.

Ella looked around the room, vases of Edna's flowers stood in each corner; they looked beautiful. 'The flowers smell lovely. This is a different room to the one we found this morning. I just cannot thank you enough.'

'That's the spring you can smell,' Walt said, starting up the stairs. 'We can move onto your bedroom tomorrow. When are you moving in?'

'Oh, I completely forgot, I meant to ring the solicitor and my landlord's agents and I still don't know how much money I'm getting from work. I've quit my job, did I say?'

'I'm not sure you did, young Ella. But never mind, you've plenty here to keep you busy. Why don't you go and make your calls. Tomorrow is another day.'

'Of course, of course. Thank you so much.'

Walt gave Ella a broad grin as she let him out of the cottage. She collected up her change of clothes – work clothes, which she wouldn't be needing again – locked up and drove home.

* * *

'Well hello, Ella,' Hal's liquid voice said, as Ella barged in through the communal door.

Ella inhaled his exquisite odour, she wasn't familiar with the aftershave he used but it smelled expensive; intoxicating. He grinned at her, crinkling his eyes, it made her knees go weak. He wore dark trousers, a white shirt tucked in to show off his perfect V-shaped body and a dark jacket slung over his shoulder. Ella gave him her best smile, desperately wishing that she had taken the time to wash the paint off her face.

'That's a fetching little outfit,' Hal said. 'I think I even prefer it to the frog one.'

Ella laughed. Flirty laugh.

'Oh darling, what happened to you?' Another voice said with a shrill laugh, and Phoebe appeared behind Hal. She also smelled expensive and looked immaculate in a cream designer floaty creation.

'Been decorating,' Ella said. She felt ugly, scruffy, embarrassed.

'Why don't you wait in the car Phoebes, I need a word with my neighbour.'

Phoebe cast a critical eye over Ella, shrugged and teetered out to the car.

'So,' Hal said, leaning in towards Ella who inhaled his deliciousness further. 'Have you been to your cottage?'

'Yes. I've given up my job and I'm just going to sort out the details. I have to the ring the solicitor now.'

'Good move. Well done. Will you be there tomorrow? Painting in this sexy little number again?' He pulled the neck of the boiler suit, at the same time pulling Ella even closer to him.

'Oh yes. There's a lot to do. Fortunately I've got lots of help. My neighbours and some other villagers have been amazing.'

'If I get time tomorrow I might drop in,' his voice was husky now. 'If that's all right?'

'That'd be great,' Ella said, her voice almost a squeak. She coughed, before continuing. 'Anytime.'

'Maybe we could fit in a bit of dinner tomorrow evening. I have to do this work thing with Phoebes, otherwise I'd suggest tonight. Until tomorrow.' He leaned in and kissed her on the nose.

Ella stood on the stairs inhaling his trailing odour for a full two minutes after he had left.

Ella messaged Sam to ask if seven-thirty would be okay, it took Sam an hour to reply, by which time it almost was seven-thirty. *Okay*, was all the reply said.

'Hi,' Ella beamed at Sam's front door. She waved a bottle of wine in the air. 'No alcohol.'

Sam smiled, but it was a brief automatic smile; she stood aside to let Ella in.

'A lot's happened since I last saw you.' Ella's voice showed her excitement. 'You won't believe what's going on at the cottage.'

Sam nodded but didn't say anything. She took the no alcohol wine into the kitchen and came back with two full glasses, placed them on the coffee table.

'Is everything okay with you?' Ella began. 'Hopefully that stupid business with Gwynnie didn't cause too much trouble for you. I have to say, they didn't take much convincing; it was a lot easier than I expected. That silent HR Director was in the room, that freaked me out, but true to form, he never said a word. Not one.'

'Everything's fine now. Thanks.'

'So you okay? Only you seem a bit quiet. Hey, I never told you about the police stopping me that night I came to pick you up when Charlie's car broke down. I was wearing my frog onesie. Really embarrassing.'

Sam rolled her eyes, shook her head. 'That's typical you, isn't it?'

'Suppose.' Ella laughed, took a sip of the wine, wished it was alcoholic.

'Bit like what you were wearing today.'

'Sorry about that. I didn't plan to turn up dressed like that. Who would? It was just that I didn't realise the time, if I'd changed, which was my intention, I even had my clothes with me to change, my one business suit, no less, I would have been late. You said, don't be late. So…' Ella waved her hands around. 'Sorry.'

'Doesn't matter. It just made you look a fool. And me by implication.'

'Sorry. I didn't think.' Ella laughed again. Sam didn't.

'Bit like the way you jacked in your job.'

'What do you mean?'

'Well, if you'd spoken to me about it first, we could have worked something out.'

'I hadn't planned to do that, it just sort of happened. Gwynnie pushed me too far. You should have seen her and Tiffy's faces when I threw old Rueben's smelly dog rag at them.'

'Yeah, I bet it was hilarious,' Sam said in a flat tone.

'It was, actually. Anyway it was a crap job.'

'It was a good job, Ella. You used to love it.'

'That was before Gwynnie took over. Before she decided to pay Tiffy more than me and effectively make her my boss. Controller, ha, what the hell is that? I couldn't go on like that. It was eating me up.'

'So now you've decided to go live in that cottage.'

'Yes. Took me a while to see its merits, but I'm really glad I did. Those magazines really helped. Thank you.'

'Mmm. Did they?'

'Is everything okay with you? Baby okay?' Ella suddenly had a horrible feeling she might have missed something.

'Baby's doing really well, thanks for finally asking.' Sam stroked her little bump.

'Oh sorry, Sam, I know I'm babbling on about the cottage, but it's ages since anything good has happened to me. You know what a shit time I had when my mum was ill and then, well… you know.' Ella drew a quick breath, then started talking again. 'My mum would have loved that cottage, even if it has come from my dad's side. Though my mum has seen it before, she used to visit with my dad and me, when I was little. Still…' Ella stopped talking.

Sam didn't say anything.

'So, what have you been up to? What's been going on with you since I last saw you? Apart from the work stuff – so glad that's all cleared up now.'

'No thanks to you,' Sam spat out.

'What? I came and gave evidence today.'

'Yes, but if you could have kept your mouth shut in the first place I wouldn't have had to suffer all that crap. It was humiliating, Ella. Having my integrity called into question. That's my reputation you've trashed.'

'I am really sorry, Sam. I can't say that enough.'

'No, you can't.' Sam reached for her glass, took a sip, grimaced and put the glass down.

Ella deciding to ignore that, changed the subject. 'I told you about Hal, my neighbour, didn't I? Well, he's coming over to the cottage tomorrow. He's already seen it when he took me out to dinner, but he's coming round to help. The cavalry will be there, but the more the merrier, eh? Hey you and Charlie should come round too. Of course, you don't have to do any painting.'

'Charlie says that place is worth far more than this.' Sam nodded her head around the room.

'No. That can't be right. Your place is this exquisite designer pad with all the latest gadgets; you've got wifi music and lights in every room. You can probably flush all the loos from here by remote.' Ella laughed. 'My place has only got one ancient and temperamental toilet.'

'Poor Ella,' Sam said.

'What do you mean?'

'You've only got one toilet in your half a million pound, listed cottage. I feel sorry for you.'

'Listed. Is it? No one's said. Anyway, I'm sure it's not worth that much, and I can't sell it anyway. You know that.'

'But you can live in it and get paid for the privilege.'

'I thought that's what you wanted. I thought you were pleased for me. You were all keen, full of encouragement. You bought all those magazines.'

Sam didn't say anything.

'Aren't you pleased for me?' Ella watched her friend's face.

Sam shrugged. 'I did think that before you made these life changing decisions you might have thought to chat to me about it. I am supposed to be your best friend. In fact, Ella, I'm probably your only friend now. How long is it since you saw any of the girls?'

'My mum's funeral, they were all there then. There hasn't been much time since. And, of course you're my best friend. Of course you are.'

'What about this Hal? Isn't he your new best friend?' Sam made a phut noise.

'Not best friend, no.'

'Boyfriend? Really?' Sam made a *you must be joking* face.

'No. No. Of course not. It's early days. We're just…' Ella's voice trailed away, just what were they? Nothing yet. But did Sam really need to be so mean?

'Oh, and by the way,' Sam said, knocking back the wine now as though it *were* alcoholic. 'Charlie's heard from Nathan and that song was not about you.'

'Oh. I thought no one knew where Nathan was.'

'No, but Charlie messaged him and he replied. I know you think everything is about you, Ella, but that wasn't. It was about some slapper who came between him and the woman he really loved, in a pub car park. Not very romantic, I know, but that's Nathan.'

'But I…' Ella's voice trailed away again. It was about her, she was convinced of that; so now she was a slapper. That was worse, not better. And she thought she had put Nathan behind her, forgotten about him, his rock star hair, the way he looked through his eyelashes, the way he rarely smiled so that when a smile did come it was so special, so amazing. And the way he kissed, as though he were reaching into her soul, melting all her fears and worries away, just making that moment, that single moment the centre of the universe.

'Ella,' Sam snapped. 'I said what are you doing for money now?'

Ella pulled herself back together, shook off Nathan. 'I have to move into the cottage end of next week, as soon as I do they'll put my monthly allowance into my bank account. Until then I'm living on what I've got left from my wages. Actually I still don't know what I'm owed from Gubbins.'

'Ring Sally,' Sam said, her tone flat.

'Well, I rang the solicitor today and I'm going to need every penny at the moment because although I have to move into Spring Cottage, and it has to be a proper move, furniture, everything and sleeping there every night, I have to wait until the end of the month to serve notice on my flat, then it's another month. So I have to pay for that grotty bedsit when I won't even be living in it. The agent said she'd ask the landlord if we could reach an agreement, but she wasn't very hopeful.'

'Poor Ella.'

'Well, I'll manage,' Ella said, trying to sound cheerful.

'I'm sure you will. Especially when you get that lovely fat allowance – is that what you called it?'

Ella's mouth dropped open. 'What's wrong, Sam? Why are you being like this?'

Sam pursed her lips. She looked away.

'Spit it out, Sam. You've obviously got something to say.'

Sam took another swig of wine but still didn't say anything.

'Come on, Sam. Tell me what the problem is.'

Sam shook her head, she blinked back tears. Ella reached over and put her hand on Sam's, but Sam pulled her hand away.

'Sam?' Ella's voice was quiet, almost a whisper. 'Sam? Ella said again.

'You've had it all handed to you on a plate, haven't you, Ella. When the rest of us have to work hard, scrimp and scrape, you just get what you need, when you need it. Just like that. Out of the blue. Charlie's had to work two jobs for years, making extra money playing in the band, dragging me around with him. I don't even like what they play. I had to work in the bar at the Swannie, remember, just to get some extra cash…'

'Two nights, you lasted two nights,' Ella cut across.

'Yes and every penny from those two horrendous nights went into our savings. How do you think we can afford this house if it's not by saving, saving hard. We've been saving ever since we met, since the day we met, Ella. Imagine that.'

'You said Charlie played in the band because he

loved it; you said he never made any money from it.'

'Of course he makes some money from it. Anyway, that's not the point, the point is we've saved and saved and gone without and you…' Sam waved her arms in the air, 'you just get it handed to you, just like that.' Sam stood up, walked across to the other side of the room.

'Do you think I had it handed to me on a plate when my mum got cancer?' Ella said. 'Do you think that was easy? Do you think it was easy when my mum died? Have you any idea how that feels? No you haven't. You're jealous Sam, I can understand that. I've been jealous of you for years. I've never said anything, of course I haven't, I've never admitted it to myself, not in so many words. I always thought you had the charmed life, that you got everything easily, but I've never begrudged you, yet now you begrudge me. I've always envied your relationship with Charlie, how much he cares for you, how much you love each other. You're having a baby, how do you think that makes me feel? But I was thrilled for you. Now I see that when you had everything and I had nothing that was just how you liked it. Now it's changed, instead of being happy for me, you're eaten up with jealousy.'

Sam glared at Ella, her face looking ugly, but she didn't say a word.

Ella stood up, grabbed her jacket, marched to the door. 'I never thought I'd say this, Sam and I'm really sorry I'm going to, but you're smug and married yet you're jealous of me.'

Ella slammed the door behind her.

Ten

Ella spent a sleepless night tossing and turning and having nightmarish dreams which mingled swirling waters with the nasty words she and Sam had exchanged. She couldn't believe she'd fallen out with Sam; they'd been best friends for years and never had a row, not once. It was obvious to Ella that Sam really was jealous, how could she be? Sam had everything Ella didn't. Why was Sam begrudging Ella a little bit of good fortune?

Ella dressed in the boiler suit again, twisted the turban on her head and left home without any breakfast. She drove quickly and almost recklessly to Spring Cottage, she tried to focus on the good stuff, the cavalry, the cleaning, she tried to forget about the row with Sam.

'Hello there, young Ella.' Walt's big cheery face greeted her on the doorstep. 'Others just coming. And we've found some more white paint, so, as long as you want your bedroom white, we can get on with it today.'

She'd have to repay him for the paint because she didn't for a moment believe they kept finding unopened pots of paint. If she'd had the cash she'd have paid him right then, but she didn't and she could hardly pay him with a credit card. Ella gave him a hug, he was so kind. She held on to him just a little too long, heard herself sniff as she pulled away.

'What's wrong?' he said. 'You're not your usual chipper self.'

'It's nothing,' Ella said, cuffing her nose with her sleeve – not very ladylike.

'Well it obviously is. Open the door, let us in then tell your Uncle Walt all about it.'

Walt sat patiently on the stairs as Ella paced back and forth across the hallway. She hadn't intended telling anyone about it, but somehow it all came tumbling out. When she had finished, Walt stood up and patted her on the back.

'Better?' he said.

'Well. Not really. But at least I've said it all out loud now, so maybe.'

'Let's go down and put that sorrow in The Spring of Life.'

'What?'

'You read it from the hatch, *WHEN EVIL VISITS, WELCOME IT. WHEN SORROW VISITS, REPEL IT. FEED THE SPRING OF LIFE, RESPECT THE SPRING OF LIFE.* So let's go and put your sorrow in the spring, feed it.' He was already taking the key from Ella, jiggling it in the lock and guiding her down the stairs.

Ella wasn't quite sure where this was leading, but went along with it anyway. Once in the cellar, they released the bolts and cranked up the hatch, then stood watching its waters moving calmly beneath them.

'Say the words,' Walt said, nudging Ella gently in the ribs.

'What words?' Ella heard herself give an embarrassed giggle.

'You know the words. From here.' Walt patted his chest and waited with raised eyebrows.

'Um,' Ella said, wondering what the hell he expected.

He urged her on with a nod.

'Um,' she began again, 'I wish Sam wouldn't be so jealous of me, that she would be happy for me and that we can be best friends again.' She glanced at Walt, who nodded, smiled then looked down at the spring. The waters were swirling violently now, splashing, rising up, slapping against the hatch rim; Ella felt spray on her face.

'Quick. Shut the hatch. You've fed the spring; don't let it go to waste.' He ran over to the handle and wound it furiously until it was closed, then threw the bolts across. 'Better now?'

Ella stopped, listened to her head, listened to her heart. 'Yes. Yes. I do feel better. That's weird.'

'That's The Spring of Life. Put badness in, get goodness out. Well done. You need to bring your friend Sam down here, sounds to me that she has a lot more sorrow than you.'

Ella laughed. He was joking, wasn't he? Badness in, goodness out. It was bonkers and as for getting Sam there – well Ella could only hope that one day Sam would get over her jealousy, but she didn't see that happening anytime soon.

The cavalry arrived and the old lady warbly singing began; they were singing *Milkshake* by Kelis, it sounded obscene with every word carefully enunciated.

By noon the bedroom walls and ceiling had had one coat, and the window had been declared beyond hope.

'You'll have to get Gilbert to give you a quote; all the windows are probably the same, good job we're coming out of the winter and not going into it. Here's their card, keep it handy, they'll do any odd jobs that crop up as well as total refurbishment. Very reasonable rates for locals.'

'Am I a local?' Ella said, almost to herself, pushing the card into the top pocket of her boiler suit.

'Of course you are. Your family blood has been in this cottage since it was built, many generations and hundreds of years. So you're very much a local, more local than many who call themselves locals.'

The whistle sounded in the kitchen and the soup appeared again; Ella was starving and ate two full bowls.

During lunch the chimney sweep arrived, pronounced the bedroom chimney clear for use. Ella was relieved because she didn't have the money to pay him to sweep it anyway; fortunately he took a bowl of soup as payment for his assessment. He sat at the table with the others; he was middle aged, so apart from Ella the youngest at the table. Yet they all looked perky, amazingly so, in fact they seemed to be getting perkier as the days passed, as though the work was rejuvenating them.

After lunch, another coat of paint on the walls and ceiling, a very light sanding of the floor then all the wood which wasn't painted was oiled or waxed. Finally the brass bed was polished. By four pm the room was finished and the cavalry were complaining that there hadn't been a cake break today. Edna promised there would be tomorrow.

Tomorrow, Ella thought. What were they planning for tomorrow?

'You need help bringing that mattress in?' Walt asked.

'You spotted it wedged in my car then?' She laughed. 'No, I can manage. I'll get it soon. I've got new bedding too.'

'Well done, young Ella.'

With the paint brushes and rollers washed out in the old kitchen sink and dripping into a bucket outside, Edna and Walt said their goodbyes. Ella walked down the cottage path with them, Walt offering help with the mattress again.

'No, I can manage, really I can,' she said, wondering if that was actually true. She heard the rev of a high powered car as it pulled into the lane. It was Hal. Hal. 'And if I can't my friend has just arrived, he'll help me.'

Edna hugged her, then Walt hugged her, then they left.

'Are they related to you?' Hal said, nodding at Edna and Walt's retreating forms as he locked his car.

'No, they're just really friendly. And kind. And helpful. And lovely.'

'I'm sure they are,' he said, leaning over and kissing her on the forehead.

Oh God, he smelled gorgeous.

'Only what with you all dressed as little *Teletubbies* I thought you must all be related.' He laughed and Ella play-punched him on the arm. 'Come on then, show me your palace, let me see these improvements.'

'I need help with this mattress first.' Ella opened her car boot.

Hal peered in, looked down at his clothes and Ella saw a flicker of hesitation before he smiled and reached in for it.

Together they manhandled the mattress up the stairs

and into her bedroom, then wrestled with the plastic, finally ripping it off and letting the mattress unroll itself on the brass base. They bounced simultaneously onto it, laughing, looking up at the freshly painted ceiling.

It was a lovely room, especially now it was clean and fresh. The ceiling pitched a little where it joined the walls. The window, even though it needed replacing, was pretty with its little panes.

'So, Ella, this room is looking good. When are you moving in?' Hal leaned over her, stared right into her eyes. She inhaled his deliciousness, worried about how she smelt herself after a day painting and sweating. As if in answer to that question he pulled away sharply.

'Next week. I have no choice on that,' Ella said, sitting up. 'That's why we're working so hard to make it habitable. Of course the big jobs like the kitchen, the bathroom, the windows, they won't get done for months. And I want to put central heating in, I can't really cope with these little coal fires everywhere. They look pretty though.'

'There's no central heating. How did your relatives cope?'

'They were obviously made of sterner stuff than me.'

'Well good for them.' Hal laughed and got off the bed. 'Come on, give me the tour.'

She showed him the other bedrooms, similar in size to her own, clean but in need of redecoration. Ella thought that she might not paint them all white. She imagined each room having its own theme, perhaps named after a flower. Images of flowers hand painted onto the lovely oak tongue and groove doors floated before her eyes. She would call her own room daisy because it was white and she would accessorise it with yellow and green. She smiled to herself as she realised that the new bedding she had bought was yellow with a green stripe. She must have already made that decision without being conscious of it. One of the other rooms would be bluebell, another lavender, and the fourth, maybe carnation.

'You're miles away,' Hal said, interrupting her daydream.

'Sorry, I was just thinking about the colours I'm going to decorate these rooms in. Have a look at the bathroom,' she said, opening the door to a big beast of a bath, a giant sink with a crack in it and the high-level black plastic cistern complete with rusty chain.

'Smart toilet,' Hal laughed.

'Yes, and it doesn't work properly either; apparently it's not the original cistern, it should be white and china. And it's the only one.' She gasped, thinking of how she and Sam had bitched at each other over the toilets in their respective homes.

'Are you all right? You're not in pain, are you?' Hal's brow furrowed in concern, he looked even more attractive.

'No. No. I'm fine. Just had a falling out with my best friend; you could almost say that toilet is to blame. Well, partly anyway.'

Hal raised his eyebrows inviting more.

Ella smiled but didn't elaborate; since throwing her sorrow into the spring that morning, she hadn't felt too bad about the row and she didn't want to rake those feelings over again.

'Come on, let me show you downstairs.'

They walked through the rooms, which despite being thoroughly cleaned still seemed dark and drab, not helped by the light outside beginning to fade. These rooms might need to be white, Ella thought as they made their way into the kitchen.

'This is um…' Hal started to say, then stopped.

Ella looked at him, smiled, caught his eye.

'I think the words you're looking for are absolutely revolting,' Ella said, and laughed loudly. Hal joined in. 'To be honest I don't know where to start. That thing over there, I call it The Beast,' Ella pointed to the big old solid fuel range cooker standing between two bizarre little cupboards. 'It's truly hideous but apparently works really well. They've been warming up our lunchtime soup on it every day. And tomorrow, Edna says she's going to bake a cake in it, just to prove to me how good it is.'

'Rip it out,' Hal's tone was very decisive. 'Rip it all out, get something sleek and modern and white, with reflective surfaces to brighten it all up. It's like living in the dark ages.'

'I know. Look at the sink.'

They turned around and looked at the opposite wall. The sink was long and shallow and brown. The taps hung above it, their pipes running along the length of the room and disappearing through the wall.

Hal grimaced. 'Like I said, rip it out. Start again. Have you got hot water? There are two taps.'

'Not sure. There is a funny coal boiler in another little room, but it's not to be used. I want proper central heating, radiators, everything; I want to be cosy in the winter. And my water is supplied by my own spring. Have you ever heard of such a thing?' Ella laughed.

'What do you mean?'

'I have my own spring, beneath the cottage. That's why it's called Spring Cottage and it supplies my water and sometimes it supplies water to some of the other cottages. They're all really excited about it. They say the water is good for you.' Ella laughed again, 'I think they're all mad.'

'So where is this spring?'

'Downstairs, in the cellar. Come and see. We've painted it out, it had to be first. It's very important, apparently.'

Ella unlocked the door and showed Hal the way. He stood in the middle of the cellar and did a slow circle, taking it all in.

'Why all the flowers?' he asked.

'I don't know. We have to respect the spring, and stuff…' She glanced over at the hatch. 'It's written on there, if you can make any sense of it.' She was being dismissive, and she wasn't sure why. When Walt and Edna and the cavalry had been here it had seemed perfectly normal, now it seemed silly.

Hal walked over and read the inscription on the hatch, raised an eyebrow in question.

Ella shook her head and shrugged.

'When evil visits, welcome it,' Hal read out. 'What does that mean?'

Ella shook her head again.

'When sorrow visits, repel it. What does that mean?'

'I don't know,' Ella said, thinking of how much better she'd felt when she'd put her sorrow in spring. She didn't want to tell Hal about it, and now, with just the two of them down there, it felt as though she was mocking the spring. And that felt wrong. 'Come on,' she said, turning to walk back up the stairs before he read any more out.

'Aren't you going to show me your spring,' he said, his voice was low and he made it sound like a seductive invitation. He stepped next to her, nuzzled her neck and she felt her knees weaken.

'Another time, maybe.'

'Come on, Ella,' he said, kissing her neck. 'Show me your spring.' He kissed her neck again, moved up to her ear, kissed the lobe.

'Okay.' Ella pulled herself away from him.

She walked over and unlocked the little door in the wall, lifted the handle that threw the bolts. Hal's attention was fully on the spring now, his face rapt as Ella started to wind the hatch open. She could hear the waters passing beneath them; they were calm again, like they had been before Ella threw down her Sam sorrow. Once the hatch was fully open she stood next to Hal and stared down into the spring.

Hal was mesmerised.

'That's a lot of water running under your cottage,' he said, after watching it for a few minutes.

'I know. But it's always been here, so I'm not going to worry about it. Hundreds of years or something.'

'And it's drinkable? It must be if it supplies your cottage,' Hal mused.

'Yes. Actually the cavalry were all drinking it yesterday when they were painting. Look there's a cup on a stick especially for it.' Ella retrieved a copper mug on a long rod. 'They called it the sipping cup and they think the water's good for them,' she laughed. 'They call it The Spring of Life.' She put the sipping cup back in its corner.

'No, bring it here. Let's try it.' Hal held his hand out and when Ella handed it to him he leant over the spring and lowered it in. The calm waters swirled a little as he pulled the filled cup out. He fed the rod through his hands until the cup reached his mouth, tilted his head back and tasted it.

'Urgh God, that's awful. It's bitter. Have you tasted

this? Here.'

He handed the cup to Ella. She took a little sip.

'It tastes sweet to me,' she said, 'and that's what they all said. Have you been eating something spicy?'

'No. Who owns the spring?'

'I do. I suppose. Well, as much as anyone can own running water. I'm not connected to the mains.'

'You could bottle that, sell it. Make a fortune.' Hal smiled.

The spring started to swirl and churn, a sudden spout leapt up high into the air, Hal stepped back sharply, a look of disgust on his face.

'I have to shut it quickly when it does that. I shouldn't let the evil out.' Ella half laughed and hurriedly wound the hatch closed.

'Seriously, Ella,' Hal said, when they were back upstairs, 'you should consider it. People will always buy natural spring water. Even if it does taste disgusting.'

'It doesn't.'

'Anyway, think about it. I could help you with that. Extraction, bottling, marketing. We could call it Ella's water.'

Ella frowned.

'No, maybe that sounds like you've peed in it. What about Ella's Spring Water?'

'It's called The Spring of Life and I can't sell it.'

'Or course. Spring of Life. Perfect.'

'I can't sell it. I can't profit from it. I have to respect it. Anyway, I don't think, at least I hope, that I won't need the income.'

'We could put you and your *Teletubby* friends on the label. That could be its USP.' He chuckled to himself.

'Its what?'

'Unique selling point. Differentiate you from the rest

of the market; they're all about mountain springs, freshness, natural.' He nodded his head from side to side, considering his idea, then smiled to himself. 'I think we should seriously consider that one. Or, wait, I've just had another idea – your fetching little frog outfit, you could wear that on the label.' He paused for a moment. 'Mmm, maybe not, that might suggest pond water.' He laughed.

Ella laughed too, nudged him in the ribs to let him know she knew he was teasing her.

Then he grabbed her, pulled her close, held her head in his hands, looked straight into her eyes. She blinked. He smiled a kinky, sexy, one-sided smile that made her knees wobble. Then he kissed her, hard, long and compellingly. Ella joined in as wholeheartedly as she could, but the voice in her head was telling her what a mess she looked and how smelly she was.

He pulled away and Ella looked down; she felt embarrassed. She had fantasised about kissing Hal, but in her dreams she was wearing a slinky dress, heels, her favourite perfume, not a stinky boiler suit. She studied him, his immaculate clothes, his gorgeous smell; what a mismatched pair they were.

'Come on, let's get you home and cleaned up,' he said, confirming what Ella was feeling. 'Then what about dinner? We could make a night of it, I know a great little club, only an hour's drive.'

Ella smiled at him. 'Dinner sounds great. I'd love that. But I've got an early start tomorrow back here with the cavalry.'

'Why do you call them that? Do they have horses?'

'No. It's what they call themselves; it's just sort of caught on.'

He nodded; he didn't look amused or particularly

interested. 'Okay, just dinner.'

Ella went upstairs to find her coat and handbag while Hal waited in the kitchen. As she wandered past the bedrooms her heart really did soar; it was starting to feel like home, her home. 'Look at me now, Mum,' she whispered, looking up.

When she came downstairs Hal was in the little boiler room next to the kitchen studying the ancient pot-bellied stove that sat on three legs. It had red and white 'do not use' tape wrapped around it.

'So this heats the water,' Hal said, 'which also comes up from the spring?'

'So I'm told.' Ella put her coat on. 'But it's been condemned. Definitely not safe to use.'

'No. When you take it out, let me know. I might know someone who would be interested in it as an interior design piece. Just decorative, not functional. Might get twenty, twenty-five pounds for it.'

'Okay.'

'So what are you going to do for hot water if you're moving in next week?'

'I'll pop round to Walt and Edna's for baths and showers and boil the rest on The Beast. And Edna says I can use her washing machine, so it should be fine. It's only temporary, until I can get the work done.'

'When does it start?'

'Oh, I haven't arranged anything yet. I do have a contact for a local builder, I need to call him.' She thought about the card in her pocket, wondered if she'd have time to do that when she got home, between having a shower, washing her hair, plucking her eyebrows and possibly other places and generally anointing herself with sweet smelling oils, just in case.

'Who is this local builder?'

'Oh, I don't know, just a company everyone in the village uses. Apparently, they give good rates to locals.'

'Probably doesn't get much business elsewhere,' Hal muttered. He closed the boiler room door and followed the pipes through the wall and into the kitchen all the way to the sink taps. 'Which is which?'

Ella thought about it for a while. 'I can't remember.' She could only think now about getting clean and dressed in something more glamorous than a boiler suit. Ella buttoned up her coat, shouldered her handbag and turned away.

The clonking noise was horrendous. Hal had turned on a tap. Ella could tell it was the left one because it was rattling furiously on its mounting. They exchanged alarmed looks then Ella shouted, 'turn it off.'

Hal glanced at it as though it were a dangerous animal, then reached for the tap. It wouldn't turn. Ella dropped her handbag on the floor and lurched for the tap, grabbing and attempting to turn it off, all the while the tap shook violently and the noise increased.

'It won't turn off,' she cried above the noise.

'You don't say,' Hal said. 'But at least there's no water.'

The tap hissed, then spluttered. Then there was water. It gushed out at a furious rate, hitting the shallow stone sink and quickly filling it before it started to overflow. Ella tried harder to turn the tap, it wouldn't move, she looked round for something to give her extra traction, grabbed a tea towel Edna had left and wrapped it around the tap handle.

'It's giving,' she called to Hal – who had stepped well away from the sink – as the tap began to turn. Slowly the flow diminished, until finally it stopped. Ella breathed a sigh of relief, then looked down at her feet.

It was just as well she was wearing her ancient trainers as they were now soaked. She stood in a puddle, Hal, however, was on dry land. Well, at least his lovely shoes weren't ruined.

'Sorry about that,' Hal said.

'Not your fault,' Ella said, between gritted teeth. It wasn't his fault, but she wished he hadn't touched it.

'I guess that's the hot one then, from the condemned boiler.'

Ella shrugged. 'The sooner it's all replaced, the better.'

'Yes.' Hal's eyes followed the line of higgledy-piggledy cupboards finally stopping at the puddle Ella stood in.

'I need to mop this up so it's dry in the morning,' Ella said. Suddenly she felt dog tired, she really didn't want to spend time mopping up the kitchen.

'Anything I can do?' Hal said and Ella imagined him slopping a mop around his designer shoes.

'No. I can manage. Thanks.' She paddled over to the mop and bucket in the corner and opened the top part of the kitchen stable door to let some air in to help dry the floor. She started to mop, squeezing the water out into the bucket, then mopping again.

'Look, if there's nothing I can do,' Hal said, his car keys already in his hand, 'I'll get off. Shall I call for you at seven? Will you be ready by then? I think I owe you an extra special dinner after this.' He smiled his gorgeous smile, heart-melting.

'Yes. Of course.' Ella smiled back at him. 'I'll see you later.' She watched Hal let himself out of the front door and saw him walk down the path and get into his car. Then she turned back to the kitchen floor. It only took another ten minutes for her to finish mopping and then she emptied the bucket down the sink. Even after sloshing around on the floor the water still smelled sweet. She put the bucket back in its place and glanced around the kitchen once more; the floor was already starting to dry. She picked up her bag, slung it over her shoulder.

Swish. Swoosh. What the hell was that? She turned. The tap was rattling again. But how could that be, it was turned off.

The top of the tap hit the ceiling, then flew into the corner of the room. The water gushed out at phenomenal pressure and also hit the ceiling. Screeching, Ella grabbed the tea towel she had used to turn the tap off and ran towards it. She tried wedging the towel in the top of the tap, soaking her coat sleeve in the process; but the pressure was too great and the tea towel hit the ceiling and was pinned there by the water jet. Suddenly the pressure dropped then picked up again and this time the tea towel, still pinned to the ceiling, diverted the water straight at her. It felt as though a bucketful had been thrown over her, she was drenched.

She ran out of the water's way and had to force herself not to cry. What the hell should she do? Go and get Walt? Then she remembered the card he had given her, she unbuttoned her soaked coat, and fished in her pocket.

The voice at the other end of the phone was a woman's. Ella explained what had happened and begged them to send someone. The woman said she would send one of the men immediately. In the meantime she suggested that Ella try and find the stopcock.

'The whatcock?' Ella said.

'It might be under the sink. If not, try following the pipes. It looks like a tap, but it will be on the pipe.'

Ella put the phone down, looked under the sink, couldn't see anything then tried following the pipes into the boiler room. She couldn't find anything that looked like a tap. She went back into the kitchen just as the water pressure dropped again then picked back up and the water spout was diverted straight at her yet again. She screamed as the icy water hit her full in the face. She managed to escape and stood dripping onto the floor.

She felt like crying, in fact she thought she might be; it was hard to tell with so much water everywhere.

There was loud rap on the kitchen door. It must be the man from the builders; that was quick, thank God. She turned towards the door, saw the man resting his arms on the bottom half of the stable door, no doubt taking in the devastation. Then she saw his face at exactly the same time as he saw hers.

'You,' they yelled in unison.

Eleven

Ella blinked. Nathan blinked. Neither spoke. Ella took in Nathan's cropped hair, his white T-shirt, his muscles. She felt his mocking eyes running up and down her body so that she was acutely aware of her own appearance; the dripping hair, the soaked coat exposing the paint-splattered boiler suit beneath, the snot bubble now forming on the end of her nose.

'Just go,' she screeched, and this time she *knew* she was crying.

Nathan shrugged, turned and walked away but not before he cast a quick glance over his shoulder. Did he just smirk?

She turned back to the tap, its fountain still hitting the ceiling. She tried to stuff a sponge from the draining board into the tap pipe – a vain attempt to dam the geyser. It shot out and joined the tea towel pinned to the ceiling.

'Oh, oh,' Ella heard herself bawling like a baby.

The water pressure dropped. The tea towel dropped to the floor. The water went off. Ella moved as far away as she could before the pressure picked up again.

She waited. Nothing. She waited. Nothing. She took one step forward and peered at the tap; she was ready to spring back if it started again.

'I've switched it off,' Nathan said, coming into the kitchen from the hall door. 'It'll be fine now.'

Ella stood looking at him for a moment. 'Where did you come from? How did you get in?'

'I came back in the front door, it was swinging open, I've closed it.' He turned to walk away, then turned back. 'Someone's been tampering with that condemned boiler, haven't they? This is what happens. It's condemned for a reason.'

Ella blinked at him, felt like a naughty child suitably told off. 'Not me,' she muttered.

Nathan looked her up and down again, said 'You're welcome,' before turning away.

'You owe me,' Ella blurted to his back.

He turned round, looked her in the face. 'Actually, I took all your old tat down the tip, so I think you owe me. Twice. I can't think what I might owe you for.'

He was out of the kitchen door and down the path while Ella was still trying to form a response. Finally, it came to her. She squelched across the kitchen, stepped outside just as he was getting into his van and shouted, 'That shitty song.'

If he heard, he didn't reply, just glanced at her and lifted his chin.

'Arrogant bastard,' she shouted after him.

'Everything all right, young Ella?' Walt was standing behind her. Had he heard her swearing? She shook her head slowly. Walt stepped forward and gave her a hug. She pulled away quickly, remembering how sodden she was, no need to soak him too.

In the kitchen Edna was wielding the mop and

bucket.

'How did you get in here without me seeing? Is the front door still open?'

'I just walked past you, but I think you might have been occupied elsewhere,' Edna said. She had almost finished mopping up.

Ella looked up, the force of the water had taken great chunks out of the ceiling; the soggy pieces spread out in the sink. Yet, somehow the sponge still stuck fast. 'Look at that,' Ella said; she could almost see the funny side of it. Then the sponge fell down, hit her full in the face. Ella wavered between laughing and crying again, laughing won, especially when Walt and Edna joined in.

'Is he the only builder in the village?' Ella said, as they were leaving.

'Yes, it's a family firm. But Gilbert fell from some scaffolding, broke his leg in three places, so Nathan came back. Nathan has taken over the running of the firm until Gilbert is better,' Walt said, smiling. 'I got the impression you two had met before.' There was a hint of mischief in his tone.

'You could say that,' Ella said, but she didn't elaborate.

* * *

As she showered, washed her hair and dressed, Ella couldn't stop thinking about Nathan. How dare he invade her life? How dare he turn up in *her* village and spoil it. When she thought of that song, that shitty little song, she could scream. One thing was for sure she would not, most certainly not, be using Nathan's building firm for the renovation of Spring Cottage. She was also annoyed by his looks. Gone was his rock star hair which Ella had always found particularly attractive, she'd loved the way he peered enigmatically from behind it, yet his new cropped hair cut was even better, he looked so devastatingly male. She thought about how muscled up he was, something she'd never noticed beneath the grungy dark clothes and heavy leather jackets he always wore in the band. And what was the white T-shirt about? White. Really? For a builder?

Stop it, stop thinking about him; Mr Bastard Shitty Song.

Ella had just finished drying her hair when Hal knocked on the door. She was dressed, but she hadn't put any makeup on – did she have time? She glanced around the grotty bedsit – no, she definitely wasn't inviting super cool Hal into this mess.

She opened the door and stepped out at Hal's feet. He leaned in for a quick peck on the lips but Ella misread his movement and turned her face aside, it looked as though she were avoiding him.

Don't apologise, she told herself, it will make it worse.

Hal was wearing a soft cashmere jacket over a designer shirt. His now familiar aroma filled the stairway as they walked down together.

'I've booked a table at Gino's,' Hal said, holding the communal door open for Ella, 'I hope you like Italian.'

'I love it,' she smiled. She was so hungry she would have eaten anything, but Italian was her favourite. Clever Hal.

He opened the car door for her, waited while she got in and then closed it. Such manners.

'Tap all right after I left?' he asked.

'Not really. Well, okay in the end.'

‘Good.’ He smiled and concentrated on driving.

‘It did sort of explode again. I got soaked. Had to call for help.’

‘Your neighbours?’

‘No, the local builder.’

‘Good. Best to get the experts in.’ Hal drove past the spot where Ella had been stopped by the police. She opened her mouth to tell him, then decided against it. No need for him to know she had been out in public in the frog onesie.

In the restaurant the staff danced attendance around Hal, he laughed and joked with them and enjoyed their attention.

‘Don’t tell me you own a part of this business too,’ Ella said.

‘No. I just dine here rather a lot.’

How nice for him, Ella thought, and for me now.

Ella ordered Tagliatelle al Salmone, Hal ordered a steak. Hal also ordered bottled mineral water for them both – no offer of wine tonight.

‘I’d be quite happy with a jug of tap water,’ Ella said, as the waiter opened the bottle and began to pour. He stopped, waited for instructions.

‘Please pour,’ Hal said, without hesitation.

After the waiter had gone Ella reiterated her comment. She took a large gulp. ‘It’s very expensive and it doesn’t really taste any different.’

‘You’re quite right about the price. The taste…’ he shook his head from side to side, made a face, ‘not sure I agree with you on that.’

‘Bottle’s pretty though,’ Ella said, fingering the tall, tapering bright blue bottle.

‘Yes, it’s all about the packaging.’ Hal smiled and finally the penny dropped for Ella.

'I've told you, I cannot sell it. I cannot make a profit from it. I have to respect the spring. I was specifically told that I cannot bottle it and sell it.' Ella looked into Hal's eyes, they were blank for a second or two then he smiled. God he looked gorge, his warm brown eyes bored into her soul. Ella shook herself.

'Who says?' Hal said.

'It's part of the covenant, one of the rules.' Ella's stomach rumbled as her tagliatelle arrived. 'Mmm, this looks good.'

'Covenant, rules, these things can be challenged. We can get my law man on it. You're sitting on a goldmine there, Ella.'

Law man? Did he mean solicitor? 'I'll be fine for money once I move in and the inheritance goes into my account.' Ella took a large mouthful of pasta, it was so good, the sauce was so creamy and tomatoey. 'This tastes as good as it looks.'

'You have tomato sauce on your chin,' Hal said. He leaned over and wiped it with his napkin. Ella smiled her thanks and blushed with embarrassment; at least he hadn't let her sit there all evening with a saucy chin.

'I'll talk to my law man about it,' he said again, cutting into his steak. 'We can be partners.'

Ella's heart leapt, what did he just say?

'I'll provide the business expertise, the marketing solutions, the branding, the strapline, our unique offering and you can supply the water.' He laughed as though he'd just told a joke. So he meant business partners. Stupid Ella.

'I'll think about it,' Ella said, not wanting to spoil what might be going on between them.

Hal looked at her, his mouth formed a thin smile then he leaned over and took her hand, brought it up to his mouth. Ella's stomach did a little flip.

'Don't look a gift-horse in the mouth, Ella.' He laughed. 'I'm sure we can work out this covenant thing. You could be a very rich woman.'

Ella smiled back at him, he still had hold of her hand and she liked it, she just wasn't too sure about selling the spring water. And as for being rich, financially she had more money than she'd ever expected to have and a potentially lovely home – even she was beginning to realise Spring Cottage could be amazing.

'Well, you know what I've been doing all day, what about you,' Ella said, keen to change the subject.

'I've been securing the finance for my latest venture, just a few more things to finalise then we'll be ready to roll.'

'What was that again? You did tell me.'

'It's a spa, as I said, run down but a great deal of potential. There's a small hotel attached to it, so we'll be able to offer what Phoebe calls *Stay and Spray*.' He finished his steak and called the waiter over to remove the plates.

'Stay and Spray. What's that?'

'Hen parties, even stag dos. A few nights' accommodation, the girlies get their nails and faces done and a spray tan, hence Stay and Spray.' Hal stopped for a moment, looked away, thinking. 'Hey, maybe we'll get a tattoo artist in for the stags. I need to think of a catchy phrase for that, or get Phoebes on it.'

'Ink and Stink,' Ella said, thinking aloud.

'Ha. Maybe not,' Hal said, 'I think you'd definitely better leave the marketing to me.' He topped up his glass from the blue water bottle. 'So, what are your plans for tomorrow?' Hal said.

'More of the same, the cavalry will be over to help;

they've been great. And I need to see about a builder. Oh, can you recommend anyone?'

'Yes, I'm sure I can. He got his phone out, started flicking through his contacts. I'll message you the info.'

In the car on the way home Ella fought hard to suppress her yawns; she was so tired. All this physical work was exhausting; she wondered how on earth the cavalry found the energy.

At the top of the stairs Hal stopped outside Ella's door. He smiled. She smiled. And he waited. Ella wondered if he was going to kiss her goodnight – that would be nice.

'We didn't have coffee,' Hal said, prompting Ella.

'Ah. Right. Do you mind if I don't invite you in. My place is small and a bit of a mess.'

Hal didn't look offended. He reached for her hand and pulled her close. 'Another time,' he said. 'I'd invite you upstairs but Phoebe's there.'

'That's okay, I'm so tired anyway. All this cleaning and painting.'

Hal pulled her in closer. Looked into her face and kissed her. It was really rather nice and this time Ella wasn't grubby and smelly.

'Good night. Sleep tight,' he said. 'And let me know how you get on with the builders. Make sure to mention my name.'

Once in bed, Ella got her phone out and went through the three builders' numbers Hal had sent her. It was too late to ring them now, but first thing tomorrow morning, before she even left for Spring Cottage, she'd call them.

She got into bed with a smile on her face; things were starting to come together. Then she thought about Sam and the silly row they'd had. How was she going to resolve that? She couldn't just let Sam slip out of her life over a silly bit of jealousy. She just couldn't.

* * *

Ella was up early, dressed in her boiler-suit-turban combo and on the phone as soon as the clock hit eight-thirty. She left voice mails for the first two builders but struck lucky with the third – a real person answered the phone. She gave a brief outline of the work involved, explained how she was there all day, every day, so available whenever he needed to come round to assess the work and the builder sounded really interested.

'I know that village,' he said. 'Old Gilbert Jessop's firm usually does all the jobs there. I heard he was laid up.'

'Yes,' Ella said, grateful for the get out. 'He's broken his leg in three places.'

'Ouch. That must be tough for him. Okay, I can come round this afternoon; otherwise it'll be over a week 'cos we're starting another job tomorrow. Three be okay with you?'

'That'd be fab,' Ella said smiling to herself. Sod you Nathan Jessop.

'Where did you get my name from?' the builder asked. 'Was it out of the Gazette? I only ask so I know what advertising works.'

'No. No. A friend gave it to me. Hal,' Ella said, then realised that she didn't actually know his surname.

'Hal. Not Hal Heddington?'

'Might be,' Ella said. 'Sorry, I don't know his surname.'

There was a silence, then, 'Sorry love, I've just checked my dates again. Even if I price it up today I won't be able to start it for six months or more.'

'Oh.'

'So there's not much point in me coming really. Sorry.' He ended the call without another word and left Ella standing open mouthed staring at her phone.

But there wasn't any time to dwell on it because her phone started to ring – maybe he'd changed his mind. But it wasn't him; it was one of the builders she'd left a voicemail for. She went through the same description of the work to be done and agreed a time, eleven that morning.

She made the bed, folded it back into a sofa and tidied up, just in case Hal popped round – she wasn't going to get caught out again. She was on her way out when her phone rang again, but it wasn't the other builder she'd left a voicemail for, it was the letting agent. She told her that the landlord wasn't prepared to accept such short notice and Ella would have to pay for the extra month that the flat would sit empty.

'I'm sorry,' the agent said. 'It was always at the landlord's discretion and it is on the letting agreement.'

'I know. It's just I'm so short of cash at the moment.' Ella could hear the sigh in her own voice. She'd be moving out soon, at least it would give her plenty of time to clean the place up and make sure she got her full deposit back. And, once she moved into Spring Cottage her inheritance would come through.

Just as Ella was getting into her car her phone rang again.

'Call central,' Ella said, expecting it to be the third builder this time, but it wasn't. It was Tiffy.

* * *

As a result of Tiffy's phone call Ella arrived at Spring Cottage much later than she had planned. She felt a little bit disappointed that the cavalry weren't queuing up outside like they had been the previous day. They'd probably given up and gone home.

She walked up the path with the keys in her hand but just as she reached it, Walt opened the front door from inside.

'Young Ella. At last.' He stepped aside to let her in. 'Hope you don't mind, the kitchen door wasn't locked so we're getting on with the jobs.'

'Oh God. With all that water everywhere I must have forgotten.'

'Not to worry. It meant we could get in.'

'I'm so sorry I'm late. I expected to be early but I've had one phone call after another.' She didn't tell Walt about the landlord's meanness, or about Tiffy's odd call. 'And I've got a builder coming round at eleven.'

'Twelve,' Walt corrected. 'Look we've started on the back sitting room, or will you be using it as a dining room?' He laughed.

'You can't have found another pot of white paint,' Ella said, seeing that they had painted the ceiling and two walls already. 'I'm going to reimburse you as soon as I can afford it. I cannot have you subsidising the materials as well as the doing all this work.'

'All this work is keeping us young,' Walt joked. 'You pay me back when you can.'

'What did you say about the builder coming at twelve?' Ella said, going back to the previous conversation and wondering how and why he'd contacted Walt.

'I saw Nathan in The Giddy Goat last night, agreed the time. Hope that's all right, young Ella.'

'Well,' Ella began, looking into Walt's earnest face. 'I've got someone else coming at eleven.'

'Oh he won't like that.' Walt turned away and picked up his paintbrush.

'I don't care whether Nathan likes it or not. It's my cottage and I'll decide who does the work. I'm going to ring and cancel him.' Ella shuddered at the thought of Nathan telling her what needed doing. She fished her phone out of her bag. 'I can't believe this, the battery's flat. That's Tiffy's fault. Has anyone got a charger?' Ella looked around the room, the old ladies carried on humming and Walt shook his head.

'Not one that'll fit that phone,' he said, without even looking at it.

Ella went into the kitchen to find Edna baking a cake in the old range cooker. 'That smells lovely. Have you got a charger I could borrow? My phone's gone dead.'

Edna glanced over at Ella's phone and shook her head. 'Cake'll be ready in about ten minutes. Then I need to let it cool. I think we could be eating it after our soup.'

'Well can I borrow your phone? I need to cancel Nathan. I don't want him turning up here.'

Edna turned back, smiled then looked beyond Ella.

'I think it's best to let Nathan come. You'll need more than one quote anyway.' Walt's voice said from behind her. His voice was a flat monotone.

'Okay,' Ella heard herself say and although she was annoyed at giving in so meekly she didn't have the heart to argue with Walt.

'Good. That's settled then. Let's get on.' Walt was instantly back to his normal cheery self.

The next hour went very quickly, Edna's cake came

out of the oven, the men were dispatched to the garden to see what could be salvaged and dig up the rest, and the builder arrived to see Ella.

'I'm Jim Scott,' he said, shaking Ella's hand.

She welcomed him in, showed him around Spring Cottage, explained about the precarious plumbing, the probable rewire, the kitchen and bathroom refit and asked what else he would recommend. He had some ideas about knocking some downstairs room together, which hadn't occurred to Ella. She wasn't too sure about that.

'Let me show you the cellar,' Ella said, looking round for the keys, she was sure she'd left them in the kitchen. 'All the water is supplied by the spring below so you'll need to see it.'

Jim Scott stood patiently waiting in the hallway while Ella called out to ask if anyone knew where the keys were. Finally one of the cavalry found them in the bathroom. Ella had no idea how they had got upstairs.

She selected the correct key and turned the lock, turned the knob but the door wouldn't open. She called Walt, he tried – rather half-heartedly Ella thought – then shook his head and made a can't help face. Jim Scott had a go too, but nothing worked; the cellar door was stuck fast.

'This door has a mind of its own,' Ella muttered, as she made another unsuccessful attempt.

'Let me try,' Nathan's voice said from behind her.

Ella spun round. Was it twelve already? She had one more futile go at the door, then stood aside and waved Nathan towards it. She stood with her arms folded and dared the door to open.

'There you go,' Nathan said, opening it with ease.

Ella glared at him. He smiled back, but it wasn't a

warm smile.

'You're Gilbert's lad,' Jim said, recognising Nathan. 'I'm Jim Scott.' Jim held out his hand to Nathan. 'How's he doing? I heard he took a fall,' he said as they shook.

'He did. He's on the mend now, thanks'

'You here to quote for this job?'

'Yes.'

'Not much point me continuing then, is there?' He turned to Ella. 'You'll go with Gilbert's lad, so I won't waste any more of my time.' He turned to walk out the door.

'Hey,' Ella called after him. 'But we haven't finished. I'm not going with Nathan. I want you to quote,' she called, as Jim reached his car. She ran up to him. 'Please, I want you to quote.'

'Look. There's not much point. I shouldn't have come out here. I only came because Gilbert is off sick, I didn't realise his lad was back.' He got in his car and drove away, leaving Ella standing on the pavement, her mouth gaping. 'What is this?' she muttered. 'Builders' mafia?' A question she repeated when she went back into the cottage to find everyone, including Nathan, in the kitchen sitting down to soup. No one answered her question but Nathan did at least laugh.

'Sit here, Ella,' Walt said, patting the empty seat between him and Nathan.

She glanced up and down the table; there was nowhere else to sit. Short of taking the chair away and putting it on a corner – which would have looked petty – she had no choice.

The cavalry chatted to Nathan about his dad's health, how the building business was going and then about his music.

'Did you know that Nathan's a musician?' one of the old ladies said. 'He did a song or two in The Giddy Goat this week.'

'I bet he did,' Ella said. 'I've heard him perform before.'

'You've never heard me sing,' Nathan said, helping himself to another bowlful of soup.

'I've heard your songs. I've heard your words, even if you get others to sing them.'

'Talking of Charlie, I hear that you have upset Sam.' Nathan tore off a hunk of bread.

'Actually, she upset me. So get your facts right. Though I don't know what it's got to do with you.'

The rest of the table went silent. Eyes flicked between Ella and Nathan. Ella felt uncomfortable. Nathan carried on mopping his soup bowl out with bread.

'Anyone for cake?' Edna said. 'Fresh baked this morning in Ella's very own oven.'

Nathan had two pieces, then he finished Ella's off when she couldn't quite manage it all. Ella couldn't imagine sophisticated Hal eating someone else's leftovers.

Everyone got up from the table; lunch had taken over an hour, mostly because they all seemed to be fawning over Nathan.

'Let's get this done,' Ella said. 'Let's start in the cellar since you're the only one who can open it today.' She stomped down the stairs and Nathan followed her.

Ella headed towards the cupboard so that she could lift the hatch and show him the water, but Nathan headed off to the far side of the cellar, pressed the wall then lifted a panel out. Behind it were an array of pipes and valves.

‘I didn’t know that was there.’ Ella peered over his shoulder as Nathan inspected the pipe work.

‘And now you do,’ he said.

Ella made a face to the back of his head.

He pulled a little torch out of his pocket and shone it into the recess to get a good look, then got down on his hands and knees to inspect the pipes further.

‘I can’t be completely sure until I test it properly, but this pipe work is looking good. I think my dad replaced this about ten years ago, so it should be okay.’ He stood up. ‘The rest of the house is a different story, I think.’ He moved across to the stairs.

‘Do you want to see the spring, or not,’ Ella said, her voice sounded horribly sulky.

‘I might as well while I’m down here. But I can tell it’s good by everyone’s perky faces. It came through to my parents’ cottage this morning. It’s tasting pretty sweet. My mum was feeding jugs of it to my dad.’ He laughed and shook his head.

Ella didn’t know what to say to that.

She shot the bolts and cranked up the hatch. Beneath them the waters swirled. They both stepped to the rim and looked in.

‘It’s calm down there today,’ Ella said, inhaling the spring’s sweet aroma. ‘When I showed it to my…’ she hesitated, ‘friend yesterday it shot a big angry spout out.’

‘At you or your friend?’

Ella frowned at Nathan. ‘I don’t think it was at anyone,’ she snapped, turning back to wind the hatch back down.

They went upstairs next; Nathan inspected the electric switches and what he could see of the wiring. He went up in the loft via a tiny hatch above the stairs while Ella held onto the ladder he had brought in from his van.

'Come up and have a look,' he called. 'The underside of the thatch is amazing.'

'No thanks,' Ella shouted back, thinking of the spiders and God knows what else that might be up there.

He inspected the bathroom, made copious notes and took photographs on his phone. He checked out the windows and measured them. They were still upstairs when Walt called up to say they were finished for the day.

Ella called back her thanks and wondered what the time was.

'What *was* all that with the other builder? He said I'd choose you anyway, so he didn't want to waste his time.'

'Our firm's long established, goes back generations. We do all the work in the village.'

'But I might not choose you.'

'You probably will, we're good and we're great value for money.'

'But someone might be cheaper.'

'I doubt anyone will undercut us,' Nathan almost laughed.

'So it *is* like a builders' mafia then.'

Now Nathan did laugh.

'I want central heating,' Ella said, when they reached the little boiler room.

'Yes, there's room here for a proper boiler, but it will have to be oil or bottle gas, there's no mains gas in the village. I'll warn you now, this is a big job, costly, to modernise it while keeping the character.'

'My friend says he can get me twenty pounds for this

stove, so that will offset it.' Ella laughed.

'Worth a hundred scrap,' Nathan shrugged. 'Where are you going to live while the work's done?'

'Here. I have to live here.'

'You're moving in before it's done?'

'I have to. That's why everyone's been helping me with the cleaning and painting. I have to move in next week.'

'Can't you stay with a friend or something?'

'No. I have to be here. It's one of the rules.'

'Rules?' Nathan frowned.

'The cottage comes with a whole list of rules. That's one of them.'

'I always thought that was just a story.'

'You know about the rules?'

'I've heard of them. I thought they related to the spring, looking after it, feeding it, that sort of thing. I think the whole village knows about that. But I didn't realise there were rules about living here.'

'Well there are,' Ella said, feeling tired. 'What did you mean about feeding the spring?'

'Oh, nothing really. Just stories.'

'What stories?'

'I don't really know.' Nathan turned to leave the boiler room but it was so small he bumped into Ella. She felt something she could only describe as a sharp electric shock, like static. She jumped away, so did Nathan. 'Sorry,' he muttered.

In the kitchen he took more photos, more measurements and added to his growing pages of notes. Ella followed him around, answering questions and trying to match this Nathan with the one she'd kissed in the car park, the one who'd written the shitty song about her.

'What sort of kitchen do you have in mind?'

'Um, something glossy white,' Ella said, thinking of Hal's advice, 'so it reflects some of the light back in.'

'Glossy white, in here?' Nathan shook his head.

'Why not?'

'Parts of this place are seventeenth century.'

'So I have to have a seventeenth century kitchen, do I?'

Nathan shrugged, muttered, 'your place,' then closed his notebook.

'Actually,' Ella said, seeing his point. 'Sam gave me some magazines…'

'Let's have a look, I can tell you what kind of thing will fit in here.' He stopped. 'I mean size wise, not style obviously. I know it's not for me to tell you what to have. The ceilings are low; you won't be able to go for tall modern cabinets.'

Ella enjoyed watching him squirm. 'They're in the car.'

'Show me on the way out, it's getting late.'

Ella made sure every door was locked before she left and followed Nathan outside. She pulled the magazines out of her car and laid them on the bonnet. There wasn't a glossy white kitchen in any of them. She pointed to a cream kitchen with solid wood tops.

'Yes, that would fit,' Nathan said. 'That would work too.' He pointed at another one, pale blue.

'Mmm, that is nice.' Ella's head bobbed up when she heard the now familiar roar of Hal's car. He pulled up sharply and skewed his car in front of Ella's.

'Hal,' Ella called out, rushing towards him.

'Fuck's sake,' Nathan muttered, and when Ella looked around, he was already in his van and driving away.

'Hello, *Teletubby*,' Hal's liquid voice said, as he lifted Ella up and hugged her. 'And who's your rude friend?'

'Oh, that's the builder.' She wanted Hal to kiss her. Right there. In the street.

'I don't recognise him.'

'Not one of yours. He's local.'

'What's his name?'

'Nathan.'

'Not Nathan Jessop?' Hal asked, dropping Ella as though she were a sack of potatoes.

'Yes. Do you know him?'

'By reputation. He's a bastard, Ella. Keep away from him.'

Well, I already know that, thought Ella. You don't need to tell me.

Twelve

'So you do know Nathan?' Ella stood back and frowned at Hal.

He shrugged, then shook his head. 'Like I said, I know of him.'

'Only he seemed to know you.'

'I don't think we've ever met. Well, not that I remember anyway.'

'He's been right through the place, been very thorough. Made suggestions, made notes and taken measurements.'

'Builders do that, Ella. It's their job. Try my guys.'

Ella wondered if now was a good time to tell Hal that one of his guys was too busy, one hadn't replied at all yet, and that the other had bowed out to Nathan. Maybe not. 'Come and have a look round,' she said, changing the subject. 'We've painted another room.'

Hal nodded his approval in all the right places as Ella guided him around the cottage. She had to stop herself from talking about Nathan's suggestions or how Nathan was going to tackle the jobs. Whatever had gone on between Hal and Nathan it was obvious the feeling was mutual even if Hal maintained they'd never met.

Hal put his arm around Ella's shoulder. 'Are you all ready for your move?'

'Sort of.' Ella thought about the few pieces of her mum's furniture in Sam and Charlie's garage. She sighed.

'What was that for?' Hal asked.

'Just thinking about my friend Sam, we had a big row.'

'What about?'

'Just stuff. Stupid stuff really.'

'Never mind, you've got me. I'm your friend now.' Hal laughed and wandered towards the cellar. 'How's the spring?'

'Fine,' Ella said, buttoning up her coat. 'Shall we go? I need to change.' Maybe she would ring Sam tonight. Maybe she should just pop round. 'What's the time?'

'Nearly six,' Hal said, after consulting the Rolex on his wrist; everything about Hal was expensive.

'I didn't realise it was so late. Someone's ringing me at half-six.'

'Your friend, no ex-friend, Sam?'

'No, my ex-colleague, Tiffy the Troll.'

Hal laughed; Ella adored his laugh, so deep and throaty, it managed to sound both sexy and friendly at the same time. It made her feel warm inside.

'Phoebes is out tonight, cinema or something with her girlfriends, so I thought I could cook dinner for you,' he paused. 'At my place.'

'That sounds great,' Ella said as she got into her car and Hal closed the door behind her.

'About eight,' he said, after she'd wound the window down.

Ella wondered if she'd last that long, she felt exhausted.

She nodded and started the engine, watched Hal saunter over to his car.

She just made it through the door and plugged the phone into the charger when it rang. Tiffy. Right on time.

Tiffy started with small talk, how was Ella, what was she doing, was everything going well, wasn't the weather getting nicer? Ella was tired, too tired for this nonsense.

'Tiffy, why don't you just tell me what you want. Make both our lives easier.'

'Right. Well. Where to begin.' Tiffy sounded flustered now. She coughed. 'We want you to come back, Ella. We need you to come back. You're such an integral part of the team. We miss you. We all miss you.'

'Yes, you said all that this morning. Look, Tiffy, I don't know why Gwynnie has put you up to this, but I've already told her, I'm not coming back.'

'Gwynnie hasn't put me up to this.' Tiffy coughed again. 'Excuse me, I just need some water.' Ella heard Tiffy swallow. 'The truth is I *need* you to come back. We all do.'

'I can't believe you miss me that much. It's not as though we were best friends, is it?' Ella considered ending the call; would that just be too rude?

'No. I suppose not.' There was a silence followed by Tiffy's meek sounding voice. 'I need you to come back, even if it's only for a short time because you're the only one who knows how to do the work.'

Well, there it was. It wasn't a startling revelation; Ella had announced that to everyone herself. What was surprising, shocking even, was that Tiffy was admitting it. 'But there are written procedures, haven't you looked at them?' Ella asked.

'Yes. But…' Tiffy's voice trailed off. 'They might have been mislaid when you left.'

'Mislaid? What do you mean, mislaid? They were in the folders, in the cabinet.'

'All your stuff was,' Tiffy paused, 'cleared away, when you went.'

'You mean binned, don't you? Well that's not my fault. I left clear documentation; it's always been my thing, very clear documentation. What did you do when I was off?'

'We didn't have the volume or complexity of work then. I'm begging you,' Tiffy said, 'on behalf of the whole team. We need you to come in and show us what to do. Especially me and Gwynnie.'

'Oh. I don't know what to say.'

'Please say yes.'

'Did you say Gwynnie didn't put you up to this?'

'No. It was my idea, but she knows I'm ringing you. Please, even if you only come in for a few days, at least you could give us a good overview of what we need to do.'

'But how did you manage when I wasn't there?' Ella persisted. 'When it was just you and Gwynnie, when I was off because of my mum?'

'We bluffed it. We didn't have any major projects on like we do now and we bluffed it. We can't do that anymore. We need you.'

My God, that was honest, thought Ella. But she really didn't want to go back, not even for a week, not even for a day. And she still hadn't had notification of how much they were going to pay her, or not pay her on payday.

'Ella,' Tiffy said, 'Gwynnie has authorised me to offer you double pay for that week.'

'Ha. It's not the money, not now.' Ella smiled to herself. That was the irony; if Gwynnie had paid Ella fairly in the first place, she would probably have continued to carry Gwynnie and Tiffy. She may have resented it, but she would have done it. Who knows, she might even have turned down Spring Cottage.

Would she?

Maybe not.

'I can't do a week.'

'A few days?' Tiffy said, sounding hopeful.

'I need to think about it. I have a lot on at the moment. I'm moving house.'

'Oh. Then the extra money would come in handy,' Tiffy reasoned.

'It's not about the money.' Ella said again, though some cash right now would be useful.

'Gwynnie is prepared to apologise, if that's what it takes.'

Ella laughed, she couldn't help herself. 'I don't know. I don't really have the time.'

'Look, Ella, I'm begging. We both are. Please. At least sleep on it, let me ring you tomorrow morning.'

Ella didn't speak for a moment while she thought about it.

'Ella, you still there?'

'Yes, I am. Okay. Ring me tomorrow. But I'm not promising anything.'

'Thank you,' Tiffy's voice sounded more hopeful. 'And I'm sorry about your friend Sam. I hope she gets better soon and everything.'

Sam. What was wrong with Sam? Ella felt alarmed.

Had something happened to Sam. Had something happened to the baby?

'What with her being rushed into hospital and everything,' Tiffy continued, 'I expect you've got a lot on your plate. But please, please, help us.'

Ella caught her breath, she wasn't about to admit to Tiffy that she didn't know about Sam.

'Ring me tomorrow morning, half eight. I'll let you know then.' Ella put the phone down and immediately called Sam, but her phone went to voicemail. So did Charlie's. Ella left a message.

* * *

It was Phoebe who answered when Ella knocked on Hal's door twenty minutes later. Ella was showered and changed into clean clothes. She had her coat on.

'Darling,' Phoebe simpered, 'you're very early and you won't need a coat. Hal is cooking for you. Hal,' she called behind her, 'your little neighbour is here.'

Hal came to the door frowning, even then he managed to look hot. 'Ella,' he said, 'I thought we said eight.'

'Yes. No. Well, my friend is in hospital. I need to see her. I'm sorry. Will it keep? Can I come later? I'll message you.' She was already running away, heading back down the stairs.

'Yes. It'll keep, don't worry. I hope your friend is all right.'

Ella went straight to the hospital as agreed with Charlie; thank God he had rung her back. Charlie had assured Ella that Sam was fine, but Ella wasn't convinced, the concern in his voice was apparent even over the phone.

She steeled herself as she went through the hospital main entrance; the last time she'd been in there was when her mum died. That had been a miserable, horrible time and Ella shuddered at the memory.

She stood in the lift with ten other people, packed in tight and all impatient to reach their floor. A man coughed, a deep hacking cough that elicited dirty looks from the other lift users and a collective move away from him. Ella found herself crushed into the corner and a man who looked nine months pregnant himself stood on her toe. Ella let out a loud involuntary howl. Everyone in the lift now glared at Ella and moved away from *her*. Good.

Ella stood in the corridor next to the maternity ward. She took a deep breath. What would she find? Despite Charlie's assurances Ella knew that Sam wouldn't be in here without good cause. A man came towards her clutching the hand of a small boy who was gripping a helium balloon. *It's a girl* flashed by her in a haze of pink.

I should have brought something; grapes, chocolate, anything. Ella felt flustered, annoyed with herself.

'You came then,' a voice said from behind her.

Ella spun round.

'Nathan. What are you doing here?'

'Same as you, I should think. Unless you're having a baby, which obviously *I'm* not.'

'Not funny. And I wanted to see Sam on my own.'

'And so you shall. I'm just leaving. You'll have to shoo Charlie away, but I'm sure you'll manage that.' He turned and walked down the corridor towards the lift.

Cussing him under her breath, Ella watched his retreating form; he looked over his shoulder and caught her staring. She marched through the ward doors and stopped.

There were four beds and Sam's was by the window. She lay in bed, the covers pulled up. She looked small and pale. Ella felt a catch in her throat; her mum had looked small and pale.

'Ella,' Charlie called, seeing her hesitate at the door.

Ella watched as Sam's head turned slowly towards her, her blue eyes widening. She smiled.

'I'm so sorry,' Ella rushed forward. 'I didn't know. I would have come sooner. Is everything okay? Why didn't you message me?'

Sam shrugged, didn't say anything, just kept her lips together.

'Everything is okay, isn't it?'

'Everything's fine,' Charlie said. 'Just a scare. Now you're here, Ella, I'm going to grab a coffee.'

Ella smiled her gratitude at Charlie, watched him leave, then turned back to Sam.

'I'm so sorry about what I said, it was stupid and mean.'

'Me too.' Sam said, and Ella noticed Sam's sad eyes, her doleful expression. Sam patted the bed suggesting Ella sit on it.

'Am I allowed?'

'Of course. Sit down.'

'So what happened? Why are you in here? It wasn't because of our row or the work thing, was it?'

'No. It happened at work the next day. I just fainted. Next thing I know I'm here. They say I have to stay in for a while, complete bed rest. If I'm good, they might let me come home in a few days.'

'I'm so sorry.'

'Stop saying that, Ella. It's not your fault. I've not felt right for weeks. I hope they let me home soon though; it's very boring being stuck in here. They only let me out of bed this evening, prior to that it was,' Sam's voice dropped to a whisper, 'bedpans. Can you imagine the indignity?' She shook her head.

'Oh God, that sounds awful.'

'It was. Anyway, on the bright side, I won't be going back to work again before the baby's born.'

'I might,' Ella said, almost to herself.

'What?'

'Go back to work. Tiffy rang me; they're desperate.'

'Serves them right.' Sam reached over and grabbed Ella's hand. 'You were always too good for that job.'

'I loved that job. Well, I did until…'

'You were always exploited; you carried old Don Perkins too.' So now Sam wasn't being her usual HR diplomat.

'Oh, he was all right. At least he never treated me as though I was an idiot. And he never brought in any creative days like Pink Day and Think Day.'

'Or Stink Day,' Sam added, laughing.

Relieved, Ella joined in with Sam's laughter. 'They're prepared to pay me double my normal rate. They'd be grateful even if I can only do a few days. Ironic isn't it? Now I don't need the money they're flinging it at me. I haven't got the time either; I have to move in soon.'

Sam gasped, put her hand to her mouth. 'I'd completely forgotten. How's it going?'

So Ella told her, exactly how it was, including Hal and Nathan's apparent hostility.

'So they know each other?' Sam was puzzled.

'Hal says not. But Nathan swore when he saw him and stomped off in a huff.'

'Bit strange.'

'Anyway, Nathan is listing all the work that needs

doing and estimating the cost but Hal has told me not to use him.'

'What will you do?'

'I'll see what the estimate is. Then *I'll* decide what *I* do. Oh Sam, we've done so much painting and cleaning, as soon as you're out of here, you'll have to come and see.'

Sam sighed. 'It might be a while before I can venture that far.'

'Sorry, Sam, I wasn't thinking. You just stay here and get better and keep growing my little God child.'

Sam smiled, but it was a sad, faraway little smile that made Ella feel uncomfortable.

'Anyway, enough about me,' Ella said, feeling selfish.

'No, keep talking. Your adventures are a lovely distraction from this.' She waved her arms around the ward; a loud snore came from the corner.

'I saw Nathan outside,' Ella said.

'Yes, sweet of him. Have you seen his hair? I hardly recognised him. He looks pretty hot.'

'Yeah. No.' Ella said, thinking of how much she had liked his enigmatic rock star look.

* * *

It was after nine by the time Ella got to Hal's, she'd messaged him, so he knew when to expect her. He opened the door wearing an apron; it said *World's Best Chef*.

'Is that true?' Ella said, pointing to it and laughing.

'I'm the best everything,' he said, bending down to kiss her briefly on the mouth. He tasted of brandy. 'How's your friend?'

'Okay. I think.'

'Good. I hope you're hungry; I've made my signature steak. I call it Steak au Hal.'

'Sounds intriguing.' Ella forced a big smile, in truth she wasn't hungry at all, she'd lost her appetite the instant Tiffy had dropped the bombshell about Sam. Even seeing Sam hadn't restored it.

If Hal had planned an evening of seduction he soon gave up when Ella fell asleep at the dining table while he was bringing the dessert. The true gentleman that he was he escorted her back to her place and even helped pull out the sofa bed, then kissed her softly on the mouth and left her on her own.

'Sleep tight,' he called, then laughed. God, he had such a sexy laugh.

Ella fell asleep with Hal's face floating in her dreams. Sweet dreams.

Her phone went off and she was suddenly, horribly awake. She reached for it only to discover that it wasn't the alarm but Tiffy calling. Was it eight-thirty already?

'Morning, Ella,' Tiffy's voice said, with a layer of jolly cheerfulness that didn't suit Tiffy or the time of day.

'Hi,' Ella said, getting out of bed and walking the few feet to the kitchenette to get herself a drink.

'Did you have a nice evening?' Tiffy was starting with the small talk again.

'Yes, I will come back in. Only one day this week. Friday.' Ella said, without wasting any more time. 'After that, we'll see how it goes.' I want cash in hand – at least then she could repay Walt for the paint he kept *finding* – and I want to know exactly how much I'll be getting paid on payday. So get Gwynnie organised on that. I'll see you Friday at half-eight.'

'Thank you. Thank you so much.'

'That's okay. Bye.' Ella put the phone down, rubbed her eyes and knew, even though she wanted to, that she couldn't go back to bed.

* * *

The following days went in a whirr of activity at Spring Cottage, more ceilings were painted – Ella had to stop them from painting the walls because she didn't want everything white. There was more digging in the garden, not by Ella, but she was being given a comprehensive lesson in vegetable gardening by Walt. Ella winced every time he took her outside to instruct her further; she was growing to love the cottage but the garden was something else. Gardening was for old people.

'Do you think they'd like to take this on permanently if I paid them?' Ella said, nodding at the two old men who seemed happy in their digging work. 'And you, for your expert advice.'

Walt pondered awhile. 'Yes, I think they might. We'll have to ask them. But you don't need to pay me for my advice.' He clapped his hand on Ella's shoulder and laughed.

She wrapped her arms around him while he hugged her back. She was grateful but it was more than that; he was like a father figure to her – a father figure she'd never really had.

'They'll be ready to plant on Friday. We'll get on with it while you're working. There's not much more we can do inside now.'

'What are they planting?'

'All sorts. Don't you worry about it.'

'Who's paying for the plants, the seeds or whatever it is?'

'Don't you worry about it.'

'Right, Walt. I want you to list out everything you've spent, including all those pots of unopened paint you keep finding.' Ella gave Walt a *don't think you're fooling me* look. 'I am going to repay you. It's the very least I can do.'

'Don't worry, Ella.'

'No, Walt. I mean it. I want to know exactly how much you've spent. It's bad enough that you are all giving me your time and energy, without you spending out of your own pocket.'

Walt shook his head.

'If you don't give me the list, today - after lunch if you can – I'm going to lock you all out.' Ella pursed her lips.

Walt laughed. 'All right, all right. Talking of lunch, I think it's arrived.'

'Talking of lunch,' Ella said, running to keep up with him as he marched back up the garden towards the house, 'include the cost of that too.'

'I'm not paying for lunch. I told you, the pub is very happy, very, very happy to donate it.'

'Then I'll have to pay them back.'

'No. Don't. They'll get it back tenfold.' Now Walt pursed his lips and the look on his face was enough to tell Ella to leave it at that.

* * *

Ella woke up early on Friday morning. Too early; it was still dark. She showered, then dressed in her work clothes, made her face up – which was something she'd never normally do for work and surveyed the result in the mirror.

'You'll do,' she said to her reflection.

Grin and bear it, the voice in her head chimed back.

She arrived at the office at exactly eight-thirty, but they were already waiting for her, all of them. Ben gave her a sly smile which Kevin echoed. Tiffy beamed like a Cheshire cat and Gwynnie smiled with her mouth but most certainly not her eyes.

'We're so happy you've come in,' Tiffy said, rushing towards Ella. 'Would you like a coffee?'

'No, thanks. I've just had one.' This was not how it used to be.

'When you've settled in,' Gwynnie said over Tiffy's head, 'can we catch up for ten mins.' The words were phrased as a question, but the intonation made it clear it was a command.

'Sure.' Ella smiled, thinking that if Gwynnie started with her, she'd just get up and leave. They had no hold over her now, she was here as a favour.

After about thirty minutes during which Ella had given Tiffy a very comprehensive run down of one small process and was now supervising her doing it, Ella glanced over at Gwynnie. She was concentrating, her brow furrowed as she compared figures on her screen with notes she had made. Ella couldn't suppress a smile, she knew what Gwynnie was doing, checking potential new lines on the inventory against scrappy notes she had made. Ella knew there was a better way to do it, and she would explain it, but not yet.

'I'm ready when you are,' Ella said, watching Gwynnie jump.

Gwynnie stood up, grabbed a folder from her desk drawer, waited for Ella then walked with purpose to the nearest vacant meeting room. Ella wondered what was coming next.

Gwynnie opened the door for Ella and then closed it behind them. She leant against the door.

'First Ella, I'd just like to say how very mature it is of you to come in and help us out. Thank you.'

Ella smiled her response.

'Also, here is your payslip, we don't get paid for another week or so, but HR agreed you could have this now, so at least you know what you're getting. And...'

Ella held up one finger, silencing Gwynnie, then tore open her payslip. If the amount wasn't what she considered fair, she'd be off right now. She looked at the figure, read the accompanying explanation; paid to the end of the month and a month's pay in lieu of notice. Much better than expected.

'That seems to be in order,' Ella said, trying her hardest to contain her delight.

'Good. Finally we agreed that you'd be paid double in cash today. Here it is.' Gwynnie handed over a brown envelope.

Ella opened it, counted the notes and smiled. 'Thank you.'

'I'm trusting you, Ella, because obviously you've only been here less than an hour, but I'm trusting you to stay all day. It's...'

'Stop,' Ella said. 'Firstly, I'm here for the day. That's what I agreed, that's what I will do. After that, we'll see. I've taken time out of my busy life to come here, time I could put to much better use. I came after Tiffy begged me and from what I've seen so far, you'll all benefit from what I can teach you. Secondly, don't patronise me, don't think you're doing me a favour. I realise it must really stick in your throat to have me here, but it's of your own doing. If you had paid me fairly we wouldn't be in this situation.'

'But…'

Ella held up her finger again, silencing Gwynnie. 'Thirdly, I don't want to waste my energy on fighting with you, so let's just walk out of here, smile and be pleasant to each other. When I've finished with Tiffy, there are a few things I can show you to make your job easier. Okay, let's go. Smile.'

The two walked side by side back to their desks, grinning inanely, and got on with their work.

* * *

'How was your day?' Hal asked, when he knocked on Ella's door early that evening.

She'd had the foresight to tidy up so wasn't too embarrassed to invite him in.

'Better than I expected,' Ella said. 'I've agreed to go back next week, which is pretty good of me really.' She allowed herself a little smug smirk.

'I forgot you wouldn't be at your cottage and called round. The old people were gardening and singing, weird singing.' He shook his head. 'That jolly one, the leader, he gave me this to give to you.' Hal handed over a brown envelope – her second one today.

Ella knew what it was, she'd been expecting it. She didn't open it in front of Hal, just pushed it into her handbag.

'Dinner. I'm taking you out right now, while you're still presentable and don't have to rush off on some emergency, then you can tell me all about it.'

Over dinner, Ella did tell Hal about her day. How she'd enjoyed lunch with Ben and Kevin, how she'd made some sort of peace with Gwynnie and Tiffy, and most importantly, how she no longer resented them, because now everyone knew the truth.

'You can put it all behind you,' Hal said, giving her a devastating smile.

'And I intend to.'

'I've been talking to my lawyer pal,' Hal said, 'about your predicament.'

'What predicament?'

'Your spring. He thinks there's a way round it.'

'Round what?' Ella tucked into her pudding – chocolate fudge cake.

'Being able to bottle and sell it.'

'I'm not sure I want to do that. It's against the rules.'

'That's what I'm telling you. He thinks you can have those rules relaxed.'

'Oh, I don't know. I'm not sure selling it is a good idea. Anyway, did you know that I still have to pay water rates on it? I thought it would be free, but apparently not.'

'All the more reason to sell it then. I've thought some more about the marketing, the name has definitely got to be Spring of Life, then maybe some fountain of youth image. All green. Everything should be green, green bottle, green label, green lid.'

'I don't know, Hal. I'll have to think about it.'

'Then think about it, Ella. It's a great idea.'

'How's your spa going?'

'Still sorting out the finance. These things always take time.' He turned to call the waiter, ask for the bill. 'I can't hang about after this,' he said, 'I have some business to attend to early tomorrow morning.'

'On a Saturday?'

'Yeah. That's what it's like when you're in business

for yourself.' He laughed and raised his eyebrows.

'That's okay, I've got a busy weekend myself; packing and moving.'

'Damn, I probably won't be able to help you.'

'That's okay, my friend Charlie is arranging transport for the furniture I have in their garage and the rest will fit in my car. Might take a couple of trips though.'

After dinner Hal drove them both home and, in his usual well-mannered way escorted Ella to her door. He kissed her; delicious. Then he said goodbye, looking back as he turned to walk up the stairs to his flat; he gave her a knock-out smile and blew her a kiss.

Once inside her own place she thought about Hal. He kissed her like he meant it, he took her out to dinner and always insisted on paying, but he didn't seem to want to take their relationship – if that's what it was – any further. Ella wasn't too sure how she felt about that.

She got ready for bed – freshly washed frog onesie on because it was cold in her place and pulled the brown envelopes from her handbag. Plenty of cash in one; it felt like a bribe, which it was, of sorts. She'd be paying Walt back for the paint pronto. The second envelope contained a very detailed breakdown of all the work needed in Spring Cottage, including the costs – eye-watering, and a handwritten note from Nathan. *E, Suggest we discuss further. Also suggest we do the work in stages, especially as you will be living in it. N.*

He seemed very sure he'd be getting the job, and he couldn't even be bothered to sign his full name, or write hers in full either. Arrogant bastard.

* * *

Ella woke up feeling excited. Today was the start of the big move to her new life. She looked forward to seeing how the few items of furniture she had kept from her mum's house would look in Spring Cottage. There wasn't much, a sideboard, a table, a few chairs, bedside tables and some lamps.

Charlie messaged to say the furniture would be at her place at eleven.

Ella messaged Sam, hoping she was well and thanking her for Charlie's help. Sam sent good wishes back.

It was going to be a great day.

Ella made her first trip to the cottage with as many things as she could stuff into her car. All her mum's boxes balanced precariously in the back, pots and pans and everything from her kitchenette. They would be ridiculously lost in the cottage kitchen.

She'd just arrived with her second load and was unlocking the front door when she saw a van approach. Charlie. Great. He was right on time.

The van pulled up outside and Ella turned and waved. But it wasn't Charlie who got out of the van, it was Nathan. And he was on his own.

Thirteen

'I was expecting Charlie,' Ella said as Nathan opened the van's back doors.

'He's a bit busy, doesn't have a van and is office worker weak.' He laughed. Ella didn't. 'I was joking,' Nathan said, when he saw Ella's face. 'Sam might be coming out of hospital today, so he wanted to get the house all spic and span.'

'Oh.' Sam could have messaged her. 'I thought she'd be stuck in there for weeks.'

'I don't know.' Nathan shrugged. 'Where do you want this stuff?'

Ella's furniture was stowed inside and wrapped in old blankets.

'I think that should go in the dining room.' Ella pointed to the sideboard.

'Okay. And which room is that?'

'Um.' How ludicrous, she hadn't really thought about the purpose of each room. There were several downstairs rooms and since access went around in a circle almost any could be the dining room. 'I'm not sure.'

'Go for the one at the front. That way you can have the back as your sitting room and keep it nice and private. Also, isn't that where the best fireplace is?'

'Yes. I think so. Good idea. We can always move it in the future if it doesn't work there.'

He raised his eyebrow and smirked.

'I mean *I* can always move it in the future, obviously.' Ella felt her face redden. 'It would have been good if Charlie had let me know he wasn't coming,' she said, to cover her fluster.

'Tell Charlie,' Nathan said, as he moved the sideboard to the front of the van.

'Do you need me to help?' Ella looked on in alarm as the sideboard teetered over the back edge of the van.

'No, you go inside. I can manage. I have a trolley.'

Ella hoped his faith in his abilities wasn't misguided but went back into the cottage, back to the kitchen where she began to unload her pots and pans and put them away in the horrible – though clean – cupboards. She unpacked the contents from her bedsit fridge, but without a fridge in the cottage she wondered how long the milk would last.

Five minutes later Nathan called her to the dining room where he'd placed the sideboard against the far wall. A thin shaft of sunshine shone on it like a spotlight. Ella smiled. She couldn't help it. She ran her hand over the sideboard's oak surface, breathed in the scent of home.

'It's a good piece,' Nathan observed.

'Thanks. It was my mum's. She inherited it from her mum.'

'Fits well in here.' He headed back out to the van and Ella went back to the kitchen where she filled her kettle from the cold tap, careful not to even look at the hot tap – fearful it might turn into a fountain again – and plugged it into the only electric socket she was able to use.

When she returned to the dining room to ask Nathan if he would like a cup of tea she found that he'd arranged her mum's oak table and chairs in the room. It looked lovely, it would look even better after a good polish. Ella felt a lump rise in her throat and tears prick the back of her eyes. Her mum would have loved this cottage; it was so unfair.

'Fits well. All this furniture looks like it's always been here.' Nathan stood beside her, his hands on his hips, surveying the room.

'Yeah.' Ella's voice sounded wistful.

'You said this was your mum's stuff. Doesn't she want it anymore?'

'My mum died a few months ago. That's why I've got it.' She turned to walk back to the kitchen. She didn't want Nathan to see her face but he followed her.'

'I'm sorry, Ella. I didn't know. It must be tough for you.'

Ella nodded. She didn't want kind words, it made the grief worse. She sniffed loudly, took a deep breath. 'I've made tea,' she said with false brightness. 'I think there's some of Edna's cake left too. We could eat in my new dining room.'

'Sounds good,' Nathan said. 'I'll just get the last bedside cabinet in and lock the van up.'

When he came back Ella had laid the table – she'd found a tablecloth in the kitchen dresser, it was blue and white, hand embroidered. It was very similar to her mum's, the one she'd used to cover the boxes.

'I remember this tablecloth,' Nathan said, sitting down to his tea and cake.

‘Really? How?’

‘Used to come here as a kid, with my gran.’ He picked up the cake and took a large bite. ‘That’s good. The cakes here were always good.’ He laughed and took another bite.

‘I’ll have to get some practice in then. But maybe I’ll wait until my kitchen is sorted out.

‘Have you had time to look through my estimate?’ Nathan poured himself another cup of tea, adding a liberal amount of milk and sugar.

‘Yes. Not in any great detail though.’

‘I know it’s a lot of money. Just to put your mind at rest you should get other quotes, but I doubt any will be better.’

‘Okay.’ Ella didn’t want to tell him she’d had no luck with other builders.

‘I would suggest we start with the heating, install a new boiler first, that way you’ll have hot water. Rewire at the same time. Then the kitchen, then the bathroom.’

‘Yes,’ Ella said, her voice sounding mechanical. It was overwhelming.

‘Don’t worry; our guys will keep the mess to a minimum. They’ll only work Monday to Friday, office hours, so most of it will happen when you’re at work. ‘I’ll ensure they leave it tidy every night.’

‘I don’t go to work any longer,’ Ella said. She cut herself another slither of cake and offered Nathan one.

‘Oh. I thought you worked at Gubbins with Sam.’

‘I did. I don’t anymore. I don’t need the money so much now and I hated it.’

‘Well, I’m sure we’ll still be able to get the work done without disturbing you too much.’ He didn’t sound convinced. ‘Assuming, of course, that you choose us.’ He got up and took his plate and mug out to the kitchen, washed them up in the sink. Ella followed him.

He was wearing a white t-shirt again and she could see the muscles on his back stretching and tensing as he washed up.

'Do you always wear white t-shirts?' she said, thinking aloud.

He turned and frowned, then laughed. 'Yes. Mostly.'

'Don't they get, you know, dirty, with your job and everything?'

'Yes. But they wash easily too. Anyway, I don't do the really dirty jobs.'

'No?'

'I'm a musician first and foremost, if you remember.'

'Yeah,' Ella said, turning back to her unpacking and remembering that shitty song.

Nathan dried his hands and went upstairs. Ella heard the toilet flush. When he came back down he was smiling.

'I think you're going to have a great place here.'

'I hope so,' Ella said.

'I notice you've still got some boxes in your car, shall I bring them in?'

Ella was about to say no, but then thought better of it. If Nathan was going to do the work in the cottage – and that seemed highly likely – she needed to get on with him.

'Yes. That would be great. I'll just find the keys.'

Nathan emptied Ella's car and when he had finished he put the seats back into their proper configuration. He even shook the mats; Ella watched him from the dining room window then darted into the kitchen as he came back in.

'Do you still have stuff at your old place?' he asked.

'Yes, another car load or two should do it.'

'Well I'm free at the moment; would you like me to help you? We can use the van, only one load then.'

Oh God. What should she do? A part of her more than welcomed the prospect of help but she didn't want to be beholden to Nathan. He'd already given up his morning.

'I can't take up anymore of your time.'

Nathan shrugged. 'Okay.' He handed her car keys back, said goodbye without looking at her and left.

As she heard his van start she was already regretting her haste. 'I wasn't planning on sleeping here tonight anyway,' she said, out loud.

'Well, that's a shame, young Ella.'

'Whoa,' Ella shouted, as she spun round to see Walt's jovial face. 'Where did you come from?'

'Nathan let me in. Hope you don't mind.'

'Course not. It always a pleasure to see you.' She hugged him.

'So you're not moving in today then?'

'No. Tomorrow. I still have more stuff to bring over, mostly clothes. Then I can just clean up my old place.' I won't be handing the keys back just yet, I'm still paying for it for another month, Ella thought but didn't say so to Walt.

'Well, if you need any help, you know where we are. And you can always count on Nathan.' He turned to go.

'Mmm,' Ella said.

Walt turned back. 'Do I detect something amiss between you and Nathan?'

'Oh, it's nothing; I know him from before I came here.'

'And he did something to you?'

'He wrote a song about me, it wasn't very flattering.'

'Ah yes. He's quite the musician. Good of him to give it up for his family.'

'Has he?'

'Well, he's running the business. It's quite a responsibility. They employ about thirty men. I doubt he'll have as much time for singing and stuff.'

Later, after Walt had left, Ella thought about what he had said about Nathan. The responsibility part didn't fit with what she knew of Nathan, the grungy guitar player in a part-time band. She compared him to Charlie, who loved performing but saw it as just a hobby because he loved his well-paid job and the home it provided more than being a musician. According to Sam, Nathan worked in a call centre. That Nathan and this village Nathan didn't match up. Especially since he'd cut his hair so short and wore white cotton instead of black leather.

Ella locked up and headed back to the bedsit. Her car almost looked as though it had been valetted; another thing she couldn't imagine grungy Nathan doing.

She drove out of her little lane and onto the main road, passed the duck pond and the infamous toilets then headed out of the village. The car dropped down into a pot hole and then wouldn't steer properly. Struggling and cussing she managed to pull it over to the side and got out; she had a flat tyre. Without thinking she kicked the tyre and swore aloud.

'I don't think that'll help,' a voice said from behind her. Nathan. Was he stalking her?

Ella turned and sneered. 'D'ya think?' She kicked the tyre again, but Nathan had already walked back to his van. She watched him as he sat inside chatting on his phone. She reached into her car for her own phone, wondering who the hell to call; she'd cancelled her breakdown cover when it needed renewing because she hadn't been able to afford it. She thumbed through her contacts.

'Okay,' Nathan said from behind her again, making her jump. 'One of the guys will come and sort it out later. I take it you do have a spare in the boot.'

'Yes, I think so.' Then belatedly, 'Thank you.'

'You're welcome. I'd do it myself but I'd get my t-shirt dirty.' He laughed and Ella forced a grim smile. 'So where were you going? Home?'

'Yes. I was going to bring another load back.'

'Well, as I said earlier, I'm happy to help with that. Shall we go?' He turned back towards his van.

'Won't I need to wait for your tyre man?'

'No, just leave it unlocked. It'll be fine. No one likely to steal it with a flat tyre.' He scrutinised the car for a moment too long, then added, 'Actually, no one likely to steal it full stop.'

'Thanks,' Ella said.

'Come on; let's get the rest of your things.'

Ella followed him to his van, got in and couldn't help noticing how clean it was, especially for a builder. 'Very shiny and new,' she sneered.

'Not new, just clean.' He pulled the van into the traffic and drove back to Ella's bedsit.

'Typical girl,' Nathan said, as Ella threw open her wardrobe door. 'More clothes and shoes than anyone could ever wear.'

'I wear them all, you sexist.' She laughed, mostly to cover her annoyance, but it turned to genuine laughter when Nathan joined in. 'I've got a case here, and some bin bags, oh and this.' She pulled an old backpack from the far reaches of the wardrobe.

‘Gap year?’ Nathan said, eyeing it.

‘Yep.’ She opened it up and started stuffing her shoes and boots inside.

‘Where did you go?’

‘Thailand, India, Oz. You know, the usual.’

‘Me too. Did you stroke the tiger in Thailand? Oops, that sounded like a euphemism. Sorry.’

‘I know.’ She laughed. ‘Yeah, I stroked the tiger. Well sort of. Didn’t actually touch it. Looks good in the photo though.’

Nathan laughed. ‘I didn’t even go near it, just took a photo of my mate.’

‘Do you think they’re drugged?’ Ella said, zipping up the backpack and pushing it aside, then dragging out the suitcase, laying it on the floor.

‘I don’t think so, probably just really well fed. I think they run some sort of conservation programme there, so it’s not all bad. At least tourism pays for that.’

‘I expect so. I had a good time anyway. Didn’t you?’

‘The best.’ He looked wistful.

‘Yeah. It was. What did you do afterwards? Your degree, I mean.’

‘Music,’ he said, his tone suggesting it was a stupid question.

‘Of course.’ Now she felt embarrassed. Now she wanted to ask about the call centre, the building company, but felt she couldn’t. ‘I did English, mainly because I didn’t know what else to do.’ She gave a little laugh. ‘Then I went to work at Gubbins. That worked out really well.’

‘And I went to work in a call centre so I would have time for my music; that worked out really well too.’ His laugh was a bitter one. ‘And now I’m a builder, but at least I know about it, been doing since I was a kid really, helping my dad.'

She'd over-filled the case and attempted to zip it up.

'Let me,' Nathan said. He leaned over Ella and their hands touched. They both pulled away as though they had been stung. Neither said anything.

'But you're still going to carry on with your music. That's what you said, didn't you?'

'Yeah, sure. I perform at The Giddy Goat sometimes. You should come along.'

'Yeah.' She grabbed her underwear and stuffed it into a bin bag.

'What about this furniture.' Nathan nodded at the sad sofa bed, the cheap white chest of drawers.

'Not mine. And I'll be glad to see the back of it all.'

A suitcase, a backpack and six bin bags later, and they were on their way back to Spring Cottage. Ella checked her phone during the journey. A message from Sam popped up.

'Sam's home. That's so good. She wants me to go round tonight. Oh, do you think my tyre will be done?'

'Looks like it to me,' he said as they drove past her car.

'I do appreciate this,' Ella said as they unloaded.

'Like I said, I wasn't doing anything else.'

'Still, I am grateful. I think I might even be able to stay the night here now. Actually, I'll probably have to; I haven't left much at the bedsit. Or, maybe I could stay at Sam's – no, maybe not.' Ella felt excited. 'No I'll need to go back to shower, no hot water here. I don't want to trouble Walt and Edna just yet.'

'As soon as you say the word we'll make a start on your plumbing.'

'Thanks. I am waiting for another quote. As soon as I get that…' her voice trailed away, she wondered if it was obvious she was lying.

'When you're ready,' Nathan said, and she saw him suppress a smile.

They carried most of the clothes up to her bedroom in two trips. There was just the bin bag with her underwear left and Ella insisted on getting it herself. She'd noticed the bag was already splitting and she didn't want her knickers spilling out all over Nathan's van. Nathan agreed to put the kettle on for tea while she went to get it.

'Oh no,' she screeched. 'No. No.'

Nathan came dashing out. Ella stood by the van's rear doors screeching some more.

'What's wrong?'

'Someone's rifled through my unders,' Ella said, feeling as stupid as she sounded.

'Your unders?'

'Yes. You know. Underwear,' she snapped. 'Don't you dare laugh.'

'I'm not,' he said, choking back his amusement as they surveyed Ella's bras and knickers trailing out of Nathan's van. Ella stooped to pick up a pair of jumbo comfort knickers and stuffed them into what was left of the bag. Nathan began to gather up garments too.

'Just leave it,' Ella snapped again. 'Who would do this? Some dirty perv. Why?'

'Probably Feral Billy.'

'Oh that's all right then,' Ella snapped, as she knotted the top of the bin bag together and attempted to pull the sides in. 'Feral Billy can do as he likes. Weirdo. Needs locking up.'

'Needs catching first,' Nathan said, as he leant in and expertly gathered the sides of the bag together, then lifted it out of the van.

He carried it up to Ella's room and placed it on the bed, careful to prevent it from bursting open. Ella nodded her thanks then surveyed the room – bags of clothes everywhere.

'I could put a rail in that alcove for you until you get a wardrobe,' Nathan said, nodding at the large alcove between the chimney breast and the window. 'I could do it today. We'll have the necessary bits in the yard.'

'You've already done too much for me.'

'Please yourself.' He shrugged and turned away. 'It's a genuine offer.'

'Yes please,' Ella said in a sheepish voice, as he stepped through the doorway.

'I'll be back soon.'

'Thank you,' she called after him, but he was already at the bottom of the stairs. She heard his van start, heard him drive away.

While he was gone Ella put all her underwear away, utilising the only drawers she had, the small ones in her bedside tables. One of her more glamorous bras was missing. She hoped Billy the Perv didn't have it. Typical, he had chosen the most expensive one and it was hardly worn. She screwed up the burst bin bag and tied it in a knot ready for the dustbin. She took it downstairs with her. In the kitchen she re-boiled the kettle; Nathan had already put teabags in the teapot and set a tray with cups and plates, he'd found the cake tin too and taken it through to the dining table. So, they were living on cake and tea today. She doubted he maintained those muscles on cake. Stop thinking about his muscles, she chided herself and wondered how long he would be.

She took the bin bag out to the dustbin. As she turned back to the kitchen door she glimpsed movement in the corner of her eye. She turned; there was nothing there. She looked away, sensed movement again. She turned back, still nothing. She went in, closed the door behind her.

At first she thought it was Nathan knocking on the door, but the knocking went on for too long and was too loud. She was back upstairs so it took her a minute or so to reach the kitchen door.

'All right,' she called, 'I'm coming.' But the knocking didn't stop. Instead it increased, sounding as though someone were battering the door. Maybe it was Nathan; maybe he was carrying heavy tools and couldn't open the door. And yet… and yet she felt apprehensive. She leaned across and opened only the top of the kitchen stable door. It flew open with a force behind it.

Ella screamed, her high pitched yell ringing in her ears. But it didn't bother Feral Billy.

'You're a goat,' she shouted, once she'd got over the initial shock. 'And you've got my bloody bra. Give it back. Give it back.' She lunged for the bra which was looped through Feral Billy's horns. He bleated at her and let his long, pink tongue loll out of his mouth. Then he blinked, turned tail and galloped off. Ella threw open the bottom half of the door and gave chase. But Feral Billy's four legs were faster than Ella's two. He stopped and looked over his shoulder, a glint in his eye, then galloped on again, like a dog playing chase. 'Give it back,' Ella shouted again. Feral Billy bleated and galloped on.

Nathan's white van pulled into the lane just as Ella shouted again. He stopped, took in the situation and jumped out. He tried to head Feral Billy off. Billy bellowed and turned around, hurtling towards Ella. If she was lucky she could side step him at the last minute and grab her bra back. If she was unlucky he would butt her with his horns.

He thundered towards her, his large pink-eyed goaty face looked devilish. Ella turned coward and ran towards her cottage, shrieking with fear – he was a giant goat. Nathan chased him. Feral Billy bleated. Nathan shouted. Ella shrieked. Billy was gaining on her; she could hear his hooves as they hit the ground, sending the gravel flying. She took a frightened peek as she ran, saw Nathan take a flying leap and land full on Feral Billy's back, bringing him down.

Feral Billy bleated and shook his head violently.

'Get it. Get it now,' Nathan shouted to Ella who stood motionless and blinking. 'Get your damn bra.'

Ella shook herself and reached out and unwound her bra from Feral Billy's horns. He bellowed again showing wide yellow teeth. He snapped his jaws.

'Get out of the way, I can't hold him,' Nathan shouted, as the goat shook him off. Nathan leapt out of the way; Ella ran inside and closed both sections of the door behind her, leaning against it, panting.

Knock, knock, knock, knock. Feral Billy again.

'Ella, let me in.'

'But you might be the goat.' As soon as she said it she knew how stupid her words were. She flung open the door and Nathan fell through it, also panting.

'He's gone,' Nathan said when he'd got his breath. 'Why did you think I was him?'

Ella shrugged. Shook her head. Tried not to giggle. She was still clutching the bra to her chest. Nathan's eyes passed over it. He smirked, then he laughed.

'I hope that bloody bra was worth it,' he said through his laughter.

Ella nodded; tears of mirth ran down her face. 'It's

my best bra; it was very expensive.'

Nathan snorted.

'It was so funny when you jumped on his back. I thought you were going to ride him.'

'He thought so too. That's why he was shaking me off so violently.'

'I never realised goats got so big. He's enormous.' Ella wiped her eyes with her sleeve, not very ladylike but she didn't care. She slumped down into a chair, still laughing, still clutching the bra. Her stomach ached.

'After all that excitement I could do with that tea,' Nathan said.

'Good idea,' Ella replied, between giggles.

* * *

While Nathan put the clothes rail up in the alcove Ella unpacked her clothes and sorted them into piles on the bed. It didn't take very long for Nathan to finish the rail, showing it off to Ella by hanging a coat hanger on it and spinning it from one end to the other.

'I could build you a shelf above, if you like. I've got the wood in the van.'

Ella looked at the piles of clothes, glanced around the room wondering where she was going to put them otherwise.

'Could you? That would just be amazing. Of course, I'll pay you.'

He gave her a sideways look followed by a thin smile and went out to his van. Ella wondered if she had offended him by offering to pay. Ten minutes passed and he hadn't come back. Ella got up from the bed and looked out of the window. His van was still there.

'Sorry that took so long,' he said, appearing in the

doorway. 'I had to cut the wood to size.' He showed her the shelf.

'Looks great,' she said, not knowing what else to say.

He looked at her and flashed a crooked smile. 'You'll be pleased to know that Feral Billy wasn't lying in wait.'

'Would he do that?'

Now he laughed. And Ella joined in and they were giggling about the goat escapade again.

Nathan fell silent as he concentrated on putting the shelf up. Ella watched him as he worked. The white t-shirt was still spotless; she wondered how he did that. He was the complete opposite of her; she slopped everything down her clothes. But then, he was the complete opposite of the Nathan who played guitar. She heard herself sigh, hoped he hadn't heard. He turned around and smiled, she smiled back, a little amused by the tool belt hanging loosely around his waist.

'What's that?' Ella said. She could hear an odd tune playing outside, it sounded like a sea shanty.

'Saturday. Tea time. It's the fish and chip van.'

'The what?'

'No takeaways here, only the pub does meals, so the chip van comes round.' Nathan's stomach growled a rumble. Two seconds later hers did too.

'Where is it?'

'End of the lane.'

Ella scrabbled among the piles of clothes on the bed for her handbag, found her purse.

'What do you want?' she said. 'My treat.'

'I usually have large cod and chips.'

She dashed out of the cottage, ran to the end of the lane, cast her eyes about just in case Feral Billy was lurking.

'I got us a couple of cans of shandy too,' Ella said, when she returned. 'Oh wow.' Nathan had finished the shelf and had placed a pile of jumpers on it. 'That is great. Thank you so much.'

'My pleasure. I could probably fit doors on this alcove and then you wouldn't need to buy a wardrobe. Which one's mine,' he said, eyeing the fish and chips.

'This one.' She handed it over. 'Doors would be amazing, that's such a good idea. I think most of my clothes will fit in there now.'

Nathan sat down on the floor, leaning against the end of the bed, ripped into his fish and chips. 'And if not, there's always the other alcove,' he laughed. Ella slid down next to him; put the shandies on the floor between them.

'He wasn't there,' Ella said, as she ate.

'Who?'

'Feral Billy. I checked.'

Nathan laughed again.

'Is The Giddy Goat named after him?'

'Don't think so. It's been around much longer than Feral Billy.'

'Where does he come from?'

'Escaped from a local farm probably. He's been causing havoc for weeks now.'

'Can't something be done? RSPCA or something? Or can't the farmer come and get him.'

'I would think the farmer was glad to see the back of him. RSPCA weren't interested either. I wouldn't like to try and capture him, you saw the size of him, saw how strong he is.'

'Maybe you could ride him back to the farmer.' Ella giggled, nudged Nathan with her elbow. She watched him lick the grease off his fingers.

'Maybe you could,' he giggled back. 'And maybe you could use your bra as reins.' He nodded at the bedpost where it hung.

'I think he'd look good in one of your white t-shirts,' she said.

'Who would?' a voice said from the doorway.

'Hal.' Ella jumped up.

'Ella. I thought I'd see if you'd like an early dinner, but I see you've already eaten.' He looked down on them, his eyes scanning the piles of clothes on the bed and finally coming to rest on the bra dangling from the brass bedpost.

Nathan balled up his chip wrapper, took a long swig from his shandy can and stood up. He picked up his tools and moved towards the door, stood in front of Hal and waited for him to move. Hal stood his ground. Ella's eyes flicked between them. The two men were about the same height, both tall. Hal had a luxurious mane of well-groomed hair; Nathan had a number two crop. Hal was dressed in a designer tweed jacket and chino combo, Nathan in jeans and t-shirt. No one moved.

'Hal. Nathan,' Ella said eventually.

Hal turned, smiled a thin lipped smile. Nathan looked, didn't smile then nudged Hal out of the way with his shoulder and was gone.

'Nathan,' Ella called, but he was out of the door and down the path and getting into his van. He didn't look back.

'Good riddance,' Hal said, and he leant down and kissed Ella hard on her greasy chip mouth.

Fourteen

'Embarrassing,' Ella told Sam later. 'It looked as though Nathan was squaring up to Hal. I don't know what that's about.'

'Lucky you; two of them fighting over you.' Sam reclined on the sofa, her feet on a footstool.

'I don't think they were. Well, fighting yes. But not over me. I think they *must* know each other.'

'What happened after Nathan left?' Sam arched her eyebrows.

'Nothing. Hal made some excuse and left. But he was pleasant enough, I don't think he was sulking.'

Sam nodded. 'Anyway,' she said, 'how's it going with the cottage? Are you sleeping there tonight?'

'Pretty much have to now. I've moved everything out. I going to clean the bedsit tomorrow but I'm hanging on to the keys until my contract's up. I'm not letting them re-let it while I'm paying for it, even though they said they have a tenant waiting.'

'That's a bit mean,' Sam said, stroking her bump which seemed to have grown a lot during her stay in hospital.

'Well, they'll get twice the rent.' Ella tried not to sound annoyed.

'I didn't mean you, I meant them.'

'Oh. Sorry, I'm so hyped up at the moment. It was such a great day until Hal arrived, though I do really like Hal, he's so gorgeous. Have you met him? But that goat, I've never seen anything so funny, or so big.'

'It does sound fun. I want to come and see your place, but I've got to wait until I get the say-so from the hospital.'

'What exactly is wrong with you?'

'Just exhaustion, they said, and stress.'

Ella smiled at Sam and reached over and rubbed her hand. She didn't want to refer back to the row they'd had or the trouble she'd caused at work which had rebounded on Sam. She didn't want to mention it in case it upset Sam again, and, if she was honest with herself, she didn't want to churn up her own guilty feelings.

'How did it go back at work?'

'Okay. I'm going again next week, then that's it. It's just a handover really. It's removed the nastiness I felt about it. Funny really, I would probably have left anyway now I've got the cottage; the journey is farther than I want to travel every day and it would be a right pain in winter. But, and this is the really odd bit, I probably wouldn't have taken the cottage on if they hadn't annoyed me so much, especially Tiffy ringing me in the middle of my visit to the solicitor.' Ella gave a light, little laugh and poured them both another glass of no-alcohol wine. 'What do you think of this stuff?' Ella held the glass up. Sam made a face. 'Me too. Shall I put the kettle on?'

Ella didn't leave it too late to drive back to Spring

Cottage; she could tell Sam was tired but she was also apprehensive about negotiating country lanes in the pitch black. As she approached the cottage Walt stepped out from his home carrying a lantern.

'We're having a power cut,' he said as Ella got out of the car. 'Thought you might need this.' He offered the lantern to her; a fat yellow candle burned in the middle of a metal and blue glass cage. It was really rather pretty.

'Thank you,' Ella said, wondering how much light it would provide.

'I'll see you to your door, young Ella.' Walt took Ella's arm as though *she* were the old person.

'There's really no need. It should be the other way round. I'm the one with the light now.'

Walt pulled a torch from his pocket, switched on its powerful beam and smiled. Ella wished he'd given her that rather than the pretty lantern.

'Sleep tight and don't let the bedbugs bite,' Walt said, as he hugged her at her front door.

Why did he have to say that? After she fumbled her way in and up the stairs Ella reminded herself that there was nowhere for bedbugs to hide, the place had been super-scrubbed and the mattress was new.

Once she'd clattered about in the half-lit bathroom and got ready for bed – a cursory face wash in cold water and a quick teeth scrub – she stumbled to her room under the candle's flickering glow. She put the lantern on the bedside table and got into bed. It was so comfortable it made her smile. She debated whether to blow the candle out. It was thick and would probably last all night. She snuggled down into the bed, watched the candle make dancing shapes on the ceiling. Even with her eyes closed she was aware of those strange shapes. Supposing she knocked it over in the night. Could it use all the oxygen up in the room while she slept? *Don't be stupid, Ella.* She leant over and blew the candle out. The room plunged into complete darkness. She snuggled down once more, closed her eyes and slept.

When she awoke daylight was flooding through the window – she needed to get some curtains but she'd just had the best night's sleep in a long time. Once she'd blown that candle out she could remember nothing. And the bed was so comfortable and cosy.

She used the bathroom and wondered if it was too early to use Walt and Edna's shower or maybe she could boil a kettle and have a strip wash. Urgh. It was too cold for that.

She found her frog onesie among the clothes hanging on the rail Nathan had put up and pulled it on, then went downstairs.

She tried the light switch – hurray the electricity was back on – then filled the kettle. She had a box of cereal in the cupboard and the remaining milk next to the sink. She made breakfast and sat at her dining table. Nathan's idea to put it at the front was a good one; she could see out into the lane, see the other cottages. It felt so strange. She still couldn't believe that she owned Spring Cottage, that it was hers. It was home.

'You'd love this place, mum,' she said, looking up at the ceiling then letting her eyes fall on her mum's boxes. Nathan had stacked them neatly in two piles in the corner. She'd have to find a home for the contents at some point.

Three loud knocks on the kitchen door made her jump.

'Nathan?' she called out, jumping up to greet him.

The knocks came again.

She called Nathan's name, he didn't reply. Why would he come round unannounced anyway, and so early? She shook her head.

The knocks came again.

'Who's there?'

This time there were four knocks.

'Who's there?'

Five knocks.

She ran to the kitchen window and pressed her face against the glass but she couldn't see anything.

She ran upstairs, found her handbag in the bathroom and pulled her phone out. She rang Nathan's number.

'I think Feral Billy is back,' she yelled without even saying hello.

'Right. Okay.'

'Have you just woken up?' Ella heard the accusatory tone in her voice.

'It's seven am. It's Sunday.'

'Oh. Sorry. But he's knocking on my door.' She ran down the stairs. 'Listen.' The knocking was now incessant.

'Don't open it.'

'I won't. But what can I do? He won't go away. It's driving me mad.'

'Yeah. I know how he feels.'

'What?'

'I'll come round. Give me ten.' He ended the call.

The knocking didn't stop.

'What do you want?' Ella shouted through the door. 'Go away.'

But still the knocking didn't stop, but it did get slower, quieter and then Ella even thought it had stopped only for it to start again, louder and more insistent.

Nathan arrived, knocked on the front door. Ella jumped at the stereo knocking. They went into the kitchen, listened to the knocking.

'He's on his last legs,' Nathan said, once inside. 'Apparently he's been on a rampage, knocked down a shed on one of the allotments, head-butted a wall.'

'Why's he here? Why's he knocking on my door? Shut up,' she shouted. 'Stop it.'

'I think he will soon. When I looked at him he didn't even attempt to run at me. He's actually half sat down on your path, like a giant horned dog.'

'Urgh. Do you think he might die there? I don't want that.'

Nathan nodded slowly but didn't reply. He was wearing a clean, pressed, white t-shirt, dark jeans. He had canvas shoes on and no socks. He'd obviously just jumped out of bed. Ella noticed how long and dark his eyelashes were, she had to stop herself from staring at him. She inhaled his odour, earthy and warm, not like Hal's expensive aftershave.

'Let's go into the dining room, so it's not so loud,' Nathan said. He sounded weary.

Ella led the way. Her half-eaten breakfast was still on the table. A large pot of tea was wrapped in a tea towel to keep it warm. Nathan looked at it, then went back and got himself a clean mug from the kitchen.

'Do you mind?' he said, pouring from the teapot.

'Course not.' Ella sat down. So did Nathan. He rubbed his head and his eyes.

'Late night? Sorry, I didn't realise it was so early when I rang you.'

'Yeah, played in the pub. Just me and the guitar.

Sang my own stuff.'

Ella nodded, wondered if he'd sung the shitty song about her. 'Do you want some cereal?' she said, more to stop herself from dwelling on the song rather than because she thought he might be hungry.

'Please.'

Ella pretended not to watch him eat the cereal but she couldn't help herself.

Feral Billy's knocking was getting slower and quieter.

'This looks cosy,' he said, pulling the sleeve of her frog onesie. Was he smirking?

'Yeah.'

'Don't suppose you've got any toast?' Nathan said when he'd finished the cereal.

'Where do you think you are? A café?' Ella laughed.

Nathan shrugged. Ella felt embarrassed. It was early. It was Sunday. He'd got out of bed as soon as she'd called. He was doing her a favour. Feral Billy knocked loudly several times, emphasising the point.

Ella thought of the stale bread she'd brought with her. She had no butter.

'I could do meese toast,' she said, getting up.

'What's that?' He frowned.

'*Marmite*, cheese. On toast.' Ella waited for him to express disgust.

'Okay.' He nodded and waited.

She got the bread out, it was dry and she checked it for mould before putting two slices in the toaster. She unplugged the kettle from the socket then plugged the toaster in. Once done she spread them with *marmite* and layered them with thin slices of cheese. She did two more slices – for herself. She had to wait for the toaster to finish before she could plug in the microwave to melt the cheese.

She was arranging the meese toast on a plate when something caught her eye. She looked up. Nathan was leaning against the doorway watching her, smiling. She felt self-conscious and wondered how long he'd been there.

'We need to get your kitchen sorted out as a matter of priority, don't we? You really need a fridge; I think your milk is on the turn.' He laughed and went back into the dining room.

'If I choose you,' Ella said, following him and putting the meese toast plates on the table.

Nathan picked up a slice and watched it sag.

'Obviously it's better grilled, but…' Ella shrugged then looked him full in the face daring him to criticise.

He took a large bite and chewed. She watched him. He blinked as he ate and she watched those dark lashes sweep over his ink-blue eyes. She'd never noticed how blue his eyes were. But then, she'd never been quite this close to him in good daylight.

'Tastes good,' he said.

'Yeah,' Ella agreed.

'Despite the texture,' Nathan added. A hint of a smirk again.

The goat treated them to a final frenzied knocking session then stopped.

Ella jumped. 'I'd forgotten about him.'

'I'll have a look when I've eaten this…what did you call it?'

'Meese toast. It's *Marmite* with cheese layered…'

'Yeah. I understand,' he interrupted, standing up. 'Stay here, just in case.'

Ella didn't need telling twice, she had no intention of checking on Feral Billy. Instead she cleared the table and put the kettle on to boil water to wash the dishes.

'He's dead,' Nathan said, coming back in. He walked over to the kitchen door and started to unlock it.

'No,' Ella called, her hands in soapy water. 'Don't let his…smell, whatever… in here.'

Nathan stopped. Frowned. Shrugged. Pulled his phone from the pocket of his jeans and checked the time.

'Too early,' he said to himself, pushing the phone back into his pocket.

'Too early for what?' Ella dried her hands.

'To get help. We could do it ourselves.'

'Do what?' But Ella had a nasty feeling she knew. She really didn't want to be hauling a goat somewhere. Where? What did you do with a dead goat?

'Put Feral Billy in…' he didn't finish the sentence. His tone suggested Ella knew what he was talking about. 'Only it'd be easier while he's still…' he stopped and thought about the word before adding, 'limp.'

'What?'

'Well, he's still quite warm, so he's floppy, limp.'

'I know what limp means. I just don't know what you're talking about.'

'We have to get him downstairs. Sooner the better.'

Ella shook her head. What the hell did he mean?

'Is it locked? Where do you keep the key?' Nathan glanced around the kitchen, spied Ella's keys on the table and picked them up. He selected one and walked towards the hall. Ella heard the key in the cellar door.

'What are you doing?'

'Opening the cellar door. I think we can do it. You look like a strong girl.'

'Thanks.'

'I meant you're a sturdy girl.'

'That's not any better. And I still don't know what

you're talking about. Why have you unlocked my cellar?'

Nathan stopped and frowned. He made a puzzled face, then shook his head. 'You really don't know?'

'Know what?'

'About the spring?'

Ella shook her head slowly. She had no idea what he was talking about. He wasn't making any sense; he must have had a very late night, probably drunk too much.

'Come on.' He grabbed her hand – his warm, hers damp and pulled her down into the cellar. 'There,' he said, pointing to the inscription on the hatch and reading out the words. '*When evil visits, welcome it. When sorrow visits, repel it. Feed the Spring Of Life, respect the Spring Of Life.*'

Ella peered at the words, blinked at them, shook her head at Nathan.

Nathan turned to Ella. 'When evil visits, welcome it. Feed the Spring of Life. What do you think that means?'

'I don't know what it means. But I have a very nasty feeling now.'

'We have to put Feral Billy in there.'

'No. No. It'll contaminate it. I get my water from there, so do some of my neighbours.'

'Most of the original village houses get their water from there, mine included. That's why we need to get him down there while we can still bend him, while he'll still fit through the hatch in one piece.'

'Ha ha. That is not funny.' Ella shook her hand free from Nathan's and stomped up the cellar steps and back into the kitchen. She stood with her arms folded, seething, waiting for Nathan. He thought he was so bloody funny. Just when she thought he was all right, just when she thought they could at least be friends and put the fumble in the car park and the shitty song behind them he did this. Bastard.

When Nathan hadn't appeared after five minutes Ella went to the top of the stairs and called for him. He came up; he was holding a large, old, leather bound book. Ella turned to close the cellar door behind him.

'No,' he said, putting his foot against it to stop her. 'Leave it open. Let's get this done.'

'No. I want you to go now. Just get out. You're just making fun of me. Yet again.'

'Ella. I've never made fun of you. You need to trust me on this.'

'Just get out. Just go. You're a psycho.' Ella felt the tears welling up in her eyes but she was absolutely not going to cry in front of bastard Nathan.

'I'll get help,' he said. 'If you don't want to do it. Here, this is yours. You need to read it.' He thrust the book into her arms, it was heavy and she felt weighed down by it.

'What's this? Where did it come from?'

'Cupboard in the cellar.' He pulled his phone out of his pocket, flicked through his contacts, rang someone and waited. 'Voicemail,' he said to himself. 'Still too early.'

'Just get out,' Ella said, dropping the book onto the dresser and making the china clink.

'Careful,' Nathan said.

'I told you to go. Now go.'

'Perhaps I could help with that.' Hal's mellifluous tones filled the room. Ella and Nathan spun round.

'Hal,' Ella said. 'I'm glad you're here. Nathan's leaving.'

'I should have locked the front door,' Nathan said,

pushing past Hal, who stood holding the most enormous bouquet of flowers Ella had ever seen. 'I'll be back with help,' Nathan called over his shoulder.

'No. Don't bother,' Ella shouted back.

'Lovers' tiff?' Hal sneered.

'Never in a million years.' She took a deep breath then turned to Hal smiling. 'Are those for me?'

'A house warming gift.' He held out the flowers. 'Do you have a suitable vase?'

Ella made a face. 'Probably not, but there's a bucket under the sink. You're here very early.'

'I was going to take you out for a decent breakfast. I thought you'd probably be in need of one after your first night camping out here. But I can see I needn't have worried.' Hal glanced over at the cereal packet and milk bottle still on the table in the dining room.

'Maybe some other time. I woke up early. Had a bit of a drama.'

'With Nathan Jessop.'

'No. Not really. I had to ring him with a problem.'

'This morning?' Hal said and his voice lightened a little.

'You didn't think…no. Never. He's just a handyman.'

Hal smiled. He seemed satisfied. 'I see you're wearing the frog outfit again.'

'It's warm. I was cold.' She didn't like to tell him she'd not even had a shower, wasn't dressed properly beneath it. As usual Hal was male model fresh.

'Maybe I could take you for lunch, since you won't want another breakfast. Sunday lunch, roast beef and all the trimmings.'

'That would be nice,' Ella said. In her head she was running through what she wanted to do today. 'I need to go back to the bedsit and clean it, so maybe I could meet you there, about one.' She could take a change of clothes and have a shower too.

'Sounds good to me. Until one.' He leaned over and kissed her briefly on the mouth, then pulled away making a face, frowning.

'Sorry. Meese toast. You don't like *Marmite*, do you?'

He didn't answer her question, just gave her a quick smile. 'I'll see you later, and wear something nice. We'll go to my restaurant again.'

Ella watched him get into his car, heard it roar up the lane, then she dumped the flowers in the bucket and raced upstairs to pull on her dirty jeans from yesterday, grabbed a change of clothes and headed back to the bedsit. She completely forgot about Feral Billy who was slowly stiffening on her kitchen doorstep.

* * *

The bedsit didn't take much cleaning, a quick wipe of the few cupboards, clean the bathroom out and flash through with the mini-vacuum. It looked far better than it had the day she'd moved in. Ella took the cleaning materials out to her car; she was on her way back in when she bumped into Phoebe, who looked stunning, as per usual. Well, she was Hal's sister so it was only to be expected.

'Morning,' Ella smiled.

'Hi.' But Phoebe didn't even bother looking in Ella's direction.

Ella went back in for her shower. She washed her hair then piled it up on top in what she hoped was a sexy, just got out of bed look. Her hairdryer was at the cottage now, so her hair would have to stay wet. At least it was clean.

Hal knocked promptly at one.

'Smells very fresh and clean in here,' he said, stepping inside.

'Yes. Cleaner than when I moved in. That's it now, I no longer live here.'

'So I'll be getting a new neighbour soon.' Hal helped Ella on with her coat.

'Not for another month or so. I'm still paying rent until then.'

'But you're not living here.'

'Yes, but I'm paying rent and they won't let me off it, even though they have another tenant lined up and wanting to move in immediately, so I'm not giving the keys back until my contract expires.' Ella felt irritated just talking about it.

'But you won't be using the place?'

'No? I've got my cottage now. And the rules say I have to live there.'

'Good that you don't actually need the money,' Hal said, closing the door behind Ella and guiding her down the stairs.

'That's not really the point. You'd think they'd be happy to let me off the last month's rent in view of the fact that they've got another tenant waiting. I just hope I get my full deposit back, but I can't see why I shouldn't.'

'Well, it's just good you're not destitute.'

'What?'

'Are you hungry?'

'I am now.' Ella laughed. 'After all that cleaning.'

The roast beef was excellent; the smell alone reminded Ella of home cooking, of her mum's Sunday dinners.

'You're miles away again,' Hal said, ordering a sparkling, low alcohol wine to celebrate Ella's new home.

'Just thinking about my mum.' Ella shook her head; she really didn't want to talk about her mum too much – the memory was still too raw.

'So what's next on your plan?' Hal waved the waitress over to bring more gravy. They were sitting at the same table in the conservatory as last time, and like last time, the place was full.

'Building work. Not looking forward to that.'

'Have you chosen your builder?'

'Well until this morning it was going to be Nathan.'

'Jessop? What about my guys?'

'One was too busy, one decided it was too big a job and the other never rang back.'

Hal shook his head. 'I've used all three. Do you want me to have a word with them?'

Ella nodded slowly and smiled. Hal seemed pleased.

'What was all that about this morning.'

'Oh, it was just some local business. Nothing really.' How the hell could she tell Hal about the goat and Nathan's insistence that it should be thrown into the spring.

'Yes, you have to watch people in those little villages, Tommy two-head and all that.' He laughed.

'What?'

He leaned forward and whispered. 'Inbred.'

Ella half laughed and shook her head. She didn't think they were inbred but the business with the goat *was* very worrying.

'So do you and Nathan actually know each other?'

'Let's say our paths have crossed. Are you having a pudding? I can recommend the apple pie.'

'So what happened? Between you and Nathan.'

Hal looked up to the ceiling slowly, then took in a deep breath. 'He was Phoebe's boyfriend.'

'Your sister? Oh.' Ella wasn't at all sure how she felt about that. Leggy Phoebe with her semi-casual, semi-glamorous jobs didn't seem Nathan's type at all.

'Quite. He was a bastard and he broke her heart. Don't ever mention him in front of her.'

'No,' Ella said, wondering when that opportunity might arise. Never. She was intrigued but it wasn't any of her business.

'So, that's why I say keep away from him. Don't be fooled by his apparent pleasantness. There's nothing pleasant about him. He even took a swing at me.' Hal shook his head.

'You had a fight? Over Phoebe.' Hal the hero looking after his sister's honour.

'Not really a fight. He was drunk. It was in one of those awful pubs he plays in.'

Ella nodded. She didn't tell Hal that she'd spent many evenings watching Nathan play and Charlie sing in those awful pubs.

'I'm a bit busy this afternoon,' Hal said, changing the subject. 'Bit of business I have to attend to, but are you free this evening?'

'Um. Yes. I suppose so. But I can't be too late, I'm working tomorrow.'

Hal frowned. 'I thought you didn't need to work now.'

'It's just a handover, they pretty much begged me.'

'Don't let them take advantage of you. Anyway, it won't be a late night. I have some tickets for a little avant-garde play in a little theatre I know. Should be interesting.' He smiled at her. 'If you're interested, I could pick you up and drop you off.'

Why not, Ella thought. It could be fun and spending time with Hal would definitely be fun.

'Wear something nice. Something,' he looked her up and down, 'dressier.'

* * *

When Ella pulled up outside Spring Cottage the first emotion she felt was joy; it was such a gorgeous house in a lovely village. She was actually falling in love with it. That was quickly followed by relief when she saw that Feral Billy was no longer on her path. Thank God for that.

She carried the mini-vacuum and the rest of the cleaning gear indoors and dumped them in the hallway. She needed to find a proper home for these things – there wasn't much cupboard space in Spring Cottage. Maybe the cellar. She glanced at the cellar door. It was closed. She couldn't remember closing it, but then emotions had been running high and Hal had arrived with the flowers in the middle of the goat argument with Nathan.

In the kitchen she filled the kettle and put it on. While it boiled she attempted to arrange Hal's flowers in the bucket – not really ideal. There were vases in the cellar but they were being used. Maybe there was a vase in the dresser. There wasn't, but the big leather book was still sitting on it. Ella picked it up, it was heavy, she took it through to the dining room and left it on the table. A few minutes later she returned with her mug of tea and sat down.

The book was old, it smelled musty and the pages were yellowed and brittle. It was a history of the house written by the various owners over the centuries. She knew the house was old, that much was obvious but it seemed that the first building, the part she thought was her kitchen now, was built in the seventeenth century, just like Nathan has said. The early entries were sparse and almost illegible, faded with age and the writing poor.

She went through the book, slowly turning the pages but not attempting to read everything – there would be plenty of time for that if she really wanted to. She found the rules; the list of conditions that she was now sticking to. This must have been where her great uncle had copied them from. They were much more detailed than her version, although essentially the same. There were crossings out and little amendments marked with tiny initials.

She turned the page: The Spring of Life – instructions for care.

She laughed to herself, it sounded like washing instructions, something you'd see on a dress label. The writing here was faded too, many of the words made no sense.

A knock on the kitchen door made her jump. Feral Billy. Of course it wasn't.

The door opened and Walt's cheery smile greeted her.

'Hello, young Ella.'

'I must have left that door unlocked,' she said, puzzled, then remembered that Nathan had unlocked it to bring the dead goat in before she'd stopped him.

'We thought we'd work on the garden tomorrow, since we can't really do any more in the house.'

'Garden?' Ella echoed.

'If that's all right with you? Unless you have other

plans.' He leaned over and patted her on the shoulder. Up close Walt's skin looked really good, smooth and pink.

'I'm working tomorrow.'

'We can get on without you. There's a tap in the garden. Now's the time to get planting.'

'You don't have to start when I'm not here. I mean, I'm really grateful, but don't feel you have to.'

'We want to. Everyone is keen. Everyone is so happy you're finally here. It's all looking very bright and cosy with your furniture in.'

'This is about it,' Ella laughed. 'I need to get more but not much point until the building work is done.'

'When does Nathan start?'

'I don't know. It might not be Nathan.'

Walt raised an eyebrow but didn't question further. 'Ah, I see you've found the book. I wondered when that might turn up. Where was it?'

'In the cellar, apparently. I didn't find it, Nathan did.'

'Oh, he never mentioned it earlier.' Walt sat down and started flicking through it. 'I've never had a good look. Do you mind?'

'Feel free. What do you mean Nathan never mentioned it earlier?'

'When I helped him move Feral Billy. Heavy, that goat was. Very heavy.'

Ella felt sudden alarm. 'Where did you move him to?' But she already knew the answer.

'Into the spring, of course. We had to move him when he was still limp; he fitted through the hatch then. Better than chopping him up.' Walt turned a page in the book, he was engrossed.

'No. Stop,' Ella shouted.

Walt took his hands off the book, held them up as

though he had been caught stealing.

'Tell me you're joking. Tell me this is all some cruel joke of Nathan's that he's got you involved in. Please tell me that you haven't put that goat in my spring.'

'We had to, Ella,' came Nathan's voice from behind her, making her jump.

'No, you didn't.' She looked down at her empty tea mug. 'I've been drinking that water.'

'We all have,' said Walt. 'And very good it is too. Thank you, young Ella.'

Ella looked from Nathan to Walt and back again. They stood grinning, proud of themselves. She wanted to scream. She wanted to yell and hit something. Or someone. The whole goat saga was a nightmare.

'Can you please just leave? Both of you. Now.'

Walt and Nathan exchanged glances. And left.

Ella pinched herself. But nothing changed.

Fifteen

The village shop had just closed as Ella arrived. But the old lady unlocked the door, introduced herself as the proprietor – that was the word she used – and waddled her way back behind the counter.

'I always open when there's a need,' she said.

Ella smiled at her, didn't know how to answer that. 'Do you have any bottled water?'

'Bottled water. I think there might be some out back. We used to keep it for the tourists.' Ella watched her waddle through a door behind the counter. Tourists? Did tourists really come here? 'Here it is,' she said on her return, plonking a one litre bottle on the counter.

Ella picked it up, wiped the dust off it and searched for the expiry date. Did water go off? Did it matter? Anything would be better that dead goat water.

'How much do I owe you?'

'Five pounds.'

'For one bottle?'

'Two pounds then.'

Ella blinked, opened her mouth to speak but the old lady got in first.

'All right, one pound. You drive a hard bargain.'

'Thank you. Do you have any more?'

'No. No. Just the one. No call for it.' The old lady grinned.

Ella handed over the pound and grabbed the bottle.

'It's not good for you, that stuff. It's synthetic.'

'It's better than what I've been drinking,' Ella said, pulling the door open.

'We're all drinking your spring water now. Much better for you. Tastes so good too. Sweetest water ever. Full of minerals. Banishes evil and aches and pains. You having problems with the plumbing, that why you need that?'

Ella nodded and left the shop shaking her head. Maybe Hal was right about the inbreeding. She'd ring the water company when she got back and get the supply to all the cottages cut off before someone was poisoned.

She sat at the dining table and poured herself a glass of water from the bottle. It did taste of plastic, but at least it wasn't full of dead goat.

She looked the water company's phone number up on her phone and rang them. The line was engaged – probably half the village ringing to complain about the taste. She tried again a few minutes later - still engaged.

Idly she turned the pages in the book, smelling its now familiar musty smell. Many hands had written in it, there was even the odd recipe scribbled down; one for a soup that involved boiling fish heads in the spring water to make a *broth that is both satisfying and health giving* – it sounded disgusting. Then something caught her eye, the writing was faded and tiny but Ella thought it mentioned *enticing rats unto the spring*. Surely not. She scrutinised the words and concentrated on trying to decipher them but it was no good. She slammed the book shut and tried the water company again – still engaged. She had horrible visions of people dying from dead goat poisoning and it would be traced back to her.

Sighing she opened the book again, flicked through more pages, horrified to find a poorly drawn picture of a donkey/horse/dog creature being pushed through the spring's hatch. She shuddered but felt compelled to turn more pages. As time went on newspaper clippings were pasted into the pages, one about a plague of cockroaches that had infested the village, another about capturing a deranged dog, underneath each the initials SOL and a date. Ella hoped that didn't mean what she thought it meant.

She turned the pages and found a cutting from 1983 with the headline: *Pensioners warned to beware of bogus meter reader*. On the next page the headline was: *Police seek bogus meter reader after pensioner found dead*. Ella turned the page, there wasn't another cutting, but when she turned back to the previous cutting she noticed that someone had written SOL 13/6/83 under it. Ella's mouth fell open. Surely it didn't mean that.

Her phone pinged. She jumped. Hal had messaged. He was on his way.

Ella slammed the book shut, jumped up and ran upstairs. She went through her clothes hanging on the rail and found the one dress she hoped would be good enough. She dashed into the bathroom – used wet wipes to freshen up and the bottled water to clean her teeth – then changed into the vintage chiffon-over-crepe dress that had been her mum's. It felt good. If she stood far enough back she could see most of her reflection in the small bathroom mirror. Hair and makeup completed the look and she found a neat little handbag to go with it. She was just grabbing her jacket when Hal knocked on the door. He was wearing a light grey suit with a crisp dark shirt.

'Now that's more like it,' he said, looking her up and down before kissing her softly on the mouth. 'Almost elegant.'

Only almost, Ella thought.

Hal held out his arm and escorted Ella to his car. He started the car then put some music on. It was just loud enough to prevent them from talking, which was fine by Ella; she closed her eyes and enjoyed the ride.

'Wake up, sleepy head,' Hal said.

'Sorry.' Ella shook herself awake. 'I didn't realise I'd fallen asleep.'

'As long as you don't fall asleep during the play.'

'I'll try not to,' Ella said. 'We will be back reasonably early, won't we? I've got work in the morning.'

Hal paused before he answered. 'Of course,' he said, grinning at her. Ella hoped he didn't think he was staying the night, because he definitely wasn't.

The avant-garde theatre Hal had referred to was actually a concrete bunker in the garden of a large 1960s house. Inside the walls had been draped with velvet curtains and the seats looked as though they'd been salvaged from an old cinema. Ella glanced around at her fellow audience members; a lot older than her and Hal, they were clustered together exchanging gossip and greetings. A woman in a black velvet evening dress, a fur stole and a hat with an upright black feather, teetered up a tiny staircase onto a makeshift stage at the far end of the bunker. She peeped behind the curtain, faced the audience grinning, then started to clap her hands together rapidly to get attention. The bunker fell silent.

'Ladies and gentlemen, please take your seats, the play is about to start.'

Hal ushered Ella into the front row and sandwiched her between himself and a round man in a white dinner jacket who grinned at Ella, as beads of sweat formed on his forehead. Ella leaned away from the man and pressed herself into Hal's shoulder; he patted her on the arm in response.

Before the play began Ella hadn't been sure what avant-garde theatre was and as the play progressed she still wasn't. The set comprised oversized furniture and step ladders together with a miniature balloon complete with basket beneath. The plot, she thought, was about a man who had murdered his wife, but just before the interval his wife visited him in prison. Or it might not have been his wife. And it might not have been a prison. Ella tried to concentrate on the play but her mind kept wandering back to the goat, the spring, the book. Strange as this play was, what was going on in her own cottage was far stranger.

'Would you like some punch?' Hal's voice cut through Ella's thoughts just as the curtain dropped for the interval.

'Just a small one, please,' Ella said, fearing an excess of alcohol, as was normal with punches. She stood up and watched Hal weave his way to the back of the bunker.

'Hello,' said the round man. 'I'm Kenton Blaby, director of tonight's extravaganza. Are you enjoying it?' He grabbed her hand and enveloped it in his own; his flesh was damp and squidgy. Ella stepped back from the vinegar breath he seemed to be blowing deliberately in her direction.

'Very interesting,' she lied.

‘Kenton, Kenton,’ a female voice called. Ella turned and saw the announcer waving her soft, white arms, her black feather bouncing in the air as she wobbled down the stairs. Ella glanced around for Hal, wondered if she could excuse herself without looking too rude. Too late, the woman was there, puffing, and pink with exertion.

‘Caro Blackthorn-Struthers,’ she said, offering a gloved hand to Ella. ‘I’m the hostess of this little affair. Isn’t it just fun? Don’t you simply love it?’

Ella nodded. Another lie. She glanced around for Hal again.

‘You must be Hal’s investor. Helen, is it?’

‘No, I’m Ella.’

‘Of course. Lovely to meet you. Must dash. Come along Kenton, circulate, circulate.’

Hal appeared with two lead crystal mugs filled with a murky liquid and a prune floating on the top. Ella peered at it as Hal handed over her glass.

‘Apparently they ran out of olives,’ Hal said, a snigger on his lips. ‘I saw you talking to our hosts, the Blabys.’

‘She said her name was something else, double-barrelled.’

‘Caro likes to use her first husband’s name for effect, when it suits her.’

Ella didn’t bother to ask why, she didn’t care. She sipped the punch – high alcohol content judging by the fumes – and was careful not to let the prune escape into her mouth.

Hal smiled down at her. ‘You look very attractive tonight, Ella.’ He leaned in and nuzzled her neck.

‘Thank you. Are there any loos?’

‘Oh yes. Of course. Turn left outside the door. Portaloos.’

'Portaloos. Oh. I'll wait.'

'They're fine. Trust me.' Giving her elbow a little push, he said 'trust me' again.

Outside Ella found the portaloos, she'd expected something like the ones at festivals, discoloured plastic pods that smelt of ammonia and weed. Instead she was greeted with the *Rolls Royce* of toilets; a little staircase led to a cloakroom area. A woman was just drying her hands.

'Oh hello,' she said, smiling. 'Did you come with Hal?'

'Yes,' Ella said, eyeing the toilet cubicle and remembering the last time she used a public toilet and trusting she wouldn't get locked in this one.

'Yes, he said he was bringing an investor. Enjoy the second half.' She disappeared through the door, clattered down the steps.

'Would you like another?' Hal said, when Ella returned. 'I've drunk yours too, I'm afraid.'

'Oh, but you're driving.'

'Very little alcohol,' he said, 'mostly fruit. Prunes actually.' He laughed.

The lights went down, people stumbled to their seats. Kenton Blaby didn't return to his. Good, thought Ella.

The second half was as incomprehensible as the first. Ella's mind was still occupied with the goat fiasco, but now she began to wonder why two people had thought she was Hal's investor. Investor in what?

Ella jumped up too quickly when the play finished. She yawned, made a display of putting her hand over her mouth for Hal's benefit, but he was already fawning over Caro, congratulating Kenton. He mouthed sorry to Ella over their heads.

'I thought we'd never get away,' he said, twenty minutes later as he started the car. 'I apologise for the delay but you know how these lovey types are.'

'Not really,' Ella said.

Hal drove quickly through the dark lanes and Ella hoped he was right about the low alcohol in the punch. She closed her eyes and prayed.

She felt a hand on her knee, she jerked awake.

'Sorry,' Hal said, 'you dozed off again. We're home.'

Ella blinked herself fully awake. 'Thank you,' she said, undoing her seat belt. 'It was an interesting evening.'

'Sorry. Was it too awful?'

'No. Course not.' She wondered if she should tell him now that she wasn't inviting him in for coffee, or anything else for that matter. He jumped out of the car as Ella put her hand on her door; she managed to get out before he reached her.

He locked his car behind them and escorted her to the door. He had that expectant air about him; she'd have to say something.

'What time is it? I've got work in the morning.'

'Just after eleven, not too late.' Hal's husky voice sent a ripple through her body. It would be so easy to let him come in, let him stay. He stood close to her as she unlocked the door, he pushed it and it creaked open.

'I've got an early start, Hal. I'm not going to invite you in.'

He took a tiny step back. 'Of course not. It *is* Monday tomorrow. I, too, have an early start – investors meeting.' He tapped his nose.

'Actually two people tonight thought I was one of your investors.'

'Who?'

'Some woman in the portaloo and that Cora Struthers-Blaby-whatever her name is. She got my name wrong, called me Helen, but…'

'That explains it,' Hal interrupted. 'Helen *is* one of my investors. They obviously misheard when I mentioned you.' Hal grinned and the street light illuminated his perfect, white, even teeth; so straight they looked as though they had been trimmed along the edge. Just another facet of his general perfectness.

'Thanks for a lovely evening,' Ella said, she stepped inside and turned back to face Hal, blocking his way just in case.

'And thank you for your perfect company.' He leaned towards her, kissed her on the mouth; she felt tempted to relent and invite him in. 'Have a good day tomorrow,' he called, as he walked back to his car.

Ella stood on the doorstep and waved him off.

She ran upstairs to the bathroom, used the loo then debated whether to clean her teeth using the last of the bottled water. She would need that in the morning. Maybe she could get away with goat water for her teeth, as long as she didn't swallow it. Tomorrow she'd call in at the supermarket on her way home and buy numerous, giant bottles of water.

In her bedroom she kicked off her shoes and began to unzip her dress. The zip stuck three inches from the top. She tried to pull it down further but it wouldn't budge. She pulled it back up and began again; it stuck in the same place. She pulled it back up, then back down several times, but it always stuck in the same place. She wondered if it would be possible to get the dress off without undoing the zip. She leant forward and, with her arms extended towards the floor, tried to shake the dress over her head. It moved, then stuck; it wasn't going over her boobs, no way. She stood and tried to get the dress back on properly, it wouldn't go back completely now. Her arms were half stuck up in the air, the dress was too far up and she couldn't reach the zip at all now.

She felt a wave of panic sweep over her body, it made her feel sick. She felt hot, too hot.

She stumbled over to the window, fumbled for the latch to open it, then saw the creature. She let out an ear piercing screech.

The spider was big, not the biggest she'd ever seen, but this one was angry. Its two eyes stood out on stalks and they swivelled to look at her. She jumped back and screamed again. She was defenceless; she couldn't move her arms properly. It moved its legs – black and white stripy fur – one after the other, a scary spider Mexican wave. She jumped back towards the bed, tripped, fell onto it. The spider scampered across the window to repair the web she had broken. Urgh, she'd touched a spider's web.

What could she do? What could she do? She knew she couldn't turn her back on it, she couldn't trust it not to leap at her, embed itself in her hair. Or worse. If she could get her shoe she could crush it against the glass. That was the best option.

She got off the bed, her arms still half stuck in the air, her dress still hooked up around her neck, she backed towards her shoes, never taking her eyes from the spider. She allowed herself a quick glance at the shoes, then back to the spider. It had moved, it was on the frame now, no doubt readying itself to leap at her.

She couldn't reach the shoes without taking her eyes off the spider. But it would leap; she knew it would leap, as soon as she bent down. It was just waiting, watching with its stalky eyes. Waiting. Waiting to pounce.

She thought about the glass in the bathroom, she could trap it under that. But that would mean leaving the room, that wasn't any better than leaning over for the shoe.

The spider waved several legs in the air; it was mocking her.

She felt a cold sweat in her hairline, something trickled down the back of her neck. She screamed. But the spider was still on the window. Maybe it had a mate. Maybe that's what it was waving at. Not her at all, but its stripy legged mate as it scampered down her back. Ella could hear herself panting.

'Edna,' she suddenly said. 'And Walt.' Was it too late to go round there?

She was reluctant to leave the spider but she had no choice, she had to get the dress of, no matter what the spider did. She pushed her feet into her shoes without turning her back on it. She had come to her senses a little and decided that it was sweat running down her back, not a spidey-mate. She made her way down the stairs, taking great care not to topple over; it was quite difficult walking with her arms in the air.

Ella stepped outside, the air was cold and she immediately went from a hot sweaty panic to shivering. There was a light on in Edna and Walt's, Ella hoped it wasn't some sort of night light, but meant they were still up. She knocked on the door.

'Young Ella.' Walt's beaming face greeted her; she was relieved to see that he was fully dressed. 'What's wrong with your arms?'

'I'm stuck in my dress. Is Edna still up?'

'No. No. She's visiting her sister in Swindon, staying overnight. Can I help?'

'The zip is stuck.' Ella's teeth chattered.

'Come in, come in. I'll see if I can undo it.'

Ella followed Walt into the kitchen, grateful for its warmth.

'It's just stuck at the top,' she said, 'I got it down a bit, then this.' She waved her arms around.

'How did you get your arms stuck in the air?' Walt asked, and he wasn't laughing although Ella knew she must look hilarious.

'I thought I might be able to get it off anyway. But I couldn't. And when you've undone the zip could you come back with me and get rid of the spider in my room? Please,' she added.

'Hold still while I do this.' He pulled on the zip, nothing happened. He pulled it back up, then down again; it stuck in the same place. He made several attempts, pulling the fabric about a bit too roughly.

'Please be careful,' Ella said. 'This dress was my mum's; it's vintage.'

'Sorry, Ella, I think we might have to cut you out of it. It's just not budging.'

'No.' Ella's voice came out in a long wail.

'Perhaps I could just nip the stitches. Edna has some needlework scissors; they're very pointy. I just need to find them.' Walt stopped pulling on the dress and left the room in search of the scissors leaving Ella alone feeling more miserable and more stupid. Her arms were aching and her hands were cold because the blood was draining from them. She bent over and shook her hands to get the circulation going. Her hair, already messed up, flopped down so she had a close up view of her split ends.

‘Hairdressers,’ she muttered to herself, making a mental note to book a full on pampering appointment as soon as she could afford it.

She heard Walt approaching and stood up. He was brandishing the scissors.

‘Oh please be careful,’ she said. ‘This dress means a lot to me.’

‘I’ll try,’ Walt said, ‘but I do wish Edna was here. Maybe you could wait.’

‘What time is she back?’

‘Tomorrow. Afternoon.’

‘I can’t wait until then.’ Ella heard the whiney tone in her voice. ‘I’ve got to go to work tomorrow.’

‘Maybe I can help,’ a voice said from behind her.

‘You. It would be you, wouldn’t it? Of all the people, it has to be you. You’re everywhere. Are you stalking me?’

‘Do you want me to help or not?’ Nathan said, stepping forward and taking the scissors out of Walt’s hand and laying them on the table.

Ella felt herself becoming hot again; she was ramping up for another hot, sweaty panic.

‘Okay. Yes. Go on.’

‘Please yourself,’ Nathan said. ‘You’re not doing me any favours.’ He turned to walk away.

‘Yes, please. Please.’

‘Okay. Bend over.’

‘What?’

‘When you were bending over, wiggling your arms about, I noticed that the fabric was looser. Let’s try it that way.’

‘You were watching me? You were watching me.’

‘Not for long.’ Nathan smirked. Ella wanted to kick him. ‘Bend over.’

Seething, Ella bent over and Nathan tugged at the zip.

'Is it moving?' Ella said, sounding as desperate as she felt.

'No. Stretch your arms further forward and pull your shoulder blades together.'

'Are you joking?'

Nathan didn't answer but he put his hands on her back and pushed her shoulders blades together. Ella could feel the warmth of his hands through the dress.

'Don't move,' he whispered, then he pressed down on her back and tugged the zip.

Ella felt it move, heard it go all the way down. She let out a long sigh of relief. 'Thank you,' she said, standing up. The dress slid off her shoulders and started to fall down her front, she grabbed it, pulled it up. At the same time Nathan reached over and pushed it back onto her shoulders.

'Come on then,' Nathan said, taking his jacket off the back of a kitchen chair. 'Did you say something about a spider in your bedroom?'

Ella nodded, at the same time shuddering.

'Let's go and get it. Night Walt. I'll see you tomorrow, thanks for the chat.' He stepped aside so Ella could lead the way and as she passed him, still clutching the dress to her neck, he wrapped his jacket around her shoulders. He didn't say a word.

In her bedroom she pointed to the spider, still swinging in a carefree way on the window, then slipped into the bathroom. Her frog onesie was hanging on the door hook; she got out of the dress and into the onesie then went back into her bedroom.

'All done,' Nathan said, turning to face her.

She screwed up her eyes. Was he telling the truth?

'What did you do with it?'

'I opened the window and threw it out. Don't worry, the window is shut now, it won't get back in.'

'What did it look like?'

'A bit cross. Then it said it didn't want to go outside.'

'Ha ha.'

'You're welcome,' Nathan said.

'You should have killed it. Then I'd know it was gone. You definitely threw it out, didn't you? You're not just saying that.'

'Yes. I definitely threw it out.' He looked her straight in the eye, didn't flinch or look away as he spoke.

'Okay. I believe you. Thank you.'

'Like I said earlier, you're welcome.' He picked his jacket up off the bed and shrugged it on.

'Thank you for helping me,' Ella said, sheepishly. 'Thanks for everything.'

'No problem.' He followed her down the stairs.

'Where did you go in your nice dress?' he said at the door.

'Theatre with Hal.'

Nathan made a disgusted face.

'I know you and Hal don't get on. He told me what happened.'

'Did he? Told you what exactly?'

'Told me you broke his sister Phoebe's heart and then punched him.'

Nathan stared into Ella's face then went through the door and stepped out into the night.

'Night,' Ella called. 'Thanks for everything.'

But Nathan never answered and he never looked back.

Sixteen

The cavalry was already at work in Ella's garden when she got up; she could hear the old ladies singing. She ran down and boiled a kettle for a strip wash, ran back upstairs with it. When she came back down she hurriedly toasted her last slice of stale bread before going outside to see them. She'd have to make it brief, because she didn't want to be late on her last ever day at Gubbins.

'Young Ella,' Walt greeted her. 'I hope we didn't disturb you.'

'How long have you been here? It's only just after eight.'

'Around seven,' Walt said. 'We like to get a good start. We've already started sowing; you're going to have a bumper crop this year.'

Ella watched one of the old men carry a full watering can over to a row of canes and start watering.

'Where did you get the water from?' Ella said, fearing the answer.

'Tap.' Walt nodded in the direction of the cottage and Ella saw the tap secured to the side wall.

'Please tell me that doesn't come out of the spring.'

'Of course it does,' one of the old ladies said, as she turned it on and filled a tin cup.

'Don't drink that. Please don't drink that; it's got dead goat in it.'

The old lady smiled and knocked it back anyway, then smacked her lips, before hanging the tin cup on the tap handle and skipping up the garden path. She turned and winked at Ella.

'You get off to work; young Ella and we'll crack on with this.'

'But Walt, that water's contaminated. No one should be drinking it.'

'Ella,' said another old lady, 'we've been drinking it for years, and it's never tasted so good.' To prove the point she too helped herself to a cup full and drank it back in one go.

'Go to work,' Walt said, giving Ella a friendly nudge.

'Don't blame me if you're all dead when I come back. I did warn you,' she muttered on her way to the car. The cavalry seemed to be drinking the water in defiance of her. But she had to admit they seemed to be getting friskier by the day. She must remember to ring the water company when she had the chance.

* * *

There was an air of restraint and politeness at Gubbins that Ella found comforting. After the weirdness of the last few days she welcomed normality, however dull. She'd always hated Monday mornings – didn't everyone – but today even that feeling was welcome; it was normal. And, of course, she wasn't going to work the whole week.

The morning passed slowly, Ella alternated between Gwynnie and Tiffy, showing them the ropes and pointing out their mistakes as gently as she could. She no longer felt hostile towards either of them. In fact she didn't feel anything at all; the events at Spring Cottage seemed far more demanding and important. Ella found herself staring out of the window and wondering if the cavalry had succumbed to dead goat poisoning yet.

Her phone vibrated on the desk; a message: Sam was going to pop round for half an hour about six, with Charlie. That cheered Ella up. She'd go out to the supermarket at lunchtime and stock up on water.

The interminable morning finally ground to an end. Ella looked at her watch, it was just after noon.

'All right if I take an early lunch today?' she said to Gwynnie, who was concentrating on a tricky part of the company's system.

'Oh. No. We have plans.'

Ella looked at Gwynnie, waited for an explanation.

'Ben?' Gwynnie called. 'Is it time yet?'

Ben nodded at Gwynnie and gave Ella a big smile then jumped up from his desk and came towards Ella with a bouquet. Where the hell had he been hiding that?

'From all of us,' he said, laying the flowers across her lap.

'Thank you. Everyone. I wasn't expecting this.' Ella felt touched and a little piqued.

'And we're off to Gino's,' Tiffy said. 'You like Italian, don't you?'

'Love it,' Ella said, gobsmacked. She felt as though she was becoming a regular at Gino's.

'Our treat,' Gwynnie said. She gave Ella a brief smile.

'Thank you,' Ella said, feeling sheepish. She wished

they weren't doing this.

'Come on, you'll enjoy it,' Ben said, once they were alone in his car.

'I'm sure I will. I am grateful, I just had other plans,' she said, thinking of the water she'd planned to buy.

Gino's was busy, very busy for a Monday, but a table had been booked, so they didn't have to wait.

'Whose idea was this?' Ella whispered into Ben's ear.

'Gwynnie's. Me and Kev were a bit surprised too. You can never second guess people.'

They ordered from the quick lunch menu and when the food arrived so did a bottle of prosecco and five glasses. Gwynnie proposed a toast to Ella, thanking her for her hard work and for passing on her abundant knowledge and wishing her good luck in her new home. Ella felt herself colour up, muttered something about being glad to help and took a big gulp of the prosecco.

The food was good and because Ben, Kevin and Ella had a pudding, lunch overran. By the time they got back to the office they'd been gone almost two hours.

Ella felt sleepy, that was the trouble with a big meal at lunchtime, especially pasta, as well as a glass of wine. As she sat next to first Tiffy, then Gwynnie, imparting her *abundant knowledge*, she had to make fists that pushed her nails into the palms of her hands to keep herself awake.

Finally it was home time; finally she could collect today's money, say her final farewells and leave. She watched the clock on Gwynnie's computer as the minutes ticked away.

'You couldn't just hang on and show me this one last thing, could you?' Gwynnie said, logging onto the system.

'Of course,' Ella said. She could hardly say anything

else after the kind words, the bouquet and the lovely lunch. Ironically if they hadn't gone for the lunch they would be finished by now.

Thirty-five minutes later Ella and Gwynnie were finally done. Ella collected her money envelope, said goodbye and dashed out into the car park, she didn't even get the opportunity to go to the loo. She would just about have time to get home before Sam and Charlie turned up. She hoped the traffic wasn't too bad.

Sam and Charlie were already sitting outside when Ella pulled up. They opened their car doors at the same time as Ella did. Ella stumbled towards her friends, carrying the bouquet from work. Sam eyed it then glanced down at the one she was carrying, smaller and obviously less expensive.

'Flower day,' Sam said, offering the flowers to Ella.

'Oh thank you, they're lovely. Come in, come in, but don't expect anything too grand.'

They burst through the front door and into the hallway, Ella glanced at the cellar door just in case, but it was closed. Everything was fine.

In the kitchen Ella laid the two bouquets of flowers on the kitchen table next to the bucket containing Hal's giant bouquet.

'Flower central,' Sam said, laughing, then produced a card from her handbag.

Ella opened it. *Be happy in your new home*; Ella stood it up on the windowsill. 'I just need to run up to the loo, then I'll give you the tour. Won't be long,' she said, dashing up the stairs.

When she came back Charlie had filled the kettle and plugged it in.

'I'm gasping for a coffee. I've put the kettle on, is that okay?'

'Not for me,' Sam said. 'I'm completely off coffee and tea.'

Thank God for that. 'Well,' Ella began, wondering if boiling it would do the trick and Charlie wouldn't be poisoned. And, she could do with a cup of tea herself. 'The water doesn't taste that good. Old pipes. You know.' Should she tell them about the goat? No.

'Tastes pretty good to me,' Sam said, 'I've just had two big glasses.

What. Oh. My. God. It was too late now.

'Excuse me a minute, I've left something upstairs.' Her handbag was on the bed where she'd flung it earlier. She got her phone out, dialled Nathan and prayed he'd answer.

'Ella,' he said. 'To what do I owe the honour?'

She wanted to tell him to get a better line but didn't have time. 'Never mind all that. Sam and Charlie are here and Sam's drunk the water.'

'So.'

'The bloody goat water, from the spring. What should I do?'

'Nothing.'

'She's pregnant and you've poisoned her. She might lose the baby, or,' Ella put her hand to her mouth and gasped, 'it might be deformed. It might be… goaty.' She couldn't think straight. She heard Nathan laugh.

'She'll be fine. Probably better than fine,' he said, amid his amusement.

'It's not bloody funny. She's drunk water with a dead goat floating in it.'

'No. It'll have broken up by now; that spring is very fierce at the moment. Very active. Very hungry.' He laughed some more.

'It's not bloody funny,' she screeched again, ending

the call and throwing the phone down on the bed. She'd have to go and face them now; she'd have to tell them the awful truth.

Downstairs Sam and Charlie had seated themselves at the kitchen table. Charlie had found one of Ella's largest mugs and made himself a coffee.

'We've made you a pot of tea,' Sam said, pushing the teapot towards her.

Ella slumped into a chair, watched as Sam poured out the tea and added milk and sugar, stirred it and handed it to Ella. She took a sip, it tasted so good. Oh what the hell. Too late. The damage was done now. She might as well be poisoned along with them.

'How was work?' Sam said just as Nathan bounded in through the door.

'Doesn't anybody ever bloody knock in this damn village?' Ella shouted, spinning round to see his grinning face.

'Work that good, eh?' Sam said, rubbing Ella's hand. 'At least you don't ever have to go back again.'

'Nathan, mate.' Charlie jumped up and the two exchanged a thumping, manly handshake complete with back slaps.

'So you're allowed out now, Sam,' Nathan said, as he kissed her on the cheek.

'As long as I don't overdo it,' she laughed.

Ella glared at Nathan, then mouthed 'goat' silently at him behind Charlie and Sam's backs.

'You look good. You've got a lot more colour in your cheeks than when I last saw you,' he said to Sam.

'Yeah, I'm feeling good. Coming out has really perked me up. Come on Ella, where's this guided tour you promised us?

Ella showed them round the cottage; of course they

loved it. Sam made suggestions for décor and changes, Charlie marvelled at the age of the place. When they got back to the kitchen Nathan was leaning against the sink drinking tea.

'Help yourself, why don't you,' Ella snapped at him.

He smiled broadly in response and when she was close enough to him, playfully nudged her in the ribs.

She narrowed her eyes.

'What are you going to do in here?' Sam said, spinning around the kitchen.

'I haven't decided yet,' Ella said, a bit too sharply. 'I mean, I've got to think about it.'

'Are you doing it, Nath?' Charlie said.

Nathan shrugged, exchanged a furtive look with Charlie.

'Are you not playing music at all now?' Sam asked.

'Yeah. I play down our local, The Giddy Goat. I'm there most Saturday nights, playing my own stuff.'

'We'll have to come and watch you, when we're not playing ourselves,' Charlie said.

'That'd be fun, Ella, wouldn't it?' Sam waited for Ella's reply.

Ella thought of the shitty song. 'Yeah. Amazing fun,' she said, without even trying to hide her contempt.

'Come on you,' Charlie said, putting his arm around Sam. 'Let's get you home. You're supposed to be taking it easy.'

'Nathan's leaving too now, aren't you?' Ella spat.

Nathan didn't respond, just wandered alongside Charlie chatting to him and Sam.

The four of them stood in the lane, Sam and Ella hugged, Charlie and Ella hugged, Nathan and Sam hugged, Nathan and Charlie did the handshake thing again. Nathan smiled at Ella, Ella glared at Nathan.

‘I’ll message you,’ Charlie said to Nathan. ‘Sort out a date.’

As Charlie opened the car doors Ella heard the familiar roar of Hal’s car as it turned into the lane. He slewed the car into the kerb and jumped out. He looked, as usual, glossy magazine fresh. He strode over to Ella, hugged her, beamed a big smile as she introduced him, vigorously shook hands with Charlie, double kissed Sam’s cheeks, and ignored Nathan who stood and watched without a word.

They waved as Charlie turned the car and drove away, then Ella linked arms with Hal and guided him towards the cottage. She too ignored Nathan.

They were almost inside when Nathan spoke. ‘Hal. How’s Phoebe?’

Hal hurried Ella through her front door, closing it firmly behind them.

‘He’s such a bastard,’ Ella said.

When she looked at Hal, he looked so sad.

Seventeen

'I don't know why you let him anywhere near you, Ella. I did warn you about him. I did tell you how he broke Phoebe's heart,' Hal said, as they stood in the kitchen. He leant against the sink and Ella, remembering what happened the last time he touched her taps hoped he wouldn't be tempted again.

'I'm sorry he was here; he's friends with Charlie and Sam, that's all.' She really didn't want to explain her relationship, or non-relationship, with Nathan to Hal. 'Anyway, how was your day? Did you say you had a meeting?'

'Yes. It was,' he paused, 'interesting. A work in progress I think is how I would describe it. How was your official last day at work?' He paused again. 'That's why I came to see you. To celebrate. I thought we could take in an early dinner, have a bottle of champers.'

Ella gave him a quick glance, he had actually said champers.

'Oh, it was fine. Quite normal really. Except they took me out for lunch.' She thought about the large plate of pasta she had devoured and rubbed her stomach. 'Which was lovely but I'm still full. So I'll have to decline your dinner offer, lovely as it sounds. Perhaps we could do it another night?'

'Of course we can. We'll arrange something.' He stepped away from the sink and Ella noticed there were envelopes balanced on the side of it.

'What are these?' She stepped forward, picked up the letters. 'Charlie or Sam must have picked these up,' she said when Hal shook his head. She opened the first letter, a long missive from her solicitor telling her that everything had gone through, she was now the official owner of Spring Cottage, and that the necessary monies were being transferred to her. She should expect a meeting invitation from her accountant.

'Accountant,' Hal said, reading over her shoulder.

'Apparently. I didn't know I had one.' She ripped open the other envelope, the meeting request from the accountant. 'It's tomorrow,' she said, 'so I'll find out more.'

'What would you like to do this evening instead of dinner?' Hal asked, putting his arm around her shoulder.

Ella wondered how rude it would be to tell him that what she really wanted to do was have a hot bath – not possible – and go to bed early, on her own. But before she could answer he handed her another envelope.

'Where was this?' she said.

'On the floor. It must have slipped.' He watched her as she opened it.

'Oh, it's the quote from one of the builders you recommended. I thought he said he wasn't going to bother.' She watched a quick smirk pass over Hal's face as she flicked to the last page. The sum was far more than Nathan had quoted. She wanted to study it properly, wanted to compare it line by line with Nathan's quote.

'He's good,' Hal said. 'I'd use him if I were you. I'll probably use him on the spa renovation.'

'Oh, yes. How's that going?'

Hal sighed. 'That's what the meeting was about this morning. We need a bit more investment before we can continue.'

'I hope it pans out,' Ella said, tidying the letters in her hand and wondering where the hell to put them. She looked around the kitchen, it was a mess, cups and saucers seemed to be everywhere, nowhere to put anything. She'd be so happy when this kitchen was done. Despite having only just moved in and having very little furniture, the place seemed to be getting cluttered already. The kitchen table was covered in flowers, so she walked into the dining room and put the letters on the table next to the open book. Hal followed her then peered over her shoulder.

'The Spring of Life,' Hal read.

'Mmm,' Ella said, closing the book, remembering the last thing she'd read which implied that there might have been a human body thrown down there in the past. She didn't want Hal reading that. She yawned, then put her hand up to her mouth. 'Sorry,' she said. 'It seems to have been a long day.'

'Don't worry.' Hal laughed, putting his arm around her again. 'I can take a hint. I expect you want an early night. On your own,' he added. 'Get into your frog outfit.'

'I don't wear it all the time,'

'Of course not.' Hal wiped an imaginary fleck from his collar.

‘That’s a nice shirt,’ Ella said.

‘Thanks. It was a Christmas present from Phoebe. Pink is her favourite colour.’ He raised his eyes to the ceiling before walking back into the kitchen to pick up his car keys. Ella followed him. ‘Shall I pop round tomorrow evening? You can tell me all about your accountant visit.’ He laughed then pulled Ella close, kissed her so long and hard that it took her breath away.

‘Yeah, that’d be good,’ Ella said, when he finally let her go. She touched her bottom lip, it felt bruised. She followed him to his car, stood on the pavement as he got in.

‘Have you thought any more about my idea about your water?’

Ella frowned.

‘Bottling it. We could sell it in my spa, see how it goes?’

‘Oh, I don’t think so,’ Ella said, thinking about the goat and God knows what else that might be down there.

‘Don’t dismiss it,’ Hal said, starting the car. ‘Until tomorrow.’

She watched him roar down the road.

* * *

Ella knocked on Walt and Edna’s door. In her holdall she had shampoo and conditioner, bubble bath, clean PJs and her frog onesie.

‘Wow,’ Ella said, when Edna answered the door. ‘You’ve had a makeover.’ After the words were out she worried about how insulting that sounded.

‘Just a haircut,’ Edna said, stroking her glossy dark

grey bob. She didn't mention the dye job, but Ella was pretty sure Edna's hair had been frizzy and white before.

'Looks amazing. You look so much,' she hesitated, she had been about to say younger, but was having second thoughts.

Edna raised her eyebrows waiting for the end of the sentence.

'Younger,' Ella said, because she couldn't think of anything better.

'Thank you. I feel younger.' Edna's smile lit up her face.

Phew, it had been the right thing to say.

'So what can we do for you?'

'Could I have a bath please?'

* * *

'Would you like a cup of cocoa before you go?' Edna asked, after Ella emerged from the bathroom pink and wrinkly from her long soak. It had felt so good, she felt so relaxed. Now a nice cup of cocoa and she'd be ready for bed.

'Yes please.' Ella sat down at Edna's kitchen table. It was so cosy in there; she hoped her kitchen would be like this eventually. She watched Edna fill a saucepan with milk from the fridge and then top it up with water.

'Half and half,' Edna said, aware of Ella's eyes on her actions. 'Tastes better and not so fattening.' She laughed.

'I'm glad you're not using the tap from the spring,' Ella said.

'No need,' came a voice from the doorway. Walt.

No need. What the hell did that mean?

'I've switched the supply,' Walt said, sitting next to Ella. She looked at him closely, he looked as though he'd had a bit of makeover too, either that, or he'd lost weight.

'What do you mean?'

'Whole house is supplied by the spring now. Just like yours. Is there enough for me, Edna?'

'I've made plenty.' Edna stirred the pan, it smelt delicious.

'I really don't think we should… hang on a minute, have I just had a bath in it?'

'Oh yes.'

'What is going on here? Is this some elaborate joke that Nathan's got you all playing on me? What I don't understand is why?'

'It's no joke.' Edna put three mugs of steaming cocoa on the table. Ella's traitorous mouth salivated. 'We're all so delighted you're here, the well is being cared for and everything is back as it should be. It's been a barren few years.'

'Why do I feel as though I've dropped into some old *Hammer House of Horror* movie? Please tell me you're joking about all this. Please.' Ella could hear the pleading panic in her own voice.

Walt took a sip of his cocoa, nudged Ella to do the same. She shook her head.

'We don't pretend to understand it. We don't even pretend to know all about it. All we know is that when there is a custodian – that's you – the spring flourishes and so does the village. Have you seen your garden? We only planted yesterday but already there are shoots. And business in the pub and shop is picking up too.

Ella shook her head. It was all too much, just too, too much. It wasn't funny, it never had been. 'It's got a dead goat in it,' she said. 'That isn't right.'

'Try not to think about it. It's how it's always been. Read the book.'

'I have read the book, or some of it. I hope I'm wrong but it looks as though people have been enticed into it.'

'Only bad ones. Murderers,' Walt said, taking a loud sip. 'This is so good. Don't let yours go to waste.' He nudged Ella again. She was struggling to resist the cocoa's allure.

Edna produced a tin of biscuits, offered one to Ella, who took it and nibbled on its edges.

'But none of it makes any sense. It's all so… wrong. Mad. Illegal probably.'

'Oh well. Not to worry. It does you good,' Edna said, hugging her cocoa mug.

'How? It's not… hygienic.' Ella put her hand to her mouth. 'Oh, I haven't rung the water company yet.'

Walt patted her hand. 'No need.'

'All I know,' Edna said, 'is that since you've been tending that spring I feel ten years younger. I look ten years younger. So does Walt.'

'And the cavalry,' Walt added.

'Oh yes, and them.'

'Yeah, you are all pretty frisky for old people,' Ella said. 'I mean retired. Sorry about that.'

'We are old,' Walt said. 'I'll be ninety next year.'

'What?' Ella choked on her cocoa. Ninety? Cocoa? She was drinking the cocoa. When did that happen? Walt was nearly ninety? How could that be?

'Just take it as it comes, young Ella,' Walt said. 'Just ignore it if you like. No one's expecting you to put anything in the spring. There's plenty of us to do that for you. It's usually the man of the house who does it anyway, though I did help your uncle sometimes towards the end.'

'I haven't got a man,' Ella said, her voice sounded sad and wimpy. She felt lightheaded and sleepy as though it was the end of a long night of partying. Had Edna slipped alcohol into the cocoa? That would explain the surreal conversation.

'What about that Hal man?' Walt said.

'Oh yeah. I forgot about him.' Ella heard herself chuckle. There was definitely alcohol in that cocoa.

'Nathan's a better fit for you.' Edna got up, collected the cups up and took them to the sink.

'Nathan. Never. I hate Nathan.' Ella fought the temptation to stamp her foot. Definitely alcohol in that cocoa. A lot of it.

'Just as well Gilbert's on the mend. He'll oversee the work on Spring Cottage now.'

'What? I thought he was in a wheelchair with a leg broken in three places.'

'Spring of Life,' Walt and Edna chorused.

Definitely alcohol.

'I'm going.' Ella stood up; she didn't feel dizzy even though she had expected to. 'Thank you for the bath and the cocoa.'

On her way to bed she retrieved Nathan's quote for the building work and collected the other builder's quote from the table, intending to compare them before she went to sleep.

They were still on her bedside table in the morning – unread.

* * *

She ate the last of her cereal for breakfast and promised

herself she would go food shopping later. She started to make a list. Her appointment with the accountant was at ten, after that she could please herself. She'd pop in at the grotty bedsit and pick up any post. She put that on the list after food shopping. Maybe she'd see if she could get some bedroom curtains, dawn was breaking earlier now and she was waking up far too soon. She put curtains on the list. She picked her phone up to google curtain shops. No good – not enough signal strength. She put *get broadband* on her list. Finally she added, *compare building quotes and make decision.*

The meeting with the accountant was boring *and* thrilling; boring because there was a lot of detail about things she really wasn't interested in and thrilling because she'd probably never have to worry about money ever again, as long as she wasn't ludicrously extravagant. He explained how much would go into her current account every month, how much she had in her house account – only to be used to renovate the cottage – and how much was in her investment accounts. She would need to attend meetings with the accountant two or three times a year and he would do her tax return.

'Tax return,' she said. 'I hadn't even thought of that. I've always been pay-as-you-earn.'

'That's no longer the case,' the accountant said, standing up and shaking her hand.

Ella felt the smile spreading across her face and it was still there ten minutes later as she got into her car. She flopped into the driver's seat and fought hard against the urge to squeal with joy.

'If only you were here, Mum,' she whispered, looking up to the sky.

Morrison's car park looked full, so she drove another five hundred yards down the road and pulled into Waitrose's car park. Well she could afford it now, she told herself.

She treated herself to fresh bread from the bakery and filled her trolley with everything she fancied. She didn't even flinch when she flexed her credit card at the checkout, even though the amount was more than she normally spent in a month on a supermarket shop. It was only as she was loading it into her car that she wondered where she would squeeze it all in the cottage kitchen. Oh well. Fortunately most of it was packets or tins because she didn't have a fridge yet; she could always stack them on the table if needs be.

She pulled the list from her handbag, extracted a sticky pen from the door pocket – maybe she could afford a better car – then ticked off *accountant* and *shopping* from her list.

Next was *collecting her post*, then *curtain buying*.

She pulled up outside the grotty bedsit block and smiled. She really needed to get her post redirected, it was all right for now, but once the month was up there'd be another tenant in there. She scribbled *redirect post* on the bottom of the list.

She unlocked the door and looked down on the mat expecting to see at least one letter, but there was nothing, not even her credit card bill. Maybe it had slid right across the hallway. But it hadn't. Maybe the agent had been round, picked it up. She went through to the main room.

'What the fuck…?' a male voice yelled. The man was in bed, smoking, naked from the waist up.

Ella screamed. 'Who the hell are you?'

'And who the hell are you? What you doing bursting in here? How did you get in?' He pulled the covers up to his neck, leaned over and dropped the cigarette into a dead coffee cup.

'With a key. I live here.'

'No you don't. I live here.'

'Since when?'

'Since yesterday.'

'But I'm still the tenant here. I'm still paying rent.'

'So am I. And there wasn't any sign of you or anyone else living here. So sling your hook.'

Ella shuddered. 'I just came for my post.'

'There's some crap in the bin, take it and go.'

Ella found her post nestling under a used tea bag and an egg shell. She gagged, then put her hand in the bin and fished it out.

'Leave the key,' he growled as she passed him on her way out.

'Not with you. I'll leave it with the agent.'

'Whatever. Get out.'

Ella slammed the door as hard as she could behind her. She heard him yell out an obscenity. She leant against the wall and took several deep breaths. What the hell was going on? She'd have to ring the agent. Then she thought of Hal, wondered if he would be in.

She knocked on the door twice, no answer, which was only to be expected really, it was the middle of a working day. She turned to walk away when the door burst open.

'Yeah?' Phoebe's voice sounded husky as though she'd just woken up.

'Sorry to disturb you. I was looking for Hal.'

Phoebe blinked at Ella as though trying to remember her. She shrugged, turned and walked back down the hall leaving the door open. Ella watched her, she wore a man's shirt; it was pink like the one Hal had worn the night before. It hung half way down her thighs, golden and sleek, unlike her bed-head hair.

Ella stepped inside the door. Phoebe headed towards the kitchen; she rapped on a bedroom door as she passed. The door swung open slowly.

'Hal. Your neighbour's here.'

Ella followed Phoebe; reached the bedroom door, peered in. Hal lay diagonally across the bed, his long, elegant legs uncovered. His hair, usually so immaculate, spread out over the pillow in a mass of greasy spikes.

'Hal?' Ella spoke quietly.

'Too early,' Hal grunted.

'Hal,' Ella said again, a little louder this time. She heard Phoebe filling the kettle, switching it on; it filled the flat with its loud hiss.

'What the fuck you doing, Phoebes? It's too soon for that.'

Phoebe switched the kettle off. Wandered out of the kitchen, she was eating a piece of cold pizza, it flopped in her hand. She gave Ella a quick half smile, half grimace. 'Shut the door on your way out,' she said pushing past Ella.

Hal turned over, grunted, 'Phoebes, get your dirty body back in this bed.'

Eighteen

'That's good timing. I've just got back from the hospital.' Sam's smile spread across her face as she opened her front door. She looked pink cheeked and radiant. 'Oh my God. What's wrong?'

Ella's face screwed up. She'd kept it together so far, but now she was breaking up.

'I was having such a good day,' Ella said, after she'd finished snivelling on Sam's shoulder. 'I'd been to the accountant, all great news.' She stopped, blew her nose and followed Sam inside. She took a deep breath, pulled herself together. 'There's someone in my flat.'

'You mean the grotty bedsit?'

'Yes.'

'But you've moved out.'

'Yes. But I'm still paying the rent, until the end of the month. I know I can afford to just write it off, but it's the principle of the thing, isn't it?'

'Oh yes. Absolutely.' Sam rubbed her stomach, then patted it. 'Who's in it? How has that happened?'

'I don't know. I rang the agent as soon as I got out after I'd been…' she paused, she wasn't telling Sam about Hal, at least not until she'd had a chance to hear his side. Who was she kidding, how could he explain that away? 'Anyway the person dealing with my flat is out with a client, due back this afternoon, they'll ring me. I've heard that before, I expect I'll have to ring them repeatedly.'

'Where's the office?'

'Swindon town centre.'

'Come on, Ella, it's not like you to get upset over something so… well, it doesn't matter, does it? You've got your lovely cottage. We can easily get to the bottom of this. It's probably just a misunderstanding. Let's just go to the agents' office. That way they won't be able to fob you off. We could go and have lunch first.'

Ella frowned. 'But what about you? Aren't you supposed to be taking it easy?'

Sam smiled. 'Like I said earlier, I've just been to the hospital. They say I'm doing really well now. All my problems,' Sam waved her arms around, 'poof, gone.'

'That's great. What exactly was wrong with you? You never did elaborate.'

'Anaemia, very low blood pressure, fatigue, some other complications, bit of stress. Generally run down. Now, I'm great. And I feel great too. I started to notice the improvement just after I came round to your place. I was still quite tired and low before that visit, but it lifted me. Even on the way home, I said to Charlie, suddenly I was feeling much, much better. Great, isn't it?' Sam stood up. 'Come on, let's get into Swindon.'

'I'm really pleased you're feeling better, Sam.' She hugged her friend and wondered if the Spring of Life had anything to do with it. Dead goat. Of course not. 'Does this mean you're going back to work?'

'No. They say I shouldn't go back until after the baby's born. So I can spend lots of time with you until then. We can go furniture shopping and baby clothes shopping and carpet shopping and maternity clothes shopping.' Sam laughed and so did Ella. Every cloud…

* * *

Ella half expected the letting agents' offices to be down a dingy backstreet, but they weren't; far from it. As they walked in they were invited to wait in the plush reception and offered coffee. They both declined; they'd had a large lunch and Ella had drunk a full pot of tea. When Ella said who she was, they were shown into a functional office. The woman who greeted them was calm and professional and about Ella's age.

'Miss Taylor,' she said, offering her hand, 'may I call you Ella? I'm Jo.'

'Yes, do,' Ella said, wondering if that was wise. 'And this is Sam.'

'So,' Jo said, leaning across her desk to shake Sam's hand, 'how can I help you?'

'There's a man in my flat, and there shouldn't be. I'm still paying the rent. Just because I've moved out early doesn't mean you can just put a new tenant in there.'

'Let me check. Oh, according to our records,' Jo turned from her computer, 'we haven't.'

'You have.'

'No. We haven't. Is it possible he's squatting?'

'Maybe,' Ella said quietly, then remembered. 'No. He said he was paying rent.'

Jo clicked around on her computer, looked up at Ella and Sam. 'Not to us, he isn't. According to us, you have the tenancy until the end of the month. We haven't, *I* haven't – and I manage that property – put anyone new in. I did have a tenant lined up, but in fact, when your tenancy expires we're not letting it again; the landlord wants it back.'

'Well there's someone in there now,' Ella said, not knowing what else to say. She slumped back in her chair.

'She'd like a full refund for this month,' Sam said, smiling over at Jo. 'And her deposit back, in full, because Ella left that place spotless, better than it was when she moved in.'

'Well, we usually do a check-out against the inventory with the tenant before we can discuss returning deposits.'

'That's not possible now, is it?' Sam smiled sweetly at Jo.

Jo blinked. 'I need to ring the landlord. There's obviously been some sort of mix up.'

'Easily unmixed,' Sam said, giving Ella a sly wink.

Jo picked up the phone, referred to her computer then dialled. 'Voice mail,' she mouthed to them as she listened to the recorded message. 'Hi, this Jo,' she began, before leaving a long message implying there was some mix up with Ella's studio apartment.

'Studio apartment. That's a joke,' Sam said loudly to Ella, as Jo flinched.

'Not much more I can do at the moment,' Jo said, when she came off the phone. 'I'm sorry. For what it's worth I do agree that you should have a full refund on both the rent and the deposit, but I can't do so until I speak to the landlord.'

Ella nodded slowly.

'Okay,' Sam said, standing up. 'Well, we're not sitting here all day. You've got Ella's number, so she'll expect an update today – even if the landlord doesn't get back to you. Thank you for your time.'

'I'll let you know what I know before close of play today,' Jo said, standing up and shaking first Sam's and then Ella's hand. 'Even if there's no news.'

'Fair enough.' Sam led the way out.

'Thanks for sticking up for me,' Ella said. 'Even if you were a bit rude.'

'I wasn't rude, Ella, I was firm. I thought one of us had better take the lead. Anyway it's not like you to be so… wimpy.'

'I've got a thumping headache; I think I might just go home now, sorry.' Ella kept thinking about Hal. And Phoebe. There had to be a logical explanation, didn't there. Surely he didn't sleep with his sister.

Sam hugged her friend. 'I should probably be putting my feet up now anyway. Maybe I'll come round and see you later in the week.'

'I'd love that, I really would. I need to get some bedroom curtains, so you could help me choose.'

* * *

Ella went to bed fully clothed when she got home, closed her eyes and slept for two hours. When she awoke she lay in bed thinking about the day; it had started so well. She didn't know what to think. She tried to look on the positive side; at least Sam was better now.

Sighing and to stop herself thinking too much, she picked up the two building quotes and spread them out on the bed in front of her.

An hour later she knew that Nathan's quote was very good value. Too good.

The knock on the door made her jump. She leapt

out of bed and ran down the stairs as the door knocker banged again.

'Hal,' she said, as she opened the door.

He gave her a quick look up and down making her aware of her messy hair, her crumpled clothes. He looked as immaculate as usual, smelt divine. Then she remembered how he'd looked sprawled across the bed that morning; the room smelling of stale sex and last night's pizza.

'Ella,' he said, stepping into her cottage. 'How are you?' His eyes flicked over her clothes again.

'Been better,' she said, although the headache had gone.

'What's wrong?' He put an arm around her as though she was an old person. She stood rigid and didn't move. He let go and stepped away.

'Had a few shocks today,' she said, watching him.

'Oh. Didn't it go well with the accountant? That's a shame, a real shame. Tell me all about it; maybe I can help you sort it out. After all, you were expecting a sizeable legacy.'

In the kitchen Ella's phone began to ring. She ran to answer it. Hal followed her.

'Ella, it's Jo.'

'Hi there.'

'I've got hold of the landlord,' Jo said. 'And to be honest I'm rather confused. He claims he knows you. Claims you've come to an arrangement over the studio apartment. He says he's paid you off.'

'None of that is true,' Ella said, watching Hal as he strayed closer to her. 'There must be a mistake.'

'Well, he described you perfectly.'

'I'm average, I could be anybody,' Ella said, thinking of her mid-brown hair, her blue eyes, her medium build, her medium height.

Jo hesitated. 'Maybe,' she said, tactfully. 'Trouble is it's your word against his. I'm in a very difficult position here.'

'Me too,' Ella said.

Hal raised his eyebrows and frowned. Ella shook her head in response.

'Are you sure you've never met him?'

'Quite sure.'

'Only he lives in the same block as you, well actually he owns the whole block, so you could easily have met him on the stairs. Mr Heddington was quite adamant you'd come to an arrangement.'

'Who?' Ella felt sick. Hal smiled his devastatingly gorgeous smile at her; his perfect teeth looked freshly whitened.

'Hal Heddington.'

'I thought that's what you said.'

'So you do know him?'

'Yes. Don't worry about it. I'll handle it from here. Thank you for your help.' Ella ended the call then turned round to Hal and gave him her best, super dazzling smile. It didn't quite match his.

'Everything all right?' He was sifting through the supermarket shopping that she'd dumped on the kitchen floor when she came in.

'Give me five minutes. I just need to run up to the loo.'

'Okay. Then did you want to go to dinner?'

'Five minutes,' Ella said, running out of the room.

She locked the bathroom door behind her, lifted the toilet seat and threw up. Afterwards she sat on the bathroom floor, panting and crying as she wiped her face with toilet paper. Why was she allowing him to have this effect on her? She was annoyed with herself, annoyed at being duped. Why did he lie? Why did he bother fawning all over her?

'Ella,' Hal called up the stairs. 'Everything okay?'

Ella took a deep breath. 'Fine. Just coming.' She flushed the toilet, cleaned her teeth, hurriedly brushed her hair and whipped it into a pony tail, smoothed her clothes and took another deep breath.

Hal was hovering in the dining room, his hands stroking the old book. He lifted the cover carefully almost as though he expected it to creak.

'Ready,' Ella chirruped.

Hal dropped the book cover, turned and gave her a broad smile. 'That's better; you've brushed your hair. Are you hungry? Could you manage a steak? I know a great little steak house in the next village. Is everything sorted out with your accountant now? Only you seemed a little upset when you were on the phone.'

'That wasn't my accountant,' Ella said.

'Oh?' Hal seemed to be waiting for Ella to elaborate.

'No, it was the letting agent.'

'Ah. I wanted to speak to you about that.' So now he was found out.

'Speak away,' Ella said.

'Well, I meant to tell, ask you, if it would be all right to move someone into your old flat. It all happened suddenly, there wasn't time before he arrived and then… I wanted to tell you myself.'

'So tell me.'

'He's an old friend,' Hal said, as he started looking around the room. 'He's been down on his luck. I felt I just had to help him. There it is.' Hal spread his arms out wide and grinned at her; he was so gorge that he could almost get away with it. Almost.

'I don't really care who he is,' Ella said, grinning back at him. 'Couldn't care less. Not that I believe he's an old friend.'

'Oh but…' Hal began.

'No but,' Ella cut in. 'There are several issues here, shall I list them?'

Hal looked up at the ceiling but didn't answer.

'Let's start with you not telling me you owned my grotty bedsit.' Ella waited for Hal's response.

'It didn't seem relevant,' he said, after a long pause. 'I like to keep business and pleasure separate.'

'Why did you insist I pay until the end of the month, then re-let to your… friend?'

'I told you that was spur of the moment. My friend…'

'Stop. Let me rephrase that. I meant why did you insist on me paying you until the end of the month? I thought we were,' she paused, just a beat, 'friends.'

'The letting agency insisted on it. It's part of the contract, the rules.' He raised his hands as though he had no control over it.

'When were you going to tell me you owned my grotty bedsit, the whole block too?'

'Now. I'm telling you now.'

Ella shook her head. She wasn't going to argue with him.

'When can I expect my refund? Oh, and my deposit, in full?'

'I'll get right on to that.' Hal sounded sheepish. Then he winked at her. 'But it's not as if you're desperate for it. You have plenty of money now. Can't we just forget about all this and go out for dinner?' He dazzled her again with his teeth.

'You're quite good at forgetting, aren't you Hal?'

He frowned, shook his head, tilted it to one side.

'How's Phoebe?'

'Fine, last time I saw her. She went back to London last week.'

Ella watched his face, not a sign, not a nervous twitch. Nothing.

'You're a good liar, Hal. Very accomplished.'

He shook his head a little, a show of indignation; his magnificent mane rippled.

'I don't know what else you haven't told me, or lied to me about, but I know about Phoebe.'

'I don't know what that bastard Nathan Jessop has told you, but don't believe a word.' Hal's voice was confident, liquid, purring.

Ella shook her head. It was almost funny. 'After I discovered your *friend* I went up to your flat, that is the one you live in, because they're all yours, aren't they?'

'Mine and the bank's,' Hal muttered, more to himself than Ella.

'Whatever. I came to see you. I wanted your help. I wanted a shoulder to cry on, I wanted support, advice. I wanted you. Guess who answered your door?' Ella raised her eyebrows and waited for his reply.

'I don't know. I was at work. All day at work.'

'Work, that's a new word for it.'

'We haven't all inherited a fortune, Ella. Some of us have to work for a living.' His dazzling smile was gone now. Ella could see anger in his eyes.

'You still haven't answered my question. Who do you think answered the door to your flat?'

Hal didn't reply, but he blinked several times.

'Phoebe. That's who. The lovely Phoebe. Dishevelled, hungover, or worse. Glazed eyes. She was wearing your shirt, the one you had on last night when you came round here. You remember, the lovely pink one I admired.'

'She obviously came back after I'd gone to work. Come on, never mind about my silly sister. Let's go out. That steak is waiting. Let's celebrate your money coming through.' He moved towards her, put his arm around her waist.

Ella stepped out of his embrace, turned around, threw back her head and laughed hard. 'You are so funny,' she said. 'You never give up, do you?'

'Ella, come on. Never mind about Phoebe.'

'But I do mind. You see, Phoebe called out to you after she'd answered the door. I followed her in. And there you were, lying in bed, not at work at all. Lying in bed calling out for Phoebe to come back to bed with you.'

Hal stood in Ella's dining room, silenced for a moment. His eyes flickered from side to side; Ella could almost see him working on his next lie. He ran a perfectly manicured hand through his pristine hair. How different it had looked on the pillow that morning.

'Obviously that wasn't me,' he said. Too late. Much too late.

'Tell me you've got an identical twin brother.'

Hal's eyes flickered from side to side again; he looked as though he was actually considering it, but before he could answer Ella continued.

'Tell me his name is Hal too,' she said.

She heard him exhale slowly through his nostrils.

'Stupid bitch,' he said. He turned to leave.

'Not quite as stupid as you thought though, eh?'

He looked her up and down; his top lip curled enough to show off the over-whitened teeth. He flung the front door open, turned back to her. 'Stupid ugly bitch.'

'And you're a lying bastard. All smiles and nice smells and underneath it all you're just a shitty sleaze weasel.'

'Fucking stupid ugly bitch,' Hal said again, and stepped out into the night.

'Shitty sleaze weasel,' Ella shouted.

Hal never saw what hit him. When he awoke he was propped up in the driving seat of his car, his nose broken and bloodied.

Nineteen

'Shitty sleaze weasel,' Charlie repeated between laughs. 'What the hell is that?'

'Oh, I don't know. It just came out.'

'Suits him,' Sam said, wiping tears from her eyes.

'He called me worse.'

Sam widened her eyes, waiting to hear what Hal had said.

'I'm not repeating it,' Ella said. 'But it was worse than sleaze weasel.'

'Then he's a shitty bastard as well,' Sam said, and they all started laughing again.

'And he sleeps with his sister. If she is his sister, which I doubt.'

'Urrgh,' Sam and Charlie chorused.

'And now I've had time to think about it I think he was after my money and my water.'

'Your water?'

'From the spring. He mentioned several times how it could be bottled and sold in his spa. I didn't take it seriously, didn't think that much about it, it's against the rules anyway, which I told him repeatedly. But now I realise he thought he could convince me.'

'Sleaze weasel,' Charlie said, smirking.

'I think he thought I would invest in his business too, his spa, I think. He took me to a weird little theatre in someone's back garden. Several of them thought I was an investor; I just thought they were mistaken, but now…'

'Sleaze weasel,' Sam spat.

'Yeah, sleaze weasel with a broken nose now.' Ella grimaced. 'Serves him right.'

'So, why was Nathan lurking outside your front door waiting to punch Hal?' Sam asked, not for the first time, and Ella knew she'd keep asking until she got an answer.

'Nathan,' Charlie called, as Nathan approached with a tray of drinks. He set them down on the table; it was busy in The Giddy Goat and they were lucky to have a table with such a good view of the stage. 'What time are you on?'

'Twenty minutes or so.' Nathan put a cider in front of Ella, a lemon squash in front of Sam, a beer each for Charlie and himself, then took the tray back to the bar.

'I hope he doesn't sing that shitty song about me,' Ella whispered to Sam.

'It's not about you,' Sam whispered back.

'Yes. It. Is,' Ella said between gritted teeth, as they watched Nathan come back.

'So,' Sam began, 'what were you doing lurking outside Ella's door?'

Nathan and Ella exchanged glances.

'I'll keep asking,' Sam said.

'She will,' Charlie echoed.

'I live opposite. I could see in Ella's dining room window.'

'You live opposite? You live opposite. You kept that quiet, Ella.'

'I had no idea. Nathan always arrived in a van when he came to my place.'

'I was usually coming from the yard,' Nathan added.

'So you really didn't know he lived opposite?'

'Not until he punched the sleaze weasel.' They all started laughing again.

'Things didn't look right,' Nathan said. 'I could see right into Ella's dining room and I could tell things weren't good.'

'Hal didn't…' Alarmed, Sam turned to Ella.

'No. He may be a liar but no, he wasn't violent.' She frowned. She didn't actually know what Hal was like. 'Well, not to me anyway,' she added.

'Nathan, what could you see?'

'Body language.' Nathan shrugged. 'It looked like a row. I just sauntered over, just in case.'

'Well, wasn't that lucky.' Sam nudged Ella in the ribs. Ella moved out of range to prevent further nudging.

'Do you think he'll press charges?' Ella asked, suddenly worried at the prospect.

'I doubt it, but I don't care if he does.' Nathan reached for his pint, took a long sip.

'It's busy in here for a Wednesday night,' Charlie said, tactfully changing the subject and looking around as more and more people piled into The Giddy Goat. 'Standing room only. Who else is on?'

'It's just me,' Nathan said.

'You're popular.'

'Local.' Nathan nodded at a several people who waved to him, called his name. Someone gave him a cheesy grin and a thumbs-up.

Sam finished her drink and smiled. 'That was lovely.

What was it?'

'Just squash. It's probably the water that makes it tastes so good. It's from Ella's spring.' Nathan narrowed his eyes across the table at Ella.

Ella mouthed 'shut up,' back at him.

'Could you get me another, Charlie?'

'I'll go.' Nathan stood up. 'I need a glass of water for my voice anyway. Oil the vocal chords.' He sounded self-conscious.

'He's going to sing that shitty song, I just know he is,' Ella said, as soon as he was out of earshot. Did she sound obsessive?

Sam shook her head. 'Not everything is about you, Ella.'

Ella clamped her lips tight shut. If he sang the song she didn't know what she'd do, how she'd react. She got a bitter taste in her mouth just remembering the last time she'd heard it.

'So, Nathan is doing your work? That's good. Good to have someone you can trust.' Charlie nodded his approval.

'Well, his father's building firm is doing it. Nathan isn't doing the work personally.'

'He said he is,' Sam said. She pulled an apple from her bag and bit into it with a crunch. 'What? I'm so hungry,' she said, when Ella blinked her surprise. 'He was telling us when we were waiting for you to get here. You know, when you were late and I had to ring you to remind you, because you wouldn't let Nathan call for you.'

'Eat your apple,' Ella said.

'Yes, he said he'll either be doing it himself or be supervising. He wants to ensure the work is top quality and the disruption kept to a minimum.' Sam was obviously enjoying herself; she munched some more on the apple. Ella wondered how true it was. Wondered exactly what Nathan had said. 'I don't know why you two don't just…'

'Don't just what, Sam?' Nathan said, appearing with her drink.

'Oh, nothing. Thanks.' She took the drink and drank half the glass straight down.

'I'd better go and,' Nathan paused, 'prepare myself.' He turned, walked across the pub. He was wearing his usual white t-shirt and jeans, Ella watched his muscles flex as he walked, the muscles in his back, the muscles in his thighs. His hair was still incredibly short, she wondered what it would feel like if she touched it. Like the bristles on a brush? She imagined running her finger tips over it.

'Ella,' Sam said. She'd moved herself close enough to nudge Ella again.

'What?'

'Where were you? Not thinking about sleaze weasel, I hope.' Sam started to laugh.

'No. I really wasn't.'

'Hey, remember that first day we came to the village and you got stuck in the loos on the green. They had to get that old penny to let you out. That was so funny, wasn't it?'

'Hilarious,' Ella said. She cringed and shuddered.

'Have you been in there again since?'

'Hardly.' Ella smiled at Sam, a big *shut up now* smile.

'Did Nathan tell you about the scout?' Charlie asked.

'Scout? No?'

Sam leaned in, took another crunch out of the apple. 'Remember that odd woman who was at the pub that night, the last time Nathan played with the band. You know, when you stormed out.'

'Yes.'

'We all thought she was the drummer's friend, remember.'

'Yes. I remember.' Ella remembered all too well, the skinny woman with tattoos and a brand new Lexus. The woman who said she was happy not to know Ella's business and drove her home in silence. Bit of a lifesaver really.

'Well, turns out she's the scout, you know, the music scout.'

'Is that true? I didn't think it worked like that anymore.'

'She only does it part-time, to fit in with her family.'

Ella remembered her talking about how she'd exploded when she was pregnant. No one had taken her seriously at the time, she didn't look like a mother; she looked like a skinny Hell's Angel.

'You must be thrilled, Charlie,' Ella said. 'Well done.' She patted Charlie on the back.

'No. Not the band,' he said, smiling; he didn't seem bothered. 'Just Nathan. Not necessarily him singing, although…' Charlie smiled. 'He can sing, really sing. But it's his song writing skills she's after.'

Ella felt her heart skip a beat. Not the shitty song. Please God, not the shitty song. Ella felt sick. She wanted to run. Get out now, before he started the song. She looked around for an escape route but the place was jam-packed.

She took a large gulp of her drink.

Nathan came on. Ella watched him sit on a stool, prop his foot up on the rung. He smiled over in their direction. Sam waved back. Ella didn't. He strummed on his acoustic guitar, tuned it, introduced the song.

Ella didn't think it was the shitty song, but then, it wasn't called the shitty song and she didn't actually know what the real title was. But once he started to sing she knew it wasn't the shitty song. She relaxed, listened to his soft, melodious voice; the hairs on the back of her neck stood up. He was good. Completely different to Charlie, but so good. It was fast paced, jolly. People were humming along with him, they knew it.

'*He* wrote this.' Sam leaned over to Ella. 'And everyone here knows it. Look at them.'

Ella nodded. They were loving him, smiling and clapping along with him.

When he finished the applause was loud, cheery, heartfelt. They were applauding one of their own. He sang another song, quieter, slower, thoughtful words. Followed it with a faster paced song. He sang ten songs one after another without a break, the audience whooping and whistling.

Finally he stopped. He hadn't sung the song. Ella let out a long breath. He stood up, took an exaggerated, playful bow. Everybody laughed. Clapped him more. He turned to go, but of course they were shouting more, more, encore, more. He bowed again, glanced over at Ella, gave her a shy smile. She forced a smile back, by way of a thank you. Stupid Ella.

He picked up the guitar, sat back down. Grabbed the mic and started to talk.

'This one is dedicated to Ella.' He looked over at her again.

Ella heard a horrible loud hiccough. Someone laughed. Charlie patted her on the back. 'Oh my God, was that me?' she whispered into Sam's ear.

Sam nodded, laughing.

'I wrote this song for Ella,' Nathan was speaking

again.

'Way to go, young Ella.' Was that Walt's voice?

'But the last time it was performed, she ran out before she could hear the whole song. I hope she'll stay and listen this time.'

Bastard. Bastard. Not only was he going to sing the shitty song, he was telling everyone that it was about her. She tried to stand up, tried to escape but the pub was so full now, everyone packed in so tightly that she couldn't even push her chair back far enough to straighten her legs. They had all been summoned for her ritual humiliation.

She slumped back down into her seat, her face reddening, her eyes stinging. She felt hot, clammy hot. She felt sick.

'Don't sing it, please don't sing it,' she called out, but at that exact moment Nathan strummed the guitar and the pub filled with applause and Nathan never heard her plea. There was no escape. Ella put her head on the table and let the tears flow. What a bastard. What a bastard.

Nathan started to sing. The familiar words felt like needles on her skin; every word hurt. '*…drunken fumble in a pub car park, icy breath that tastes of gin, an angry girlfriend in the background.'*

Ella tried her hardest to drown out the words, but every one was crystal clear. Every word worked its way into her brain, every single syllable. 'Bastard, bastard, bastard', she said to herself, hissing to stop his song getting in. But it didn't work.

She put her hands over her ears, starting humming to herself. Finally, she could only feel the rhythm, finally the words were muffled. She hummed away the song, willing it to finish. She had to stop, had to take a breath, but if she was quick she wouldn't hear too much.

'*...Psycho Phoebe...*' What did he just say? She didn't hum anymore, she listened. '*Regretful, awful one night stand, stalker with a heavy hand...*'

Ella gulped. This was the part she'd never heard. Had he said Phoebe? Or had she just imagined that?

Nathan had paused now. He had reached the end of the song. Someone clapped, someone else shushed the clapper. Nathan turned to look Ella full in the face. The audience was silent, expectant. Ella watched Nathan's chest rise as he took a deep breath, then he plucked at his guitar strings, then he sang, letting his voice fill the silent pub.

'Because Ella, it was only ever you I wanted. Only ever you I loved.'

The pub crowd hooted and hollered, whistled and cheered. Those who could stood up to continue their ovation. Ella looked on, confused, mesmerised, shocked.

She watched Nathan get down from the stage, watched him head in her direction. He was fielding handshakes and pats on the back, even an autograph hunter. He was laughing and smiling and continually looking over at her, checking she was still there, checking she hadn't escaped.

'You were right after all; that song was about you,' Sam said. 'I wasn't expecting that, were you?'

Ella shook her head slowly. 'I'm very confused,' was all she said, just as Nathan reached her.

'Sorry for embarrassing you,' he whispered, leaning in close to Ella's neck. 'And thanks for hearing me out.'

Ella nodded again, moved away from him so that they were facing each other. 'So,' she said, 'Phoebe?'

'I'm not proud of myself.' He reached over and wiped the drying tears from Ella's face with his thumbs. 'It was a shabby, drunken one night stand. A one-off, I thought. But Phoebe, who I think might not be completely stable…'

'Psycho was what you said in your song,' Ella interrupted.

'Yes. Maybe that's not fair. Maybe I need to change that. Anyway, she decided she wanted more. I don't know why. She started following me around.'

'Stalking,' Ella said, referencing the song again.

'Poetic licence,' Nathan said.

'I never recognised her from that night in the pub car park. You know, the *drunken fumble*.' She watched his face.

'Poetic licence,' he said again, letting his eyes stare straight into hers.

'Well, whatever. I never connected that girl to Hal's,' Ella paused, looking for the right word, 'sister.'

'Obviously, not his sister,' Nathan said. 'Though anything is possible. You can't believe anything he says.'

'No.' Ella was watching Nathan's lips now, watching as they moved over his teeth when he spoke. He was close enough that she could inhale his warm, earthy scent.

'After the scene, after you'd gone,' Nathan continued, 'Hal appeared. We almost had a fight.'

'Why didn't you tell me? When you saw me with Hal, why didn't you tell me then?'

'Badmouth your boyfriend. How would that have looked? What would you have thought?'

Ella shrugged. 'He wasn't my boyfriend.'

It was Nathan's turn to shrug. 'It must have looked so comical, him taking a pathetic swing at me, me pushing him out of the way. The smokers enjoyed it, they roared with laughter.' Nathan reached for Ella's hand, pulled it towards him.

'They get a ringside view of everything,' Ella said.

'Not everything,' he said, pulling her close and kissing her. And it was a heart-stopping, knee-buckling, loin-churning kiss.

And the pub crowd clapped and cheered and laughed.

THE HAPPY END

(although there is a sequel…)

A Onesie
is not just for
Christmas
A novella sequel to
Blame it on
the Onesie
CJ MORROW

What happened in the beach hut was
supposed to stay in the beach hut...
Mermaid
Hair
and I
Don't Care
CJ MORROW

CJ MORROW
Save the Date
A heart warming and witty tale of unrequited love

She just wanted to be alone...
Escape to Christmas Cottage
CJ MORROW

Printed in Dunstable, United Kingdom

64716067R00188